NECESSARY
PROOF

Book 4.1 in the Sonoma series

&

UNSHAKEABLE
PURSUIT

Book 4.2 in the Sonoma series

Camy Tang

Camy Tang
P.O. Box 23143
San Jose, CA 95153-3143
www.camytang.com

Publisher's Note: This is a work of fiction. Names, characters, places, and incidents are a product of the author's imagination. Locales and public names are sometimes used for atmospheric purposes. Any resemblance to actual people, living or dead, or to businesses, companies, events, institutions, or locales is completely coincidental.

Book Layout ©2013 BookDesignTemplates.com

Ordering Information:
Quantity sales. Special discounts are available on quantity purchases by corporations, associations, and others. For details, contact the "Special Sales Department" at the address above.

Necessary Proof & Unshakeable Pursuit/ Camy Tang. -- 1st ed.
ISBN 978-1-942225-16-4

Contents

NECESSARY PROOF

Book 4.1 in the Sonoma series

Camy Tang

1.

For the second time in his life, Alex Villa was accused of a crime. Except that this time, he didn't do it.

He crept through the underbrush, trying not to crunch the dry grass under his work boots, with his eyes on the figure of the lean man in a dirty T-shirt and torn jeans who strode confidently through the trees thirty yards ahead.

It was difficult to stay hidden from the man because the trees here on Harman Ridge in Sonoma County were scraggly, and even the hardy oaks and laurels looked a little shriveled after the dry winter. Soon, the spring rains would turn the California foothills green again, but today the sun beat hot, and the dry undergrowth threatened to give away Alex's presence to the man he was following.

At first glance, the man had looked like a Hispanic migrant worker, with darkly tanned skin and straight midnight hair. But every so often, his shirt would hike up and reveal tattoos across his lower back of strange writing. The letters weren't the standard English al-

phabet, and certainly not Spanish. The swirling sym-
bols twisted with the movement of the man's torso as
he clambered over manzanita and slithered between
juniper bushes.

This man had started the stories about the meth
lab near Graves Peak, the stories that had begun
Alex's recent troubles. This man was the one who had
framed him. This man was the reason Alex was facing
prison. Again.

He had to pause to take a deep, sharp breath.
Prison had been a brutal place, and the memories were
like dark ghosts that hovered at the edges of his vision.
But prison had also been a place where his life had
taken a drastic turn and he'd found peace for the first
time in years. He'd found love. He'd found Christ.

The memory calmed the churning in his stomach,
and he hunched lower and crept after the man. He'd
been feeling mildly nauseated since Detective Carter
had reluctantly revealed the "evidence" against Alex.
He'd been released, but he wasn't about to wait
around to see what other planted evidence would surface that would enable the Sonoma police to convict
him.

The trees grew thicker here, and he hung back even
more. If this was a second meth lab site, there would
be more people around guarding it.

But there weren't other guards. The man headed
directly for a mobile home that seemed sunken deep
into the scrub brush. A narrow, deeply rutted trail ran

from the building back down the other side of the ridge, where the distance to the nearest road was several miles. In contrast, he and the man had been walking cross country from the opposite direction for only about twenty minutes.

With no guards and only a few people aware of this remote location, this lab site would be difficult for law enforcement to find.

Not anymore. He would inform Detective Carter about this meth lab, too, just as soon as ...

He clenched his jaw. Just as soon as he cleared his name. He'd forgotten about his predicament for a pitiful moment. He was no longer a trusted confidential informant for the Sonoma PD. Instead, he was implicated in a police officer's murder.

He circled the mobile home. An acrid toxic gas burned his nostrils, and he gagged at a combination of cat urine and rotten egg smells that wafted over him, emanating from the chemicals in the lab. The drone of a generator almost drowned out the sound of voices, and he crept toward the other side of the trailer. He lay on his stomach and peered through the weeds.

The man he had followed was talking rapidly to two other men. After a few minutes, Alex recognized the language as Filipino. He'd known several Filipino gang members in prison, and after he came to Christ, he was still friends with some of them, visiting the two still in prison and doing what he could to help the others stay out of jail. Two of them had come to church with Alex once.

He had suspected the language of the man's tattoos were Filipino. It looked like a Filipino gang was involved. Not a big surprise. Alex was friends with many of the local farm workers, who had mentioned seeing more and more Filipino strangers in the area in the past couple years. It matched what Detective Carter had told him about the Tumibay Filipino gang, based in San Francisco, who had been ramping up meth production in the rural areas outside of Sonoma.

The two men he talked to were a study of opposites. One was taller, dressed in a dirty, long-sleeved shirt and jeans despite the heat, sweat running down his shaved head. He was lean, and some wicked knife wound scars running across his left cheek made him look as if he had a permanent one-sided sneer.

The other man was shorter and even more slender, but with paler skin and long black hair pulled into a ponytail. His polo shirt and shorts, while casual, were expensive, as was his watch. He wore glasses, although they couldn't have been very strong because they barely distorted his heavy-lidded black eyes.

Both men responded in Filipino, and the shorter one gestured to a nearby folding table and chair set up several feet away from the mobile home, near the generator that powered the meth lab. A laptop stood open on the table.

The men argued for a few minutes more, then the one he had followed turned and stomped away, back the way he'd come. Alex flattened himself further into the grass, glad he hadn't remained behind the man. He'd have been spotted in a heartbeat.

The two men stood and talked in low voices. From their body language, they appeared to be equals in authority, despite the differences in dress. Another man's voice called from inside the trailer, and the taller one went back into the lab.

The shorter man pulled out a cell phone and frowned at it. He then lifted it up, still staring, and walked in a widening circle.

Straight toward Alex.

God, don't let him find me. He stilled, hearing his heartbeat in his ears. His dark shirt and khaki pants made him hard to spot against the undergrowth, but it wouldn't matter if the man simply stumbled over him.

The man stopped, then backtracked, still staring at his phone. He moved around the trailer and away from Alex while dialing someone. His voice carried over the sound of the generator as he seemed to be giving instructions to someone in rapid Filipino.

Alex made his decision in the space of time between one breath and another.

He leaped to his feet and sprinted to the table. He closed the laptop as quietly as he could and unplugged the power cord, which tangled among some other electrical equipment under the table which he hadn't noticed. One looked like an external hard drive, snarled in a mass of wires. He reached for it, but the man's voice grew louder again.

No time to unplug the external hard drive. Alex took the laptop and ran. He didn't bother to hide the noise as he crashed through bushes and circled around the other side of the trailer. He picked up speed as he headed back the direction he'd come, jumping over bushes and dodging trees.

Shouts sounded behind him, but he didn't look back. There was the crack of a gunshot, and he ducked his head but tried not to slow his speed. More gun-shots, but he heard the bullets hit trees several yards behind him. They stopped firing, probably since the trees made him a more difficult target to hit.

He sprinted past the tattooed man that he had fol-lowed. The man was several yards away, but apparently unarmed. All he could do was shout as Alex dashed by.

On the way to the meth lab, they'd taken a straight route through the wilderness, about a mile or a little more. The man had parked on the remote access road at the back of old Mr. Rivers's farm, but Alex, trying not to be seen tailing him, had parked on an unused farm track on Mr. Rivers's property, hidden from the road by rows of dead grape vines.

Once out of the trees, he raced for his truck. He stumbled over some clods of dirt from the unused track and nearly dropped the laptop, but he was used to keeping his balance in uneven dirt thanks to his hours working in the fields of his mama's farm and in his brother's greenhouses, and he was able to right himself quickly. He scrounged in his pocket for his car keys and hit the unlock button only a second before he yanked the door open.

As he turned over the engine, the three men he'd seen exploded from the tree line and dashed toward him. The tallest man was in front, and he now pulled out his gun and fired again. Alex ducked low as his window exploded in a cloudy spiderweb of cracks around the bullet hole. He slammed his foot on the accelerator and the truck leaped forward.

More shots, but these hit the frame of his truck. He bumped and jolted down the farm track, but quickly skidded to turn onto the access road. He looked in his rearview mirror and saw the men running toward the tattooed man's car, but he was far down the road before they even reached it. He slid onto the curvy highway that wound through the foothills, and after a few turns, pulled into the long driveway belonging to the farm of a family he knew. He parked behind a stand of trees a little ways back from the road and waited.

The tattooed man's car soon passed by the driveway.

Alex leaned back against the seat. He'd wait to make sure they didn't double back, then he'd find his way to the main highway to Sonoma.

He laid his hand on the laptop on the passenger seat. He was comfortable with electronics, but he was a hardware guy. He understood enough software to know he was a bull in a china shop, so he didn't want to fiddle with the computer in case it had a security feature.

He needed help. He needed to clear his name. His race for his life couldn't have been for nothing.

Jane Lawton nearly dropped her steaming pot of Mac-N-Cheese at the sound of a powerful fist knocking at her apartment door. "Coming!" She spooned the gooey, bad-for-you goodness into a bowl, then ran some water in the pot in the sink.

The urgent knocking sounded again. Somehow it didn't sound like one of her neighbors, wanting Jane's help with a computer problem. She looked through the peephole.

She felt a sharp pulse at the base of her throat. "Alex?" She opened the door.

Normally a walking Calvin Klein ad, he now had a grim, serious cast to his face as he hurriedly entered her apartment with a messenger bag slung across one broad shoulder. "Quick, close the door."

"What's going on?" She locked the deadbolt.

It frightened her that he looked so different now, lacking his usual smile and dimples. "I need your help, Jane."

She couldn't control the bitterness that burned the back of her throat. It seemed that was the only thing she was good for, helping the men in her life so they could leave her and move on. She swallowed and said carefully, "Doing what?"

He pulled a laptop from his messenger bag. "There's information on this that I need, but I'm not sure if there's any type of security protecting it."

"Whoa." Jane took a step back. "You're saying that's not your laptop, and you want me to get into it? What's going on?" She knew he had been in prison for a few years, but she thought he'd put his illegal past behind him.

He scrubbed his hand over his high forehead. "It's not what it looks like."

"That makes it sound even worse."

He exhaled and seemed to study her. His intent, dark eyes made her squirm. She knew she'd changed a lot in the past year. She'd only spoken to him once in all that time, a few months ago at the party celebrating his brother's engagement to Rachel, Jane's second cousin but as close as a sister. After a minute or two of chit-chat, he had been quick to leave her to speak to Detective Carter, which had given her a pang even though she hadn't been in a sociable mood. What a difference from when she and Alex had first met years ago. He had seemed interested in her, but she'd been ...

She shoved the memories aside. "I'm only going to ask this one more time. What's going on?"

"I just ... I can trust you, right?"

"Trust me with what?"

"Could I sit down? Have some coffee?" He sniffed. "Is that Mac-N-Cheese?"

"Did you want some?"

He gave her a smile that caused that sharp pulse at the base of her throat again. "I haven't eaten since breakfast."

And it was already past seven. "But it's Mac-N-Cheese. From a box."

"So?"

"You eat Mac-N-Cheese? Isn't your mother good enough to be on Iron Chef or something like that?"

The smile disappeared, and long lines were drawn on either side of his mouth. "I haven't been home all day."

The wooden tone of his voice made Jane wonder if he hadn't gone home because he couldn't, not because he chose not to. Unlike Jane, Alex and his brother had a solid relationship with their mother and would do anything to protect her.

The combination living room/dining room in her one-bedroom apartment was currently her office, so she hastily swept aside some electrical equipment and notes from the dining table and set them in a neat stack on the floor. "Have a seat. I don't have decaf coffee."

He sank into a wooden chair with a sigh. "I need leaded right now, anyway."

As she retrieved her bowl of food from the kitchen, she eyed his six-foot-plus frame, at least two hundred pounds of solid muscle. She set the entire thing in front of him. "Go ahead."

"No—" he began.

"I'll cook some eggs."

His eyes softened. "Thanks, Jane."

She tried not to think of those eyes as she started the coffee maker and whisked eggs with soy sauce. He made her feel ... special, and she couldn't trust her own feelings anymore. Rachel had accused her of becoming too cynical this past year, but could anyone blame her after what had happened?

So in her frying pan, she scrambled the eggs mixed with soy sauce and served it on some rice she'd heated in the microwave. "Shoyu-egg-rice," as her Japanese mother called it, and it was Jane's comfort food. She needed comfort right now, in preparing to deal with the handsome man at her dining table and whatever trouble he'd brought into her home.

When she returned to the dining table, he had just finished the Mac-N-Cheese, but she had anticipated that. She served him some of the eggs and rice. "Here."

He frowned at the brown-colored scrambled eggs. "What's this?"

"Japanese-style breakfast. Try it."

She bowed her head to say grace, but she felt self-conscious. Not because he wasn't Christian, because she knew he was, but she only said grace these days out of habit. She'd been feeling like a chasm had opened between her and God. She couldn't understand why He'd allowed her to be so hurt, and maybe her distrust of men had extended to Him, too.

She took a bite of salty egg, hot rice, and remembered breakfasts at home with her mom and her brother, a peaceful and innocent time before she'd been aware of how little her father had cared for her.

Of how little anyone cared for her, apparently.

"This is good." He paused from shoveling food into his mouth. "What's wrong?"

She realized she'd been frowning into her bowl. "Nothing." She stabbed at the rice with her fork. "That should be my question."

He grimaced and slowed his eating. "Look, Jane ..."

"I want the full version. Not the version you'd tell your mama."

The glance he sent her could almost have been playful, but Jane steeled herself against the dimples that appeared briefly in his cheeks. "It's a little unnerving how you can read me, Jane."

"You're stalling." She could hear the coffeemaker burbling. "You don't get coffee until you explain yourself."

He took the last bite of eggs and rice and pushed the bowl away from him. "I'm being set up, Jane, and I have to clear my name. You heard about the police officer who died in that shoot-out at a meth lab in the foothills last week?"

She nodded.

His face tightened and he stared at her wooden tabletop. "That man is dead because of me."

After a beat of shock, Jane said, "Aren't you being a little melodramatic? The paper said it was a gang member who shot him."

"I gave the police the location of that meth lab, but it was a trap."

"How did you know about the lab?"

He ran a tanned hand through his short, dark hair. "I know a lot of the farm workers around Sonoma, and some of them found out about the lab and told me."

"How'd they find it?"

"A meth lab smells pretty potent."

"Oh."

"I told Detective Carter, but there were gang members waiting for the Sonoma PD to arrive."

She could see how he might feel it was his fault. "There's no way you could have known that would happen."

"Then the next day, five thousand dollars were deposited into my bank account from an offshore account."

"From who?"

He shook his head. "I don't know. I told Detective Carter about the deposit right away, but it looks like I was paid to tell the Sonoma PD about the lab so they'd get gunned down. I'm under investigation."

"But you help Detective Carter all the time. Doesn't that count for something?" When Jane had first met Alex, she'd overheard the detective asking to speak to him about helping the police with a case. Alex's brother, Edward, had explained to her that Alex was a confidential informant for the Sonoma PD. Alex was friends with many of the farm workers in Sonoma, and if they had a concern, they told him, who would tell the detective. This roundabout way to get information to the police protected the identities of people who weren't comfortable going to the police directly.

"Detective Carter knows I'm innocent, but it looks bad." A muscle in his jaw flexed. "I'm being set up. I'm thinking that it's only a matter of time before the police find planted evidence that will get me convicted."

He must feel trapped. Suffocating. It would be intolerable to someone like him, who was full of life, full of energy, and always transparent. "I'm sorry." She touched his forearm.

She didn't feel a jolt, but something about touching him made her feel ... different. As if he'd flipped on some switch inside her.

She snatched her hand back and stood up. "I'll get the coffee."

She had to remember this was Alex, for goodness' sake. She'd known him for a few years already. What was more, when they'd first met, he'd asked her out to dinner, and she'd turned him down, admitting that she was interested in someone else.

And she had been, at the time. She'd had grand hopes of a lasting, meaningful relationship built on respect.

What a colossal idiot she'd been to think there was anything about herself that would attract anyone.

But Alex had been attracted to you, a small voice whispered.

Except she was no longer that woman he'd asked out on a date. And she never would be again.

She needed to focus on the issue right now. She put his coffee in front of him, black, the way he liked it. "Who's setting you up? Although if people know you help the police, that list might be long."

"I know exactly who it is. The Tumibays."

The Filipino gang who had meth labs scattered in the wilderness areas around Sonoma. "The police raided a few of their labs in the past few months. You told the police about them?"

He nodded. "I found out from some day laborers. Lots of people are worried about the meth. Kids are getting addicted, especially in the poorer areas."

"I know," Jane said in a low voice. "Monica was telling me that there have been more and more meth overdose cases at her free children's clinic."

"I've been following up on any leads I can ferret out about the Tumibays. They threatened me a few times." He shrugged. "They soon figured out it wouldn't work. But then they tried to attack Mama."

"When did this happen?" Jane sat up in her chair. "Is she all right?"

"She's fine. It was a month ago. I was at the greenhouses, but three of the farmhands live with us at the house, and they held the gang off until the police arrived. They arrested the gang captain in charge of the meth operation here in Sonoma."

"So shouldn't that have ended it all?"

"There's a new captain the Tumibays sent to take over the operation."

Jane finally saw what was happening. "The new captain is trying to ruin your reputation with the police. He saw that threatening you or your family wasn't effective."

"After the officer was killed, I went to talk to the farm workers who told me about the meth lab in the first place. They had heard about it from a day laborer who spoke Spanish with a strange accent. I have a couple Filipino friends who speak Spanish with an accent, and I thought he might have been planted by the Tumibays. I found the guy and followed him to Graves Peak." He told her about the meth lab and the three men he'd seen.

"So you stole the laptop from the new Tumibay captain?"

"No, it wasn't the captain. I know what Talaba looks like. These were just his men."

"Still." Jane stared at the innocuous-looking laptop. "You should turn this in to the police."

"And tell them I found another meth lab? How convenient. If they were on the fence about if I'm involved with the Tumibays, I'm sure that wouldn't change their minds *at all.*"

"But they're the *police*—"

"And they think I gave them information that got one of their own killed. I'm not their favorite person at this moment. If I hand this laptop to them, they're going to view it with suspicion. They're not going to be careful about any kind of data it might have, because I could be feeding them more false leads. If it were my laptop, I'd set up security protocols in case it was taken, some program to erase sensitive data. That means we only get one shot at this, and the data on this computer might be the only thing to clear my name." He reached out to cover her hand with his. "Jane, you're the only one I know who can find a way to bypass any security protocols."

His palm was large and warm. Derek used to touch her like this, and it had made her stomach flutter like it did right now with Alex.

She pulled her hand away from him.

Could she trust him? She'd trusted Derek and look how that had gone.

But she knew Alex. She trusted his brother, Edward. And the fact he was being set up, that people who knew him were no longer believing him, must feel like a spear to the gut. She knew, because it had felt that way when her father hadn't believed her.

She wanted to help him because she couldn't let someone else feel he was being abandoned by his friends.

At that moment, her neighbor's dog began barking. "That's strange," Jane murmured before she could stop herself.

"What's strange?" He had grown tense.

She shook her head. "I'm being paranoid after what you've been talking about."

He gave her a hard look. "Just tell me, Jane."

"Well, Wiley—the dog—hardly ever barks. Sarah's a dog trainer, and her well-behaved pets are a point of professional pride for her."

His eyes narrowed. "Now that I think about it, the dog didn't bark when I came to your apartment."

"The last time Wiley barked was when some kids were fooling around on the fire escape."

There was a heartbeat of silence, then he shot to his feet. "Jane, get down."

To her credit, Jane didn't ask why or demand to know what was happening. She stared at him with her wide, gold-flecked brown eyes for a moment, then she dropped to her knees.

"Where's the fire escape?" he asked.

"Bedroom window."

He snapped off the lights as he made his way to the dark bedroom. The dog's yapping pierced through several apartment walls to reach his ears, but he hoped it masked the sound as he eased open the sliding glass window. He grabbed a small facial mirror propped up on Jane's dressing table and stuck a corner out the window. It took him a bit of tilting to find the right angle to see the fire escape balcony.

There was a man on the fire escape, heading his way.

He had to get Jane out of here. He'd guess there was also a man heading down the hallway toward Jane's apartment. It's what he would do, in this situation.

Thank You, Father God. If the dog hadn't barked, or Jane hadn't noticed, they might have been trapped. He'd figure out later how they'd found him.

He weighed his options. The fire escape was narrow and difficult fighting terrain, but he didn't know how many men were nearing the front door, whereas there was only one outside Jane's window.

He hurried to the bedroom door and gestured to Jane. "Grab the laptop," he said in a quiet voice.

She scurried toward him, shoving the laptop into the messenger bag he'd brought with him.

"Stay down," he told her, "but be ready to follow me."

She nodded. Her face was even paler in the dimness of her bedroom, and he saw the trembling in her hands, but she had a firm determination to her chin.

He hesitated beside the open window. He had only one shot at this. He took a deep breath, then lightly leaped over the sill onto the fire escape.

His boots hit the metal with a clang. He immediately sprinted toward the man, who was only a few feet away now.

The man had stiffened when Alex appeared out of the window, and he hadn't yet recovered when Alex barreled into him. The man was shorter but still taller than average, and even though Alex had had the element of surprise when he attacked, the man was faster. His elbow snapped out, and although Alex ducked his head, the blow grazed his temple.

The two of them hit the floor of the balcony with a thundering shudder from the metal. The narrow width of the fire escape and Alex's broad shoulders made his punches awkward, and his blows were weaker than his sparring sessions at the gym with his buddies. But he only needed to incapacitate the man until he and Jane could get away.

Alex grabbed a fistful of shirt and slammed the frontal bone of his own skull into the man's face. He felt rather than heard the man's nose break, and blood spurted across his cheek. The man gave a sharp groan of pain, and Alex followed with a jab to the jaw.

The man's body stiffened, then fell back. He wasn't completely out because his arms waved feebly, but Alex yelled, "Jane!"

She was already climbing out the window with the messenger bag thrown over her shoulder. Her eyes slid over the man as she leaped over his body on the fire escape, but she didn't glance back as she followed Alex down the stairs.

They were on the ground in seconds since Jane was only on the third floor. He had his truck keys, but realized the men probably knew the make and model of his pickup. "Do you have your car keys?"

Jane pulled the keys from her slacks pocket. "Over here." Luckily, her parking slot was near the fire escape.

Of course, her car was practical and sensible, like her. The hybrid would be uncomfortable for him to sit in, much less drive. He shook his head when she offered him the keys.

She stared for a quick moment. "Really? Not what I would have expected from a guy." She scrambled into the driver's seat.

"I'm secure in my masculinity," he couldn't resist teasing. As they buckled up, he added, "Besides, I'm probably better than you at spotting a tail."

She backed out of the parking slot like a rocket, slamming his body against the seatbelt. He thought her driving might be attributed to nerves, until she got onto the street.

The woman drove like a maniac. Who knew that lurking under Jane's neutral colored, professional clothing was a *Grand Theft Auto* leaderboard winner?

"Where to?" The tires screeched a little as she took a corner onto the expressway.

"Into traffic." He searched the cars behind them. "If we're being followed, it won't hurt to be somewhere we can try to lose them."

She wove between cars, darting left and right without warning and without hitting the brakes. He had to grab the door handle so he wouldn't fly out of his seat.

"See anyone?" She finally had to brake hard when she cut in front of a minivan and behind a convertible who had just moved into the lane.

"I think we're safe," he said.

She eased up on the gas a minuscule amount. "Now where to?"

He nodded toward the backseat, where she'd tossed the messenger bag containing the laptop. "Anywhere you can get the information off of that computer."

"You're kidding, right?"

"What do you mean?"

Jane turned exasperated eyes to his. "All the equipment I needed to examine that laptop is in a place currently crawling with Filipino gang members—my apartment."

3

Even though it looked like they'd lost anyone trying to follow them, Alex closely observed the cars around them as he directed Jane outside of Sonoma toward Jorge's tavern. It was in a remote area, he had a lot of friends there, and more importantly, he'd left his computer toolbox there last week.

Jane turned into the tiny dirt parking lot in front of the brown building. It stood in a small lot between two orchards, both in bud with new fruits soon to appear as spring swept into the county. His expert gardening nose smelled cherry blossoms as he unfolded himself from Jane's car and stretched.

"Does Jorge have wireless internet?" Jane grabbed the laptop from the backseat.

"No, he's hard-wired."

"How close is the nearest house?"

"A couple miles in either direction." He nodded toward the narrow road that fronted the tavern. "There's only farms and orchards in this area. Why?"

"I'm probably being overly cautious, but I don't know what kind of security this computer has. The security program might be instructed to find the nearest wireless network and broadcast data so the owner can find it again."

"And you don't want there to be a wireless network it can find."

"Exactly. And you said you don't know anything about software." Jane's tone was almost teasing, although her eyes were still somber from the events of only an hour ago.

"I know only enough to make me dangerous." He led the way up to the narrow front porch, then opened one of the two swinging double doors to the tavern.

It had been an old farmhouse before Jorge bought it for his tavern, useless because the farmland had been sold around it. He'd torn down most of the walls on the first floor in order to put in scarred, mismatched tables and chairs, but there was still the stairs to the second floor living quarters on one side of the front hallway. There was no one inside except the deeply tanned, old Hispanic man standing behind the counter at the back of the front room, near the kitchen door.

"Alejandro!" Jorge raised his hands in greeting and waved them toward the counter.

In Spanish, Alex said, "Thanks for letting us come so late, Jorge."

"For you, anything, my friend."

Alex turned to Jane and said in English, "This is Jorge."

Jane shook Jorge's hand and surprised them both by answering in Spanish. "I'm Jane Lawton. Nice to meet you."

"You speak Spanish?" Alex asked her.

"I took it in high school." She shrugged. "And a couple of my neighbors are Hispanic, so I use it often enough."

"Are you hungry? Adelita should be almost done cooking." Jorge disappeared behind the kitchen door.

"Where's your toolbox?" Jane asked.

"Later. Adelita and Jorge rarely cook this late. They're doing it just for us."

Jane looked around the empty tavern. "Why aren't they open for dinner?"

"Jorge and Adelita started their business by making burritos and selling them cheaply to the farm hands in the fields. They got so popular that they opened this tavern, but it's for breakfast and lunch only because they still send the lunch wagon out to the fields every day. They're usually in bed by now because they get up so early."

Jane's delicate cheeks colored a strawberry pink that reminded him of some of the rare roses his brother cultivated for clients at the greenhouses. "They shouldn't have cooked for us."

"They enjoy being hospitable."

A silence fell between them that was more awkward than the silence in the car. Then, Jane had been concentrating on driving and he had been keeping an eye out for anyone following them. Here, in the quiet of the tavern, he became aware again of how beautiful she was, with her slightly slanted eyes and high cheekbones, the graceful neck exposed by her dark straight hair swept up into a twist at the back of her head. It had been perfectly smooth when he'd arrived at her apartment, but now wisps fell, probably from their mad dash down the fire escape.

Every time he saw her was like a kick in his gut, no matter how many times they happened to meet. He had been eager to ask her out when they first met, but she'd shyly confessed she was interested in someone else. He had been jealous of the guy who could put the glow in her cheeks and the golden glitter in her brown eyes.

But when he'd seen her at his brother's engagement party, he'd been surprised at the faint lines alongside her pink mouth, the deadness in her eyes. Someone had hurt her, badly. He'd wanted to ask, but hesitated because it was obvious she was still in pain. And in the end, Detective Carter had waved urgently to him, and he'd had to leave her to speak to him.

"How have you been lately?" The question seemed a bit lame, considering they'd spent the better part of the last two hours together. "The last time we met, you said you had a new job."

There was a flash of pain that tightened the skin around her eyes, and he wanted to kick himself. But she answered in a quiet voice, "It's fine. It pays the bills."

What a change from when they'd first met, and she'd talked excitedly about the startup she worked for and the voice recognition software she was helping to write. "Are you still writing voice software?"

Her jaw flexed before she answered him. "No. I'm doing IT support for an insurance company."

"Oh," he said faintly. Jane was brilliant. Why was she doing routine IT work rather than shining like a star at a tech startup?

She obviously didn't want to talk about it. "You're still helping to run your mama's farm?"

"And helping Edward with his greenhouse business."

"And being a CI for Sonoma PD. When do you sleep?" Her attempt at a joke didn't quite lighten the brittleness in her voice.

"All I do is talk to people, be friendly. It's not work." He liked feeling that he was helping the community. He could take risks others couldn't, like fighting against the Tumibays' meth production. What if he couldn't do it anymore? What would happen to him?

He didn't want to think about it. He *would* clear his name. He had to.

"Are you still dating that one guy?" He tried to sound casual, to hide the fact he wanted to know.

She stiffened, all her muscles rigid. "What guy?"

He just couldn't stop making things worse. "You, uh, told me about that guy at work ..."

She turned her face away from him. "It didn't work out," she said in a wooden voice.

"I'm sorry." He wasn't. How long ago had it been? What kind of a loser didn't appreciate the jewel she was?

Thankfully, Jorge and his wife, Adelita, entered with steaming plates of food. Adelita laid the plate she carried in front of Alex, then reached across the counter to grasp his face and kiss his cheek. "So good to see you, Alejandro."

"You smell like cinnamon." He grinned at her. "Does that mean you made me *sopapillas?*"

She rolled her eyes. "You and your bottomless stomach."

"I just like your cooking."

Adelita then turned and kissed Jane, too, which made her cheeks flush with pleasure. "Call me Adelita."

"I'm Jane."

"Eat, eat." Adelita gestured to the plates of food.

"I'll pray for us," Alex said to Jane.

Before he bowed his head to say grace, he saw the bleakness that shuttered over Jane's eyes for a brief moment. She had always been a strong Christian. Had whatever gave her that brittle, fragile quality struck a blow against her faith in God, too?

He glanced at her as he finished saying grace, but her face was a polite mask. However, that slipped to

reveal awe as she took her first bite of the bean burrito
Jorge and Adelita had made.

"That's amazing," Jane said to Adelita. "You make
your own tortillas?"

"Of course." Jorge seemed offended she would think
he'd serve anything else.

Alex hid his smile as he wolfed down a burrito. The
flour tortilla was soft and slightly crispy on the outside
from being lightly pan-seared, while the beans were
silky and flavorful with Adelita's secret spice mix.

Jorge set two bottles of Mexican orange soda in
front of them. "Now, you tell me what kind of trouble
you're in."

Alex hesitated.

"Alejandro, you must let me help you," Jorge said
quietly.

So he told them about the shootout at the meth
lab, about the money appearing in his bank account,
about following the tattooed man to the second meth
lab on Graves Peak.

Jorge's dark eyes narrowed, making the lines deepen
on his broad forehead. "I know the man you speak of.
The tattoo, the accent. His name is Rodrigo."

"You don't know his last name?"

"No. I saw him in the fields once, last week or the
week before, but never again. He never came here with
the regulars."

Many of the Filipinos Alex had known had Spanish
names, so that didn't help him much. The man had

probably been working in the fields in order to spread the information about the meth lab trap.

He told them about the laptop and the men at Jane's apartment. Adelita's chocolate colored eyes grew large, and she covered Jane's forearm with her hand. "You are all right?"

"I'm fine." Jane smiled and it transformed her, revealing a radiance that made his chest tighten.

"You stay here and rest tonight," Jorge said. "We have extra bedrooms."

"No, too many people will come for breakfast in the morning," he said.

"Leave before then," Adelita said. "No one will know you were here."

"Thank you."

"We must go to bed," Jorge said. "We wake at four to start breakfast."

"You know where the bedrooms are upstairs?" Adelita said, and Alex nodded. "There are fresh sheets in the hall closet."

She kissed his cheek again, then also kissed Jane. Her hands lingered on the girl's smooth hair. "Alejandro is a good man. He will take care of you."

Jane's neck turned scarlet, and her gaze dropped.

Adelita's words only reinforced his protective instinct toward Jane. He wouldn't let anything happen to her. He wanted to make sure no one hurt her ever again.

Jorge and Adelita said their goodnights, then headed up the stairs.

Jane and Alex picked at their food in silence for a while. Her neck was still red with embarrassment, and he didn't know what to say to smooth over the moment. He cleared his throat. "They're good people."

"They trust you, which makes me feel better about trusting you, too. I don't want to put them in danger."

The way he had put her in danger. "I'm sorry to drag you into this. I didn't think. I just knew I needed your help."

"Don't feel bad. I would never refuse to help you." She sipped her soda. "To help anyone," she added.

Ouch. But a part of him suspected that she was pushing him away as a defense mechanism, due to whatever had changed her so much in the past year.

He wanted to put his arms around her, to surround her with his strength so she wouldn't have anything to fear, but she had a quality of barbed self-sufficiency emanating from her body language that kept him in his seat.

She had always been quiet, serious, even geeky in her conversation, but she'd never before looked so ... desolate. What had happened to her? He knew she wouldn't tell him.

"How did those guys find you?" Jane asked. "You ditched your cell phone, right?"

He nodded. Jane had done the same within minutes of escaping her apartment.

"Did they follow you to my apartment?"

"I know they didn't, because I was looking out for them and I drove in circles for a while to make sure no one was behind me. They saw my truck, but the only way they could have tracked that was through traffic cameras."

Jane gave him a sidelong look. "If they have someone in Sonoma PD, they could have."

He hadn't thought of that. "They may not have been able to track your car here. There aren't many traffic cameras out near these farmlands."

"We probably shouldn't stay here, regardless. But they might spot my car when we leave the area."

"I know a way back to Sonoma through back roads." Before he had spoken to Jane, he had agonized about simply turning the laptop over to the police, but he'd been desperate and he knew the police hadn't trusted him, not after the death of that officer. Now he was glad he hadn't turned in the laptop. What might have happened to it if the Tumibays did indeed have a mole in the Sonoma police department?

He suddenly realized, "I didn't check the laptop for a GPS tracker."

"I'll check, but I doubt it. An installed GPS tracker requires a continuous connection to a cellular network or satellite, and I can't see a gang member who's doing illegal things on a laptop signing up for a GPS subscription that the FBI can trace back to them. Plus it's a major drain on the battery. Tracking software is more practical than GPS." She picked up the messenger bag and pulled out the laptop. "Where's your toolbox? I want to look under this baby's hood."

"Jorge said he'd leave it behind the counter for me." He slid off his stool and went behind the pitted wooden counter. His toolbox lay on the floor, and he hefted it up to set it before Jane.

"Why is your toolbox here?" She opened it and sifted through the small gauge screwdrivers.

"One of Jorge's kids gave him a larger memory card for his computer, so I came over to install it for him. Then I started playing soccer with Jorge's grandkids and stayed for dinner. After dinner, I left and forgot my toolbox here."

"You didn't need it at home?" She started unscrewing the back of the laptop.

"This is my computer toolbox. I have other toolboxes at home for the cars and the farming equipment." He was comfortable around computers, but Jane began unscrewing components left and right. "You're taking it apart without booting it up first?"

"I'm removing the wireless adapter and bluetooth card." She attacked something with a pair of tweezers. "I don't know what kind of security software it has, but if he was paranoid, he'd have installed a LoJack type of software in the UEFI that would connect to the internet as soon as it had a chance. It could even be programmed to delete sensitive data. I don't want this laptop to phone home and give our location away."

He winced as something snapped, but Jane wasn't unduly worried as she removed an electrical piece from the vicinity of the motherboard. "Hardware isn't my specialty, but if I can get the hard drive out, I might be able to use another computer to hack the information off of it."

He thought of her computer at her apartment. "What kind of computer?"

"I can't use just any computer." Jane stared at the hard drive in the laptop, chewing her bottom lip as she thought. "But there's one at my workplace."

"Those guys were at your apartment. They'll know by now where you work and they might be looking out for you."

"This late at night? And this soon after they raided my apartment?"

"You want to go tonight?"

She shrugged. "Part of the job is being on call for emergencies. I've had to go into work late at night lots of times."

"They still might be watching the building. They know you're with me and that we have the laptop, so they're not going to leave any stone unturned. At least, that's what I would do if I were a desperate drug gang captain."

Jane leaned forward over the countertop toward him, and there was a calculating light in her eyes. "What if we could get into the building without being seen?"

4

Jane shivered as she and Alex hiked across the manicured lawns of the Magnolia Scott Business Complex
campus, but not from the cold. There were occasional
lampposts along the cement walkways that cut between
the shadowy buildings, but most of the campus was in
darkness that had a deathly stillness to it. No night
birds, no cicadas at this time of year, just a wet cold-
ness to the air that seemed to make their footsteps
echo even louder.

He had indeed known back roads back to Sonoma,
although the potholes had made her teeth rattle. But
they avoided traffic cameras, and luckily Jane's workplace was in a business complex that nestled next to
the rolling foothills, not in the middle of a busy urban
area. They'd driven as close as they could, then parked
along the far edge of the campus to walk to the building where her company lay.

She shivered again in her cardigan, the only outer-
wear she'd been wearing when they ran from her
apartment. He noticed.

"Are you cold?" He wrapped a large arm around her shoulders, his hand rubbing her shoulders.

She had never been this close to him before. She caught the green sweetness of basil, the woody tang of rosemary, and overlying it all was the sharp, earthy scent of his musk. It made the tension across her shoulders release, while at the same time a fluttering started in her ribcage.

She could almost pretend that she was protected, that she was cherished by someone.

"You'll be warmer when we get inside," he whispered to her, his breath tickling her ear. "How far is it?"

"Building G is right there." She pointed to the looming hulk of the four-story office building at the west-most corner of the business complex, which sat next to Building H.

"That's J. Callaway Insurance?"

"No, my workplace is Building H. Building G is empty right now, but both buildings used to be used by the Jorden Corporation. My card key will get us into Building G, and there's a walkway on the fourth floor that will get us into Building H."

"They won't see us entering Building G?"

"We'll use the back entrance, which can't be seen from the parking lot."

"Let's start avoiding the lampposts." He steered her onto the grass, wet and sharp with cold dew.

They melted into the shadows as they approached the entrance doors, which were lighted by an overhead floodlight. The light couldn't be avoided, but Jane swiped her card key quickly through the card reader and the bolts for the door snapped open. She yanked at the glass door and they slipped inside.

He headed to the elevator doors in the foyer, but Jane pulled him to the stairwell. "The elevators are really slow. It's faster to walk up."

They climbed to the fourth floor, their steps echoing loudly in the spartan stairwell. She led him through a large area empty of anything but shabby looking cubicles to the far corridor that ended at another locked door. She swiped her card and got them access to the enclosed walkway to Building H.

They walked quickly, but Jane glanced down to where she could see a corner of the parking lot. There were no cars, but anyone after them could have parked in a dark corner of the lot that she couldn't see.

Building H had more carpeting than empty Building G, but it created a muffled pall that made Jane nervous. Anyone could sneak up on them.

"Where to?" he asked.

"Second floor."

They took the stairwell down two flights to the IT department, one room filled with servers and another office area where her cubicle sat against a wall. The air was cold and dry from the air conditioning keeping the equipment from overheating in the server room, and she could hear the whir of the fans. She didn't turn on the lights, however, as she made her way to her desk.

Like her dining room table at home, her desk was piled with papers as well as equipment and cables, almost burying her desktop computer. She picked up the phone. "I have to call Security to let them know I'm here."

"Aren't they in the building?"

"No, Security is across campus in Building A, but they'll have seen my card key entry already on their computer monitors."

He nodded, but his eyes were moving around the quiet room at her coworkers' desks.

Jane dialed Security, and a friendly man's voice answered immediately. "Hi, Miss Lawton. I saw your card key entry through Building G."

"Hi, James." She always chatted with James and it would look strange if she didn't, so she said, "You got the night shift again this week?"

He gave a long-suffering sigh. "Yup. Jesse's got the flu. But the overtime will pay for a new bike for my daughter."

"How's Rosa's broken arm? Did she get her cast off yet?"

"It comes off next week."

"Bet she can't wait." She saw Alex's wary expression. "James, I'm not sure how long I'll be here tonight."

"No problem, Miss Lawton. When you do leave, just to warn you, a couple hours ago, I got an error message from the card key reader for the front door of Building G. I went to check it, and it looked okay, but let me know if you have problems."

"All right. Thanks, James."

As she hung up the phone, a chill passed through her that had nothing to do with the darkness, or the air conditioning. An error message for the card key reader ... and they'd made noise walking down the stairwell ... and she'd spent time chatting with James ...

The air in her lungs suddenly felt thin.

"Alex—"

He turned toward her.

The gunshot was deafening, even with the carpet and cloth-covered cubicle walls absorbing some of the sound. His entire body jerked. "Jane, get down!"

Her scream lodged in her throat. She fell to her knees beside him, her shaking hands pressing to the dark, wet stain on his arm. It felt hot to the touch, or maybe her hands were cold.

If he hadn't turned toward her at that moment, where would he have been shot instead?

His body jolted at the pressure of her hands on his wound. "They're coming for you," he said through gritted teeth.

No, they were coming for the computer. She had an idea.

"Put pressure on it." She guided his hand to the wound, then moved to her desk. She reached for a hammer and an extra laptop hard drive. She hadn't removed the hard drive from the laptop yet, but they didn't know that.

"Stay back or I'll destroy the hard drive!"

She peeked around the edge of her cubicle wall and saw two men in the shadows of the door to the office room. One was the man who had been on the fire escape balcony. She got a better look at him this time, noting his dark hair, dark skin, wiry build, and the gun he held in his hand. His nose had been broken in his fight with Alex, and there was already dark purple bruising beneath his eye.

The second man was a stranger to her, but she remembered Alex's description of the finely dressed man at the meth lab. This man wore a polo shirt and slacks, and he didn't have a gun. When he turned his head, she saw he was wearing glasses.

"You're being ridiculous, Jane," the Glasses Man called to her, but he didn't come any closer. "You're trapped."

After tracking Alex to her apartment, he must have gone through it to find out who she was. "Trapped animals are the most vicious," she shot back. "I have a hammer and your hard drive here on my desk."

"Well, that's convenient," he drawled. He even stuck his hands in his pants pockets. "You work in IT, Jane.

Of course you'd have extra hard drives lying around. That one isn't mine."

"Are you so sure about that? The hard drive was a breeze compared to when I removed your bluetooth card and wireless adapter." She rattled off the specs of the pieces she had removed earlier this evening. "Those are yours, aren't they?"

She could see that the Glasses Man had stiffened. "Jane, you can't win. As soon as I saw your apartment, as soon as I found out what you do for a living, I knew you'd come here, to your workplace, to utilize your computers here."

"He's just trying to rattle you. Don't listen to him." Alex's whisper was right next to her ear, and she jumped. He had gotten up and was crouched next to her, blood still slowly soaking into his shirtsleeves.

"Your arm—"

"I'm fine. I have an idea. Keep him talking." He grabbed the fire extinguisher she kept under her desk and silently moved away, staying low and under the edge of the cubicles so the two men couldn't see him. The thick carpet muffled his footsteps.

"Jane, I got into a locked building just to wait for you. And no one will be able to find any evidence at the card key reader that we were here. They might even think you let us into the building. Do you see? There's nothing I can't do." Glasses Man nodded to his associate, who started moving toward the far wall.

Her heart rate picked up. Would he be able to see Alex? "One more step, and I'm going to start whaling on this hard drive."

The man didn't stop walking.

"You can't blame me for knowing Alex is somewhere planning something," Glasses Man said, "gunshot wound or not."

"I'm sure you could retrieve *some* data from isolated sectors in a broken platter," Jane said, "but not much."

Glasses Man's face became an ugly sneer, then he hissed at his associate, who finally stopped moving.

After a moment, Glasses Man regained his confident, almost-bored tone. "What are we doing to do, Jane? Sit here all night?"

Maybe she could play the stupid female role. "Your friend is going to drop his gun, and then I'm going to throw the hard drive to you."

Even in the darkness of the office, she could see Glasses Man smile. "Fine. And then we'll let you both go. No harm, no foul."

Yeah, right. "Okay." She tried not to let her sarcasm show.

Glasses Man nodded to his associate, who reluctantly set his gun on the floor close to his foot.

"Kick it away from you," Jane said.

The man frowned, but nudged the gun away a few inches with his foot. If she told him to kick it farther, he might take a step and see Alex, wherever he was.

CAMY TANG

Jane slowly stood up so the two men could see her over the top of the cubicle walls. She raised the hard drive in her left hand, while her right still clenched tightly around the hammer. "Here it is."

"Just throw it to me nice and easy," Glasses Man said.

Jane stepped out so that she had a clear line of sight to Glasses Man. She made as if to throw the hard drive, then hurled the hammer straight at his knees.

At that moment, Alex leaped up and shot the other man with a blast from the fire extinguisher. The sound roared in Jane's ears.

Her hammer struck Glasses Man's left kneecap. He crumpled, but his shout of pain was drowned by the report from the other man's gun.

Alex! Was he all right?

Jane dropped to the ground. She hesitated, but knew what Alex would want her to do. She began crawling frantically toward the door. She was tempted to get to her feet, but didn't want to become a target for the other man and his gun.

Glasses Man lay rolling on the floor and she had to circle wide around him. However, he lunged for her and grabbed her ankle. His face was contorted with rage and pain, and his fingers bit into her tendons and bones.

She pulled her other foot back and kicked at him, but his head was too far away, so she began aiming for his elbow. She slammed into it once, then twice. Finally his hand loosened and she yanked her ankle free.

He swore at her and lunged for her again, both hands scrabbling at her legs.

God, help me!

At that moment, she spotted a dark shape on the beige carpet. The hammer, where it had fallen after it ricocheted off of the man's knee. She dove for it, her fingers curling around the smooth wooden handle. She twisted around and swung it wildly at the man's hands.

He jerked his hands back, but the hammer knocked at a finger or knuckle, and he winced.

And then suddenly a huge figure crashed on top of Glasses Man, rolling them away.

"Alex!"

Alex swung a fist at the man's jaw, and his eyes rolled back, showing the whites. His body immediately became a rag doll.

Jane crawled to him at the same moment he looked up at her. "Are you all right?" they both asked at the same time.

And then Jane's hands were around his waist, her head tucked under his chin, his arms tight around her. His heartbeat galloped under her cheek, and she felt the *whoosh* of his hard breathing. The scent of his musk wrapped around her like a cape.

It was only for a few seconds, a handful of heart-beats. He released her. "I knocked the other one out, but it won't be long before they come to."

She nodded, and forced herself to her shaky legs. She stumbled back to her desk to grab the messenger bag with the laptop, then followed him out of the building.

They ran back to the car, slipping over the cold grass, their breaths faint white puffs in the air. Once inside, she gunned the engine and shot back down the residential street they'd followed to get to the business complex.

Her hands shook, and she tightened them against the steering wheel. It took her a while to realize Alex was calling her name.

"Jane. Jane, slow down."

Her jaw was clamped shut, so she inhaled sharply through her nose. As she exhaled, she eased up on the accelerator, then finally stepped on the brakes. They stopped in the middle of a lonely stretch of road under a large oak tree. Shadows enveloped the car.

His hand covered hers on the steering wheel. His palm was tacky. It took her a moment to realize it was his blood.

"We need to take you to a hospital," she said.

He shook his head. "It's only a flesh wound."

"Men always say that in the movies."

She saw the gleam of his teeth as he smiled. "This time, it really is. Trust me, I've been shot before. Besides, the hospital will have to report the gunshot wound."

"We have to clean it." She considered her cousin Monica Grant, who was a nurse by profession, but she didn't want to involve her family in something so dangerous. Besides which, Monica still lived at home with their Aunt Becca, who happened to be dating Detective Carter. It wouldn't be the best thing to run into him with a man bleeding from a gunshot wound.

And she couldn't forget the laptop. There was only one option she could think of, and it caused a violent twisting in her gut. She screwed her eyes shut, leaning her head back against the headrest. It couldn't be avoided. He needed help, and she needed that computer equipment.

She put the car in motion again.

"Where are we going?"

"The only place I know where we can clean your wound and find a computer to analyze the hard drive." She swallowed the bitter bile that rose up in her throat. "We're going to my parents' house."

Jane hadn't spoken to her father since that day, over a year ago. Even worse than what Derek and done to her had been the carelessness of her father's words, which had cut like her grandfather's *katana* sword thrust into her heart.

Taking back roads all the way, Jane and Alex drove into her parents' neighborhood just as the sun turned the sky to pale orange. Jane knew they'd already be awake.

Just go in, use her dad's computer. He wouldn't refuse her, especially not with a guest present. If he said anything to her, she could just ignore it.

She no longer cared about earning his good opinion.

They didn't drive right up to her parents' house, just in case the Tumibays were watching the front. Instead, she took a different street that wound its way through some foothills before curving back around to edge the property behind her parents' home. They parked along the side of the road next to a ditch and a fence.

When she got out of her car, a ray of morning sun kissed her cheek, and she paused, closing her eyes and feeling the gentle warmth. A lot had happened to her in the past year, and she'd spent time dealing with it. But now, she wondered if maybe she was ready to move on, for new beginnings.

Her gaze slid to Alex, who had climbed out of the tiny car and was stretching his long body. Just a few hours in his company, and she was starting to release her pain. How did he do that?

They hopped the fence, then crossed the pasture, smelling strongly of cow, to a second fence that bordered the backyard of the Lawton family home. The wide swatch of manicured grass had a flagstone border along the sides, and Jane walked slowly, noticing that the leaves of her mother's miniature rose bushes, lining the walkway, were a pale, mottled green because of the cold weather. She climbed the two short steps to the covered back porch. With a quick indrawn breath, she knocked on the back door.

Her mother answered, dressed in an apron. Rather than being surprised that her daughter knocked on the back instead of the front door, she had a slightly vague smile on her face. "Jane, what a surprise."

"Hi, Mom." Jane had to bend almost double to kiss her tiny mother's cheek.

"You're just in time for breakfast." Her mother's dark eyes drifted onto Alex, standing behind Jane, his head almost brushing the roof of the porch. He'd draped his jacket in such a way that it hid the bloody stain on his shirt.

"Mom, you remember Alex Villa? Edward's brother."

He smiled at her mother as if Jane's introduction had not been as stiff as a dead tree. "We met at Edward and Rachel's engagement party, Mrs. Lawton."

"Yes, now I remember. Well, I suppose you should come in." She turned and led the way inside.

Jane steeled herself before she crossed the threshold, as if there were some invisible barrier she had to fight through. She felt Alex's hand touching the small of her back, and turned to look at him.

His face registered more concern than curiosity. He didn't ask meaningless questions like if she was all right, because he could see that she wasn't, but he said in a low voice, "I'm right here."

The words rumbled beneath her breastbone, an oasis of calmness, a source of strength.

The back door opened into the laundry room, which in turn led to the kitchen. Her father sat at the breakfast table, reading the morning paper.

"Hi, Dad," Jane said neutrally. She knew he'd heard their conversation when Mom answered the door.

He grunted but didn't look at her, continuing to read his paper.

"Dad, this is Alex Villa."

He treated her friend like an extension of Jane, simply frowning and nodding curtly to Alex, before returning to his paper.

Yes, he was still upset at the words she'd flung at him the last time they'd spoken, over a year ago. Maybe she was more like him than she realized, because wasn't she still holding a grudge, too?

"Mrs. Lawton, could I use your bathroom?" Alex asked.

"Oh, certainly." She waved toward the hallway.

"I'll show you." Jane led the way out of the kitchen, but she detoured into the extra bedroom that had used to belong to her. She knew her mom still kept some of her brother's old clothes in the dresser, and she grabbed a knit polo shirt that would stretch to fit Alex. She gestured toward the hallway bathroom and whispered, "First Aid kit is under the sink."

He nodded and went to clean his wound.

"Scrambled eggs okay?" Her mom was at the stove, melting butter. It sizzled, and Jane realized how hungry she was.

Years of habit made her look to her father's face for signs of his opinion. He wasn't looking at her, but he wasn't frowning, so she said, "Yes. Thanks, Mom."

"Did you want some coffee?" Her mother nodded toward the coffeemaker on the counter.

Jane retrieved mugs from the cabinet and poured coffee for herself and Alex. By the time she finished, the toast had popped up in the toaster, so she put them on a plate and buttered them for her mom. She took the toast to the kitchen table along with some plates for everyone just as Alex returned from the bathroom. Neither of her parents seemed to notice the different shirt, which was a little snug on his large frame.

She and Alex sat at the table to sip coffee and munch on toast, and her father finally spoke up, without putting down his paper. "You don't have food at your own house?" Implied was the criticism that she had to come to her parents' house to get fed.

Or was she reading more into it than was there? She wasn't about to address her parental issues with Alex here. "Dad, could I use your computer? I have a hard drive I want to access."

"Where's yours?"

"Inaccessible," she replied in the same clipped tone he had used.

The paper lowered so he could regard her with a pale blue eye beneath his bushy gray brows. "What's that supposed to mean?"

"Exactly that, Dad."

"Please." Mom laid a plate of scrambled eggs on the table. "Don't fight."

Jane backed down, and her father went back to reading his paper. She spooned eggs on her toast and finished eating it before saying, "May I please use your computer, Dad?"

He didn't reply.

Jane took a last sip of coffee. "If you'd rather I didn't, we'll just go." She stood up, and Alex followed suit.

"I didn't say that," her father said irritably. He jerked his head toward his office. "Go ahead. You know the password."

Jane suspected that he'd only agreed so he wouldn't look quite so churlish in front of Alex, but she didn't care. She headed to the living room, followed by Alex's silent form, and went through to the hallway. At the end of the short corridor was the open door to his office.

Jane was struck by how much it resembled her dining room table. She'd never noticed before. She and Alex sat at two chairs in front of her father's computer, and she took out the laptop. She shoved some papers and equipment aside to have room to set it on the desk.

He surprised her with a warm hand gently massaging the tight muscles at the base of her neck. He didn't say anything, but his touch was reassuring, pouring cold water on her sizzling temper.

She paused to take a deep breath. She didn't look at him, but she touched his hand with her fingers once. Then she went to work.

She knew where to rummage in her father's desk for his screwdrivers and other small instruments she needed to open up the laptop and remove the hard drive. It was a bit tricky because a few components had been taped down, and she had to remove the tape carefully.

She was just finishing when her father wandered into his office, coffee cup in hand. He peered over her shoulder at the laptop on the desk. "Whose is that?"

"No one you know." Jane lifted the drive from the casing.

"Why are *you* fiddling with it?"

"Alex knew I could handle the security software measures."

He grunted. He'd been in IT until he retired, and his company had often looked to him for computer security questions. "Someone locked themselves out of their computer?"

"I have to bypass the security software or this data will be as good as lost."

"You didn't do something stupid like try to turn it on, did you?"

"No, Dad," Jane said through a clenched jaw.

"Because if there's security software loaded directly into the UEFI, the computer could just connect to the internet to receive instructions. It might erase everything before you get a chance to try to get in."

Which was exactly what she'd told Alex, back in Jorge's tavern. "That's why I removed the wireless adapter, Dad. And the Bluetooth card for good measure."

He peered at the open laptop casing. "You did a messy job removing that Bluetooth card."

Was it her imagination, or was he more critical of her since their argument? For most of her life, she'd have done anything to prove herself to him, to win the same kind of approval that he doled out to her older brother so freely.

But now, more than ever, she was aware of how his criticism felt like hammer blows, knocking her down.

Alex interrupted him. "Mr. Lawton, how's your son doing?" His voice was tight, but polite.

One of Dad's favorite topics. That should keep him off of Jane's back for a little while. She flashed Alex a grateful look for distracting her father.

Dad's voice took on a brighter note. "Jason's company went IPO last year, you heard about that? He and his wife bought a new house in Cupertino."

She hooked up the hard drive to her father's computer and wasn't surprised to see full-disk encryption. However, she had probably bypassed the laptop's tracking software.

Her father listed the specs of a new tablet computer that Jason's company had just released, which probably bored Alex to tears, but to his credit, he kept a politely interested expression on his face as her father talked.

Jane worked steadily. She'd heard about all this from Jason himself. Her brother truly was brilliant, if arrogant, and Jane's relationship with him hadn't been altered by her tension with their father. Jason and his wife had Jane over for dinner once a month or so, and he kept urging Jane to quit her low-paying IT job to write software for his company. Jane had considered it, but the idea of working for her brother had seemed suffocating, as if she were still working for Derek's company, EMRY. Jason would demand everything he could from her—he would use her, like Derek had.

She made a working copy of the hard drive and then started attacking the encryption with various programs and scripts. She didn't look at Alex very often. He mostly sat beside her and listened to her father. But she started to sense the tension in his muscles. His hands clenched and unclenched once or twice. His leg jiggled every so often. When she did glance at him, she noticed the hard line of his jaw.

Was he frustrated at her lack of progress? She couldn't help it. This wasn't a run-of-the-mill laptop used for emails and web surfing. Or was he trying not to be bored to death by her dad's going on about his perfect son?

"You must be proud at how successful Jason has become," Alex said to her father. There was a strange, hard edge to his voice that Jane didn't understand. She glanced at him, but beyond a glitter in his dark eyes and the rigid set of his shoulders, nothing seemed amiss.

Her father chuckled. "He's smart, but he's worked hard, too—"

"Both your children are pretty smart."

Jane winced. Her vertebrae fused together as she tried not to anticipate her father's reply. They were only words.

Dad snorted. "This one doesn't have what it takes to make it in the high tech business." He then noticed when she opened a program she'd written specifically for her work at EMRY. "What are you doing? That program is trying to force a volume to mount."

"I've looked through the visible volume, but I think there's a hidden partition."

"Why aren't you just breaking the encryption?"

"I might lose some data."

"Sure, but the hidden partition will be fine. *If* there is one."

Jane's temper flared. "There's nothing there. If it were me, I would have at least one hidden partition unmounted at all times for my most sensitive data. We need to get everything off this hard drive."

"Why do you ... Wait a minute."

Oh, no. She had said too much.

"What exactly are you doing?" His voice rose. "I thought you were just trying to help someone who locked themselves out of their computer."

"Dad, I don't have time to explain—"

"You better find time to explain."

"All I can tell you is that it's important." Jane's typing grew harder and faster on the keyboard.

"Important? What kind of trouble have you gotten yourself into?"

"I'm not in trouble."

"No? Then why are you breaking into someone's hard drive?" he roared.

She squeezed her eyes shut in frustration. "There's more to it than that—"

"This is rich, coming from you." His voice had grown hard and vicious. "After all the stuff you spouted about Derek and EMRY. I bet you're regretting your bad decision now."

"It wasn't a bad decision," she said hoarsely.

"Your problem is you think nobody knows better than yourself."

She wanted to laugh and scream at the same time. He'd exactly described himself.

"Blayne," her mother's voice called from the living room. "Your blood pressure ..."

"I'm just telling my daughter what she needs to hear. She's never going to learn if she doesn't hear it straight from someone."

There was an almost audible *snap!* in her head. Never going to learn. It was true. She had been denying it her entire life. She'd thought she could learn how to please him. But the reality was that she would never have his approval. *That* was the lesson she'd needed to learn.

The words shot out of her mouth. "I am not your daughter. I'm some puppy you like to kick around."

There was a horrible moment of silence.

Then her mother's wheedling voice, "Blayne ..."

Jane kept typing, but she heard her father leave his office.

Then the soft words from her mother reached her ears. "Leave her alone. You need to let her make her own mistakes."

Something squeezed hard inside of her. It choked her. She couldn't breathe, but she didn't care.

The slamming of her father's office door made her jerk in her seat. She gasped in a breath, and her heartbeat roared hard and fast in her ears. She twisted around to see Alex locking the door.

"You can't lock my dad out of his own office," she said feebly.

"I just did." He began pacing—more like prowling—in front of the door, his mouth hard and his eyes fierce. "Are you almost done?"

She turned back to the computer. "Sort of. The program did find a hidden partition and I'm running another piece of software to retrieve data from the exposed sectors." Her voice was rising as she babbled. "I'm working as fast as—"

"Jane." His gentle voice and the soft pressure of his hands on her shoulders made her feel as if her heart had cracked open. She swallowed.

And then he was sitting beside her, taking her hands in his. "Jane, I wasn't rushing you. I want to leave because I can't stand listening to him talk to you that way."

She began to tremble, and his fingers pressed harder against her palms.

No one had ever protected her against her father.

"He's not always this caustic," she was forced to admit. "It's only been in the last year that he's gotten like this." Before that, she had always responded eagerly to his instructions, so he had no need to be scornful. But after quitting her job at EMRY, she had become the arrogant, foolish daughter, and so was treated as such. "And I couldn't explain to him about the hard drive, so that frustrated him."

"Don't defend him," he said fiercely, which surprised her. "He's your father. He shouldn't speak to you that way."

Jane realized that Alex's hands were trembling now, too.

The computer beeped, and she pulled her hands away to get back to her work. She blinked at the screen. "I don't understand."

"What?"

"It's done."

"Isn't that a good thing?"

"Sort of ... It took less time than I thought it would." She frowned and double-checked that the software had done its job. "Let's go. I sent the data packets to my secure cloud drive." She started packing up, including the copy of the hard drive that she had made. She spotted a laptop made by her brother's company and grabbed it.

He unlocked the door and they exited the office. Jane said stiffly, "Dad, I'm going to borrow this laptop, if you're not using it?" She held it up.

He barely looked at her. He sat on the living room couch, frowning fiercely, his face a splotchy red. "Fine."

"Thanks. I'll return it."

Neither of her parents said anything as she and Alex crossed the living room to the open doorway into the kitchen.

"Thanks for breakfast, Mr. and Mrs. Lawton." Alex strode into the kitchen and out the back door as if escaping from jail.

Jane hesitated in the doorway, as she had when she first entered the threshold. Her head bowed. She opened her mouth, then closed it. What was there to say? "Bye." She left.

They crossed the field again in silence. Cows were grazing at a distance, and the animals gave them uninterested looks as they climbed over the fence.

She always felt ... efficient when she got into her hybrid car. But today, she remembered her father convincing her to buy it.

She was done pleasing her father.

She should have felt empowered, free. Instead she felt weighted down and unwieldy, like when she'd had to move an old-fashioned tube computer monitor and the large, heavy thing had nearly taken her arms off at the sockets.

As she drove back down the road, he asked, "Are you all right?"

"As fine as I can be." That wasn't true. She felt alone. She felt as if she'd always been alone.

And what had all that gotten for them? "I think there's something wrong with the hard drive."

A vein in his temple pulsed. "Wrong, how?"

"The security on the drive was relatively minimal."

"Maybe he got lazy about security. No one ever expects their computer to go missing."

"Maybe. Or maybe the information on the hard drive isn't as important as we thought." She glanced at him, nervous about conveying her fears. "What if there isn't any proof that the Tumibays set you up? What if there's nothing to convict the Tumibays of any crimes?" She swallowed. "What if all this was for nothing?"

"It's not for nothing." He put strong emphasis on his words, but Jane heard a thread of determination. Or desperation. "What do we need now?"

"I need internet access so we can look at the files on my cloud drive. I thought maybe we could go back to Jorge's tavern to use his internet." She turned onto the main road that led out of her parents' neighborhood.

"No, there will be lots of people at the tavern by now, and we don't know who might belong to the Tumibays." He was silent a moment, then he heaved a sigh. "I know where we can get wireless internet easily. The only problem is that ..."

They were passing a blue Dodge Challenger heading in the opposite direction, and it wasn't until they were almost next to each other that Jane recognized the driver.

The man from the fire escape balcony. And in the passenger seat, the polo shirt man.

6

Jane slammed on the gas.

The Challenger's tires squealed as the two men turned to follow them.

Jane's heart was drumming, her hands on the steering wheel trembled. The hybrid car had no chance against the Challenger. It was only a matter of time before the more powerful car caught up to them.

She had to even the odds.

"Jane, traffic." Alex's voice was tight, his hands white knuckled as he gripped the dashboard. "You need traffic."

There was a large shopping mall nearby. This main road led toward it, but there was also Barclay Road, a narrow, winding road that led to the southeast side of the mall. And she knew a shortcut to it.

Jane made a sudden left turn into a long dirt driveway. The Challenger had been too close, and they overshot the driveway. In the time it took them to swerve and follow them, Jane was nearly at the end of the driveway, coming up to the farmhouse. The car skidded sideways on the dirt as she turned right onto a farm road that would cut her through the farm property to Barclay Road.

The Challenger's engine roared. The men were within a car's length of her back bumper when Jane flew out of the farm road, jouncing up onto the asphalt as she turned onto Barclay Road.

As a teen, she had often loved driving this winding road at dangerous speeds, and she pulled out all the stops now. The road was narrower than a residential street, with sharp turns that rolled up and down. The hybrid caught air as she drove over the top of a rise, crashing down with a bounce that made her teeth clack together.

She didn't want to take her eyes off the road. "Are they gaining on us?"

He had twisted around. "No. But they're not falling behind."

Jane went faster.

Barclay Road finally T-junctioned with Lewis Expressway, a broad road that would take them past the mall and eventually onto the freeway. Jane took a hard right onto the expressway, directly in front of an oncoming minivan. She left the sound of the minivan's horns behind them as she accelerated as fast as the hybrid could handle.

As she had during the escape from her apartment, she wove in between cars aggressively. The expressway didn't have a wide enough shoulder for the Challenger to drive on it to catch up to them. But she needed to lose their pursuers, not just get ahead of them.

She cut sharply across two lanes into a left turn lane, then jammed in front of the oncoming cars. Tires squealed. Car horns blared in a cacophony directly into her ears as they shot down a side road.

"Did they follow us?"

"No, they couldn't. But they'll be trying to find a way back to find us again."

This road led to another residential area, with farms. She remembered that there was one family who had horses—and a large barn.

She took a few turns, including a shortcut through a small orchard, following the dirt tractor trail. She finally saw the barn coming up on her left, and turned into the driveway. The house of the family who owned the property was far enough away from the barn that they wouldn't notice if she parked behind it, which would hide their car from view of the road.

When Jane turned off the engine, she gasped as if she hadn't taken a breath the entire frightening time.

"You're okay." He clenched her hand in his. "You did great. They weren't behind us from the moment you made that left turn."

His touch was hot, spreading warmth down her hands, into her wrists. She unclamped her fingers from around the steering wheel, and he let go.

She massaged her cramped fingers. "How did they find us?"

"I think this was by accident. They were heading toward your parent's house."

"But I thought they might have already been watching the house."

"Maybe we gave them too much credit. It might have taken them this long to guess you might go to your parents' place. Or maybe they did have someone in front of their house, and those two were coming to relieve them."

Jane heaved a sigh and leaned her head back against the head rest. "We need a new car."

"We need to look through the data you pulled from the hard drive. And I think I know where we can do both."

Alex looked around, making sure there was no one in sight as he and Jane crossed the strip of forested land between the neighboring farm's access road and the east edge of his brother's property. The nearest greenhouse lay only a few yards from the tree-line.

They approached the frosted door, and he gasped the handle. It turned easily in his hand.

"You said this was dangerous?" Jane asked him as they entered the greenhouse.

"Not for us, for me." He sighed heavily. "My brother is going to kill me."

Edward stood leaning against a stainless steel gardening table, arms crossed, his face like thunder. Luckily, Mama was nowhere to be seen.

Edward noticed him looking around. "Don't worry, I didn't tell Mama."

"Praise God for small blessings."

Edward spotted Jane, and his grim expression softened. He came forward to kiss her cheek. "Hi, Jane. Are you all right?"

"I'm fine." Even with little sleep, her smile for his brother was wide, and her eyes turned to amber in the sunlight slanting through the glass panes on the roof. She was still a little pale from her ordeal with her father.

While at her parents' house, Alex had had to fight to keep his big mouth shut in order to be respectful, but he'd wanted to jump up to defend her every time the man grated out yet another harsh observation of his daughter, another worshipful tidbit about his son. The man was toxic, and while he might have gotten worse only in the last year, as Jane had said, there was something about his manner to Jane that made it obvious that he was rarely complimentary.

Alex's father had not been kind, and he had been stubborn, but he had rarely been cruel. Alex couldn't imagine what that kind of relationship had done to Jane's self-esteem. Maybe that was also why her faith had seemed to have become lukewarm lately.

"You're lucky I don't give you a thrashing," Edward said to him.

"What do you mean? I left a message on your phone yesterday."

"'I don't know how long I'll be gone, don't freak out if I don't answer my cell phone, and protect Mama'? You call that a message?"

Jane bit her lip to hide her smile, and the shadow of a dimple appeared in her left cheek.

"All this after you'd been arrested a few days ago," Edward continued. "Your communication skills suck, bro."

"I was distracted," he said. "I was trying to lose a tail."

Edward's dark brows slammed down over his eyes. "You better explain that."

He told him everything, which only made his brother more and more alarmed.

"You got shot? Why didn't you tell me that when you called?" Edward stepped forward, scanning Alex's body. "Where?"

He winced as he eased off his jacket, then rolled up the sleeve of the borrowed shirt. "Grazed me."

Edward wasn't so blasé. "You idiot. That needs to be taken care of. Stitches, or—"

"I will." He'd been shot before on more than one occasion, and although his arm hurt, this wasn't as bad as some other wounds he'd had. He needed stitches, but he also knew he could get away with waiting before he had it looked at. He'd used butterfly bandages to close the wound, which had stopped bleeding, at least.

Jane said, "I just realized there are at least two bullet holes in the walls of the IT office at my workplace."

"Maybe your coworkers won't notice?" Alex said.

"You're going to tell Detective Carter all about it," Edward said firmly. "I don't understand why you didn't speak to him about this first."

"His superiors are not happy that he defended me," he said. "I didn't want to involve him until I had proof that I was innocent."

"Because everything you've done so far has made you seem above suspicion?"

"Alex wasn't the one coming after us with guns," Jane said quietly.

Edward sighed, then tapped the computer lying on the table next to him. "I brought my laptop, as you asked."

"Good. Jane has another one, so we can both look through the data from that hard drive."

"There's WiFi here?" Jane looked around the greenhouse. It was only partially filled at the moment with the last of the latest Malaysian basil crop that Edward and Alex were growing for Rachel Grant. It certainly didn't look like an internet cafe.

"All the greenhouses have WiFi," Edward said. "The buildings have security and sensors, and Alex helped me install soil sensors for the plants. We needed WiFi to be able to monitor them all with our computers." Edward hesitated, then said, "Is there anything else I can do?"

"Do me a favor," he said, "and don't tell—"

"I won't tell Mama," Edward said. "But just ..." His mouth tightened, and his expression was anguished. "... Just fix this. Soon."

He nodded.

Edward cleared his throat and clumsily waved a hand toward a paper sack on the table. "I made you sandwiches, and there's bottled water and a thermos of coffee."

"Thanks." His head was starting to whirl from lack of sleep. He'd be glad for food and more caffeine. He hadn't been able to eat much at Jane's parents' house.

"Have you slept at all?"

"After the car chase, since we were out of sight of the road, we napped in the car for a couple hours." Then they'd been awakened by the farmer whose land they were parked on, demanding they leave his property.

Edward's cell phone beeped once, and he glanced at it. "I have to get back to work." Edward gave him a long, steady look, then left the greenhouse.

He grabbed two stools and set them at the gardening table. The greenhouses were all equipped with electrical outlets which had covers to protect them from water when there wasn't anything plugged in, so they had power for the laptops. After he had connected them to the WiFi, Jane told him how to access her cloud drive, and divided up the data she'd retrieved from the hard drive.

They worked in silence for a few minutes. He glanced at her intent face a few times. Finally he said, "Did you want to talk about it?"

"No." Her jaw tightened briefly.

"Jane, you can't pretend you don't feel anything." He had learned that lesson very well.

"It's none of your business. You shouldn't have witnessed that in the first place."

"I think I witnessed that for a reason. I think I understand better than you realize."

She sighed, bowing her head and rubbing her forehead with her fingers. "He's not normally like that. It's only been for the past year."

She had mentioned that before. "What happened last year?"

Her face hardened, and her voice was hollow as she said, "I quit my job, and Dad thought it was a bad idea."

"Why did you quit? You loved your job."

"It didn't love me." There was something odd in her tone as she said that. Something bruised.

"Jane—"

"Alex, just leave it alone."

"Look, I get it. I get not living up to your father's expectations." He couldn't stop his hands from clenching as he said it. After all these years, it still stabbed at him like a broken bone that wouldn't heal properly.

Jane had stilled. The silence hung between them like the heavy chill at the bottom of a canyon. Finally she whispered, "It never occurred to me that you and Edward never talk about him."

"The last time I spoke to my father, was an argument the week before I got arrested."

"But ... he died after you got out of prison."

"Don't get me wrong, he had every reason to yell at me. I ran with a bad crowd. I'd been bullied in grade school, so when I filled out, I vowed to protect anyone else who got bullied, but some of them were into things I should have avoided. After high school, I got even worse. That's what Papa and I argued about."

He could still hear the thundering of his father's voice, shuddering off the walls of the low-ceilinged living room. He heard Mama's pleas. Papa's normally immaculate work suit had become rumpled with the force of his anger.

"But when you became a Christian in prison ..." Jane's face was utterly confused.

"I went to him. I apologized. I told him I was a different person." His father's face had been stone. He hadn't looked at Alex. The silence had been unbearable, and Alex had finally left. "But he couldn't forgive me for the shame I'd brought on the family. On *him*."

Her small hand reached out to cover his. The feather-light touch was like the striking of a gong, causing a deep hum throughout his body.

"When he was in the hospital, he still wouldn't speak to me. And then he died."

Jane didn't try to tell him that his father had loved him. She understood how impossible that could be to believe.

"He was disappointed in me. He simply didn't care about Edward," he said. "He abandoned both of us emotionally. So Edward and I found a father's love in God, instead."

Jane withdrew her hand and turned her face away from him. "I feel like God has abandoned me. And don't try to tell me that He hasn't, because it really feels like He has."

She sat stiffly on the stool, self-contained, brittle, and alone. He wanted to reach out to her, but he could sense that if he did, she might shatter. And he'd lose any chance at helping her.

Then words tumbled out of his mouth, and he didn't understand why he said them. "Sometimes when we feel alone, we're really not. We just can't see Him behind us."

She wrapped her arms around herself and didn't answer.

"Jane, I'll be here for you." He realized how deeply he meant it. He had always liked her, always been attracted to her, but seeing her strength in the face of stress and danger made him see how amazing she really was. "And I know you don't want to hear this, but God is here for you, too. He won't turn away from you."

"He already did." She heaved a long breath that sounded like dry leaves rattling in the orchard. "I don't want to talk about it."

He had to be content with that. *Lord, only You can convince her of how intensely You love her, of how she's not alone.*

Jane turned back to her computer. "Let's just get back to work."

It was true, he needed to clear his name. He needed to stop the Tumibays from gaining a foothold here in Sonoma. But now, repairing his reputation was no longer as important as repairing the pain he'd seen in Jane's eyes. When this was over, he had to show her how her father was wrong.

Nothing. There was no evidence that the Tumibays had set Alex up.

He had been so sure there would be something. It might not have been front and center, but it would be there. But the hard drive didn't mention anything about Alex or even the Sonoma operation. It was all banking information and shipping records. "This is everything from the hard drive?" he asked her.

"I think so." Jane rested her forehead in her hand as she stared at her laptop. "I found that hidden partition. I thought for sure there would be something in it about the money they wired to your bank account."

"There's plenty of bank accounts here, although they're all in code. Can you crack it?"

"It's not my forte. You'd need a forensic accountant to analyze all this banking information in the hidden partition, to see if it's enough to convict anyone. "

"Did you find anything else?"

"He uses a secure cloud server for his email, so I don't have the actual messages on this computer, but I can see notes he's made to himself about messages he's sent. He doesn't email many people at all, and the ones he does email, he refers to by code names."

"What names?" He moved toward her and looked over her shoulder.

"Emeril is the one he emails the most."

He gave a bark of laughter. "Not very original. I'll bet that's the bald guy I saw at the meth lab, the one cooking the drugs."

"How can you be sure?"

"I've known lots of different drug gang members. A lot of them call their chemists 'Emeril.'"

"Then there's this one, Oyster."

He felt a bubbling in his chest, like a pot about to boil over. "That's the Tumibay captain in charge of the drug operations here in Sonoma. He's referred to as Talaba, although I'm not sure if that's his real name. It means oyster in Tagalog. Any other names? Maybe this accountant emailed Tumibay officers in San Francisco."

"He emailed four other people, and he refers to them as Sleepy, Dopey, Happy, and Doc."

He groaned. "Practically every gang on the planet has members with names from the Seven Dwarves."

"There's one other name." She clicked a few folders. "It wasn't in the hidden partition, it was a memo in the outer volume. I didn't pay much attention at first because the accountant wrote it all in code words, and since it was in the outer volume, there's a good chance it's not very important. But it's the only memo with a first and last name mentioned."

She pulled up a document. "It's about payment for delivery—he refers to it as a shipment of Thighbusters."

He had to swallow a laugh. "Seriously?"

Jane shrugged. "At the bottom is a bunch of notes to himself. One is to remind himself to ask Jejomar Babingao about delivery schedules."

He straightened. "That's not a nickname or a code name. That's a real name."

"It is?" Jane clicked through and started searching for it online. "Filipino?"

"Yes."

"For everything else he used code names. He must have overlooked this one. That's probably also why it was in the unprotected outer volume."

They actually found the man on Facebook. His page was in Filipino, but Jane put it through a translation program. He worked as a customs officer for a small shipping port in the Philippines.

Shipping from the Philippines. "Jane, you hit the jackpot."

"I did?"

"The main ingredient for meth production is ephedrine. It comes from the *ma huang* plant. Most gangs get ephedrine from Mexico, but some still smuggle it in from the Philippines."

"So this man might be involved in supplying the ephedrine for the Tumibays?"

"The FBI can follow him back to the ephedrine supply in the Philippines. We could cut off the Tumibays' drug production at the knees."

Jane frowned at him. "But even if we give this information to the FBI, this Tumibay captain has already destroyed your relationship with the Sonoma police. This information won't necessarily change that."

He hadn't realized how much he enjoyed working with Detective Carter until it was gone. He had always been friendly with people, but with Detective Carter's support, he had been able to use his friendships to help the community. To protect people. He liked doing that.

He enjoyed working with his brother and on his mother's farm. He enjoyed the physical work, even though it was tiring, and they were fortunate that they made enough of a profit to be able to hire help so the work wasn't so backbreaking.

But his work with the Sonoma PD had slowly become as much a part of his life as his other jobs.

Except that it didn't define who he was. And if he had to give up his work with Detective Carter in order to keep firm in his own personal integrity, that's what he'd do.

"My reputation isn't worth anything to me if I don't do what I can to protect this community," he said slowly. "But we're still in danger. The Tumibay captain—the oyster guy—and the accountant will still be after us because of what we know. They might have a mole in the Sonoma PD. They'll threaten our families to get to us."

She studied him, and seemed to know what he was thinking, because she said, "It's not your fault that my family and I are in danger."

But it was.

"So what do we do?" she asked.

"If that guy in the polo shirt and glasses is the accountant, he doesn't strike me as being very loyal. If we get to him, he might flip on the Tumibay captain in charge of the meth operation in Sonoma, the Oyster."

Jane shook her head. "From what he said to me at my workplace last night, he's not stupid. He reminds me ..." She gave a small sigh. "He reminds me of my brother, actually. Smart and arrogant. I don't think we should assume he'll turn on his captain. We need something that'll bring both of them in."

"Then let's play to the weaknesses of a smart but arrogant man. He still wants the hard drive."

Jane started clicking on windows on her computer. "I looked at the coding for the tracking software he had on the hard drive. I think I can alter it so that if he hooks the hard drive up to another one of his computers, it will alert one of our laptops with its location."

"But that doesn't help us also get the Oyster."

She looked up at him, speculation shining in her eyes. "I think I know how to get them both."

In the end, it wasn't very dramatic. Jane walked up to a car parked outside her apartment and knocked on the window. She leaned against the car frame to hide her trembling knees and told the startled Filipino man who sat inside, "I want to talk to your boss."

Alex hadn't wanted her to do this, but she'd convinced him. What choice did they have? They had reached the point where their backs were to the wall. The accountant wanted three things—the hard drive, Jane, and Alex.

Jane would guess that he'd be happy to take two out of three.

The two men took the messenger bag from her before they shoved her into the back seat of the car. The smell of garlic and onions made her gag. One of them telephoned someone, speaking rapidly in Filipino, as the driver headed out of Sonoma.

They didn't bother to blindfold her. They apparently didn't care that she saw where they were taking her.

Jane closed her eyes and tried not to panic at the implications of that.

It seemed they drove for a long time, past vineyards and fields, and finally down a deep gully. The only people they saw on the road were a few bikers in black leather and a lunch wagon on its way back from the midday business.

As they drove down a deeply rutted dirt track into the foothills, the wind in their faces carried the acrid scent of ammonia. Jane coughed and breathed through her mouth. Soon the road ended next to a mobile trailer. Several yards away from the trailer sat a generator and a folding table with computer equipment.

Glasses Man sat at the table, typing at another laptop, but he stopped when he saw the car. And when he spotted Jane, he smiled.

Jane shivered.

As she got out of the car, she said, "I want to make a deal." The chemical odors from the meth lab made her cough again.

"Of course you do."

The driver handed Glasses Man the messenger bag, and he dug out the laptop casing. "You did quite a hack job on this." He set it on the table.

He next removed the laptop Jane had borrowed from her father, flipping it back and forth in his hands. "This looks like it's one made by your brother's company. I think I'll keep this."

In the side pocket of the messenger bag, he found the hard drive and the wireless adapter and Bluetooth card Jane had removed from his laptop. There was nothing else.

He stared hard at Jane with black eyes glittering. "I know you made a copy of the hard drive. It's what I would do."

Jane stared back at him, and her jaw grew tight.

"I'm sure you don't want me to ask one of these men to search you for it."

She couldn't stop the shudder that passed through her. She reached under her shirt and pulled it out from where it had been lying between her waistband and lower back. "I want to meet with your captain. I want to work for him."

"And why would he want to hire you?" The man nodded to the two who had brought Jane there, and they got back in the car. In a swirl of dust and dead leaves, they executed a three point turn and left.

The grit and heat were starting to make Jane sweat even more. She moved from the patch of direct sunlight into the shade of a bedraggled oak tree, near the folding table. "Look and see what I did. Your full-disk encryption wasn't very encrypted."

He gave her a long look. For the first time, she noticed how young he was—her age, perhaps. He had thick dark lashes that made his eyes look like they had on eyeliner.

CAMY TANG

"Why not?" He called something guttural to the trailer, and a skinny young man—barely more than a teenager—exited the lab. His dark eyes fell on Jane with a sort of hunger that had her involuntarily taking a step back. "Happy, keep an eye on her while I work."

The young man gave Jane a feral smile, and he casually pulled a handgun from the back of his jeans. He didn't point it at her. It hung almost carelessly from his twitching fingers.

Glasses Man sat at the folding table and plugged the copied hard drive into his computer.

"What's your name? Let me guess. Doc?"

"Farmboy." He gave her a bland smile. "I bring home the bacon."

Alex had probably been right. This was an accountant for the gang.

Farmboy studied the computer, and his smile widened. "I see you didn't find the second hidden partition."

She couldn't stop the surprised twitch of her shoulders.

"You're really not as smart as you think you are. Why are you even bothering trying to play with the big boys?"

Different voice, same words. But this man wasn't her father, and she no longer cared about trying to please her dad, or any man, because none of them would ever be pleased with her. It seemed she tried so hard, and she always fell short. Why bother?

But wasn't that just fulfilling what her father had always said about her?

Farmboy laughed as he looked at the code on his screen. "Oh, that's cute. You altered the tracking software. No wonder you wanted me to look at this hard drive. Too bad there isn't a random wireless internet signal out here." He swept a hand at the twisted trees and scrub brush of the wilderness around them. "Meth labs tend to annoy the neighbors, so we had to go out a little far from civilization."

She clenched her jaw at his tone.

He feigned surprise. "Did you really think that would work? While I do have wireless internet, it has security to prevent computers from hopping on. Duh. And you really thought you could work for my boss?"

The sound of a car—no, two cars coming up the pitted road drew her attention. And then she recognized the truck in front.

Oh, no. It wasn't supposed to happen like this.

The man from the fire escape balcony drove Edward's truck, which Alex had been using. Behind him was the Challenger, driven by another man. Where was Alex?

The driver got out of the truck and lifted a hand in greeting, and Happy returned the gesture.

"Where is he?" Farmboy demanded.

The driver opened the back door to the truck cab and hauled on something heavy. Alex slid off the back seat and fell into a heap on the ground. He grunted and stirred, and Jane saw the purple bruising already starting to form around his eye. His hands had been duct-taped together.

"He was trying to follow her." The driver nodded toward Jane.

Farmboy nodded. "Thought he might."

"Let me talk to your captain," Jane said. "We can still make a deal." She had to stall. This was not going the way they had planned it.

"What do you possibly have that I would want?" Farmboy gave a short laugh. "You delivered yourself to me like a Thanksgiving turkey."

"Can I eat her?" Happy leered at her.

"Go ahead and try," Jane shot at him acidly.

A growl came from Alex's form, and he sat up with a wince. "Didn't expect that to happen," he muttered.

"You're not as good a driver as your girlfriend," jeered the driver of the Challenger.

"But you're just as stupid," Farmboy said. "I looked up the make and model of your brother's truck as soon as I figured out who you were. We've been watching for it."

Jane eyed Happy's gun, then Alex's slumped figure. Nothing was going the way Alex said it would.

Alex looked up at her from where he still sat in the dirt. "Just do it."

Farmboy spun to face her. "Do what?"

Jane glared at Alex. What was he doing?

Farmboy grabbed her shoulders and shoved her back against a tree trunk. The sharp edges dug into her spine. "Do. What."

Jane closed her eyes and exhaled. Fine. She'd do it. "It's already done."

Farmboy slammed her against the tree again, blowing the air out of her lungs. Her heart was racing like an engine.

She had to gasp a few breaths before she could speak. "The laptop."

He stared at his laptop, which sat there innocuously.

"Mine," she said.

Farmboy strode to the table and flipped open her brother's laptop. The screen was flashing, while code scrolled up the screen.

"What?" He slapped the keys. "What's it doing?"

Then the code scrolling on the screen abruptly ended, and a cursor blinked next to the words, "BAILE cloud server hacked. You lose."

Within a few seconds of him opening the laptop, it suddenly went dark.

Farmboy rushed at Jane, his fingers biting into her shoulders. Happy grinned and raised his gun, and then there was the sound of guns being drawn by the other two gang members, as well. "Hey, hey!" Alex said.

From the mobile trailer, a tall man with a shaved head emerged, also holding a gun.

"Calm down or you'll never know what happened." Alex had risen to his knees, his hands still taped together, which contrasted with the ring of authority in his voice.

Farmboy's face was close to Jane's. Anger had drawn harsh lines against his mouth, alongside his nose. His breath was hot and foul in her face.

"If you hurt her, you'll never find out what she did." Alex's voice sounded reasonable and confident. "And I sure couldn't tell you."

If they got out of this alive, Jane was going to kill him. Or even worse, tell everything to his mama, and let *her* kill him.

Farmboy shoved Jane once more, but stepped back. Happy sighed and dropped his gun, and the others did, as well.

"I hacked your cloud server." Jane's throat was dry, and she swallowed.

"I know that," Farmboy bit out. "What did you do to it? How did you do it?"

"I knew you had secure WiFi at the other meth lab, because I saw the network connection on the laptop Alex stole, although I figured you'd change the password. But your second laptop would be connected to the internet, and if I could get your guys to bring me to you ..."

Farmboy paled. His lips barely moved as he said, "What did you do?"

"I uploaded a virus that hit my workplace a few weeks ago. They're all insurance guys so they weren't very cautious about spammy emails. I altered the virus." Jane licked her lips. "It's being sent specifically to your captain."

Farmboy backhanded her across the mouth. Pain shot up her jaw as if it had been disconnected, and she tasted blood. She'd bitten her tongue.

"Hey!" Alex had climbed to his feet.

The driver of the Challenger shoved his gun in Alex's face. "Get back."

"The virus," Farmboy said to her.

Jane spat out some blood. "It'll email everyone in your captain's address book, except I altered this one to carbon copy the Sonoma police department on all those emails. So the Sonoma PD will see every person your captain has ever contacted." It hurt for her to talk.

Farmboy whipped out his cell phone, and within seconds he was talking to someone in Filipino. He repeated himself earnestly a few times, then his brow clouded in confusion.

Was it enough time? Had her program worked?

Finally he hung up the phone, then stalked to Jane. "He didn't get an email. You didn't do anything."

"Of course not—"

He drew back his hand. Alex yelled, "Hey!"

Jane cringed and quickly said, "Of course I can't hack into your cloud server ... But I can make it look like I can."

"What?"

"I didn't need to meet with your captain. I just needed you to call him." She nodded toward his hand, holding his cell phone. "I noticed your wireless was secure, but your bluetooth wasn't. My computer just hacked your phone and got your captain's cell number. The police will track him in a few minutes."

Farmboy's lips pulled back in a snarl. He strode to Happy, grabbing his gun, but suddenly stopped at the sound of a shotgun being primed.

"Drop the guns," said a deep voice with a Hispanic accent.

Jane hadn't expected them to have gotten so close to the camp. She turned to see Alex's friends with rifles and shotguns closing in on them. One had snuck up on the driver of the Challenger. With the man's rifle pressed to the back of his head, the driver dropped his gun away from Alex.

Farmboy circled around, his mouth open. "What the—"

"There's exactly twelve of us," said a tall man with a cowboy hat who had appeared from behind the mobile trailer. "Counting you five and the two guards you stationed on that ridge behind us, we've got you outnumbered."

Within seconds, all of them were disarmed and Alex's friends began tying them up with the zip ties they'd brought with them. Farmboy started cussing in Filipino as he was tied.

Jane's hands began to shake, and she clenched them together.

It was over.

"Are you all right?" Alex was in front of her, his hand not quite touching her face.

Her cheek felt hot, and it throbbed. "What were you thinking?"

"What do you mean? It went off without a hitch. Sort of." He winced.

"You weren't supposed to get caught." Her legs were starting to shake, too. She sank down onto a chair by the folding table.

His hands closed over her shoulders. His look was serious. "I wasn't about to let you walk in here by yourself."

"I was afraid for you."

He touched the puffiness at the side of her face. "If I hadn't been here, they might have hurt you even worse."

"But I knew your friends were here."

The truth hit her with a thud of her heartbeat. She'd been nervous. She'd been afraid for Alex. And she certainly hadn't liked being knocked around. But she hadn't felt alone. Because the entire time, she'd never been alone.

She knew there was something there that she would need to think about later.

"Detective Carter's on his way," said a voice in Spanish.

Jane saw Jorge clambering over brush and rocks from behind where the Challenger was parked on the pitted road.

"Jorge, you were supposed to stay in your lunch wagon," Alex said to him in Spanish. "Adelita's going to kill us."

"So is Detective Carter. I think he didn't like us cowboys doing his job."

"His job?" The man with the cowboy hat, a rancher named Emory Valdez, had an innocent expression. "We saw our good friend Alex being kidnapped by these guys and followed him to rescue him. Not our fault they drove up to a meth lab."

Meth lab. Funny how she couldn't smell the fumes anymore. Her head felt as big as a basketball. Stars began to crowd the edges of her vision.

She didn't remember hitting the ground.

8

Jane was alone again. She really shouldn't be surprised.

The rest of the day was a blur. She had woken up lying on the ground with Alex yelling at her. So she'd yelled back—or more like whispered back—for him to keep his voice down.

Detective Carter arrived within minutes. Paramedics arrived half an hour later, but by then Jane had moved to sit on a rock far away from the toxic gases of the meth lab and was feeling better. She was relieved when the paramedics dressed Alex's gunshot wound.

At the police station, Alex's mama had yelled and cried and hugged him and scolded him. She also spent a lot of time alternately poking at and then crying over his gunshot wound. His mama had cried and hugged Jane, too, and her embrace had smelled like apricots and pies. Jane hadn't wanted to let her go.

Detective Carter was dating Jane's Aunt Becca, and so all of Jane's cousins came to the station to make sure she was all right. Maybe to make up for the fact that her own parents were absent.

But Alex and his family had gone back to their farmhouse. Jorge and Adelina and Alex's friends—neighboring ranchers, farmhands, and farmers—had gone home after giving their statements. The Grants had gone back to their mansion outside of Sonoma.

Jane entered her empty apartment and began to cry.

She shut the door quickly, but her legs failed her and she slid to the floor. It was just the shock. She was responding to the stress of the past two days.

No. She was crying because Alex had been trying to tell her something, and she'd turned away. God had been trying to tell her something, and she hadn't wanted to hear.

Hadn't God failed her? Hadn't He allowed Derek and then her father to rip gigantic holes in her chest?

Why had He allowed these people to hurt her?

But He hadn't allowed Farmboy to kill her. Their desperate plan had worked. Detective Carter had said they had picked up the Tumibay captain, the Oyster, within an hour of the accountant's phone call to him.

Jane and Alex were safe.

She rubbed her cheek and jaw, still sore from the blow Farmboy had given to her. Safe, but not unscathed.

They had done a good thing today. That was worth a blow to the jaw.

She grudgingly admitted there was good that had come out of her pain from a year ago. She had broken the chains of her father's disapproval. She had discovered Derek's lies and left EMRY.

With all these things that should free her, why did she feel so alone?

She was cried out. She crawled across the floor to the living room couch, shoved some books and cables off the cushions, and climbed into it.

One of the things that dropped to the floor was her Bible.

It lay in a forlorn heap, pages rippling. She immediately picked it up and smoothed the wrinkles.

Her bookmark was still in place. She'd been reading the Bible in a year when everything happened with Derek and her father, and she hadn't opened it since. It was in Jeremiah, a book she hadn't understood very well at all.

The Lord appeared to us in the past, saying:
"I have loved you with an everlasting love;
I have drawn you with loving-kindness.
I will build you up again
and you will be rebuilt, O Virgin Israel.
Again you will take up your tambourines
and go out to dance with the joyful."

She couldn't stop reading these two verses as she lay curled up on the couch. She was loved. Derek's betrayal and her father's rejection had devastated her because it made her feel so unloveable. But she was loved with a love she was starting to realize she couldn't comprehend.

And that love could heal her. Rebuild her life.

She crushed the Bible to her chest. It was as if she were hiding in a closet and there was a gentle whisper at the closed door. *I am here for you.*

She hesitated, then said, *Come in.*

The Villa farmhouse was loud and warm from the people crowded into it. Jane would normally have felt claustrophobic, but she was happy.

One reason was because she'd finally tasted Alex's mama's cooking, and she wanted to move in so she could have that amazing food every single day. At the moment, everyone was waiting for the apricot *empanada* pies to come out of the oven, and the buttery scent of their crusts was filling the house.

Another reason was because she had a chance to thank each of Alex's friends, his own personal cavalry, who had helped last week to take down Farmboy and his associates. Some of them had known Alex in prison. Some were friends of the Villa family. They all had been glad for the chance to help stop the Tumibays.

And a third reason was because she'd had her last day at work today. As of tomorrow, she was making a go of her own business, and the party tonight was an appropriate send-off.

Throughout the evening, she hadn't had much time to speak to Alex, but now he pulled her away from staring at the oven. "The *empanadas* will come out soon. I want to show you something." He grabbed a quilt from the couch before leading her out the back door.

The motion-sensing floodlights turned on as soon as they stepped off the back porch into the yard. Fruit trees lined the yard on three sides, and half the yard was taken up by his mama's vegetable garden, where the shapes of kale and leeks were gilded by the light.

He led her to a trellised bench set in the far corner. Grape vines had been trained into the lattice, and they were just starting to mist with green from new leaves.

They sat, and he draped the quilt over them both. "Edward built this for Mama. I trained the grape vines."

"Do you get grapes?"

"Yes, but they're sour." He made a face, and she laughed. "I have great news. Detective Carter said that they managed to unmount that second hidden partition on the laptop, and it had all the information on how the accountant was going to set me up. I am officially cleared of suspicion."

She squeezed him tight. "I know that was bothering you."

"They also found the name of a police officer who was on the Tumibays' payroll."

Her mouth dropped open. "I know we speculated about the gang having someone at the station who would search traffic cam footage for my car, but it seems so much more awful to find out it was true."

"Detective Carter also said that customs official we found led the FBI to the Tumibays' ephedrine supplier in the Philippines. The gang won't be getting any more of it shipped to the Port of San Francisco."

"That'll stop the meth production?"

"I'd like to think so, but ..." He grimaced. "At the very least, it'll slow things down for them while they search for a new supplier."

"Hopefully Detective Carter will get a bit of break."

"He might try to talk to you later."

"About what?"

"I mentioned how you could have found that second hidden partition in the hard drive so much faster, and that now that you're starting your own contracting business, maybe the Sonoma PD could hire you once in a while."

"I'll take any work I can get. Uncle Aggie has hired me to write new software to integrate the reservations for both the Joy Luck Life Spa and the hotel."

"How was your last day at work today?"

"I said goodbye to everyone, which was sad, but turning in my security badge was ... great." She smiled. "I'm glad they let me give only a week's notice rather than two."

"Are you going to like writing software all the time?"

"It's what I'm best at."

He leaned closer to her. "But is it what you enjoy doing?"

"It used to be. That's why I think it can be, again."

The floodlights switched off, and he said, "Look up."

The clear night sky unfolded over them. It wasn't black, but a deep, deep blue, and the stars looked like they were hanging just over the top of the trellis. She felt his chest expand as he breathed in the night air.

"It reminds me that God is bigger than any of my problems," he said.

"It makes me feel loved," Jane said.

His arm tightened around her.

"I wrote software for EMRY up until a year ago."

"You don't have to tell me," he said.

"Do you want to know?"

He hesitated only a second. "Yes," he whispered.

"My boss was Derek Wallace, and I thought I loved him."

"Is he the one you were dating when we first met?"

"I told you I was interested in him, but we weren't dating. But he gave every indication that he was interested in me. EMRY was a startup, and we worked sixty hours a week together. We wrote a powerful voice recognition software program. Whenever I wrote a piece of code that was especially brilliant, he was affectionate and appreciative. And I kept wanting to please him. You probably know why."

In answer, his hand rubbed her arm.

"We were having a problem with the program, and I had lunch with an old college girlfriend working for a company who makes bluetooth headsets. After I explained what I was working on, she told me about a software engineer at her company who's been working on vocal optimization for their headsets, and how this engineer has found a way to adjust for slurring and incidental throat and lip noise. I told Derek I'd talk to the engineer to ask for any ideas he could give me that wouldn't violate his non-disclosure agreement with his company, but Derek ..." She swallowed. This was still difficult to talk about. "Derek wanted me to offer the engineer money to steal his software from his company and give it to EMRY."

Alex's expression was shocked. "He actually asked you to do that?"

"I refused. Derek was livid. I had thought he ... cared for me, but he said that he only pretended to like me because I was 'smarter' when he paid attention to me."

Alex's muscles had turned rigid. "So he just strung you along like that?"

"It doesn't hurt anymore. That's why I can tell you this. I think it actually hasn't hurt in a long time, but I was in pain for other reasons, and so I didn't notice."

"At least he didn't get the software, did he?"

"Derek went to the engineer himself and got it from him. He used the code to finish EMRY's voice recognition program."

"That's why you left EMRY?"

"I knew it was only a matter of time before Derek fired me, but he wanted to keep using me for my software skills as long as I stayed. Dad didn't want me to quit. That's why we argued. I couldn't stay, because that would be like pretending Derek's behavior was okay. Dad told me essentially to just suck it up. That I was exaggerating. That EMRY was going IPO soon and I'd be stupid to throw away all that money. Dad and I had a huge shouting match, and I walked out and quit EMRY the next day. A few months later, EMRY was bought by Google and my father was livid that I'd been so stupid."

"You weren't stupid," he said.

"I know, but at the time, I doubted myself. Derek wasn't done—I had signed an NDA, so he knew I couldn't say anything about what he'd told me to do, but maybe he was afraid I'd find a way around that. He spread rumors about me to other companies I might have worked for, and the only job I could find was working IT at half what I had been making. I felt so betrayed by everyone, including God. I thought God should have protected me for doing the right thing." Jane took a deep breath, and smelled rosemary and basil. "But it was right for me to leave EMRY, and if I'd gone to another software company, I would still be working for them rather than starting my own business."

She turned her head, rested her brow in the curve of his neck. His skin was warm. "Derek hadn't really loved me, and my father had showed how little he regarded me. This past year, I felt unloveable. And very alone."

"Derek is scum. And your father shouldn't have made you feel that way."

"I'm starting to realize that maybe he did. Because otherwise, I'd still be striving after his approval rather than discovering what God's love really is. I didn't understand God's love, because I'd thought it was like my father's love. But the way God loves me is different. It's real, and it's nonjudgmental, and it's unfailing."

There was a heartbeat of silence, then he whispered, "I love you, too."

She smiled.

He dipped his head and kissed her. His lips were cold, but his kiss was fervent. His hand tilted her face up, then caressed her cheek, her jaw, her neck. He kissed her as if there was nothing else in the world he wanted more, and yet there was also a tenderness as if she was more precious to him than breath.

He pulled back, but his face was still close enough that she could feel the warmth coming off his skin.

"I've never been kissed before," she said.

His smile was bright white, his dimples dark against his tanned cheeks. He kissed her again.

Much, much later, she said, "I want you to come car shopping with me tomorrow."

He gave her a curious look. "Okay ... Why the sudden urge?"

"It was Dad who convinced me to get the hybrid."

Alex grinned at her. "What car did you really want?"

"What I'm going to get tomorrow. A Mustang. Cherry red."

He leaned in for another kiss. "Why am I not surprised?"

Connect with Camy

Dear friends,

Thanks for joining me on another adventure in Sonoma, California! I love this small town with a big heart, which is also a popular destination for tourists.

Those of you who have read my Sonoma series will recognize Jane and Alex, who were minor characters in *Formula for Danger*. They were both so fascinating to me, with Jane's scarring and relationship with the Grant sisters, and Alex's painful past. They also seemed to have a bit of chemistry in *Formula For Danger* which I couldn't explore since that was Rachel and Edward's story, so I knew I had to give Jane and Alex their own story.

If you enjoyed this book and you'd like to know each time I have a new release or a sale on one of my books, you can sign up for my newsletter (eepurl.com/qT7ZD).

I love to hear from readers! You can email me at camy@camytang.com. I post about knitting, my dog, knitting, tea, knitting, my husband's coffee fixation, knitting, food, oh and did I mention my knitting obsession? at my blog (blog.camytang.com/) and Facebook page (https://www.facebook.com/CamyTangAuthor). I hope to see you all there!

Camy

Necessary Proof is book #4.1 in my Sonoma series, however each book can be read alone.

Sonoma series:
#1 Deadly Intent
#2 Formula for Danger
#3 Stalker in the Shadows
#4 Narrow Escape
#4.1 Necessary Proof (novella)
#4.2 Unshakeable Pursuit (novella)
#5 Treacherous Intent
#6 Gone Missing

You can find out more information at my website, http://www.camytang.com/.

UNSHAKEABLE
PURSUIT

Book 4.2 in the Sonoma series

Camy Tang

1

"Are you Doctor Geoffrey Whelan?"

Geoffrey looked up from the chart of the ten-year-old boy he was perusing. The woman approaching him wore nurses' scrubs, but they weren't the colorful, cartoon-speckled ones of the other nurses at the Sonoma Free Children's Clinic. Instead, they were a solid washed-out gray color that matched the pale color of the young woman's face, with the letters KSN embroidered in red on the pocket. He didn't remember seeing her here at the clinic before.

There was an expensive Rolex watch on her wrist. A graduation present? She was very young, barely out of nursing school. But then again, lately most of the nurses seemed extremely young to him. The events of the past few years had made him feel old.

"Can I help you?" he asked.

The young woman edged closer down the clinic hallway toward him, and he realized that her eyes were wide with ... fear.

"Are you all right?" he asked. "What is it?"

"I have an urgent message for you and Nurse Kinley," she whispered. She glanced behind her, then around him toward the other end of the hallway.

Geoffrey turned, but saw no one. He looked back at the young woman. "You mean Maylin Kinley?"

She nodded.

Geoffrey knew who Maylin was—in fact, he'd first met her years ago when he was doing his residency at the Merlyn Memorial Hospital down in Los Angeles.

He'd been a different man back then.

But Maylin was the same as he remembered her, still beautiful, still wary of him. She had good reason to be.

"What kind of message? Are you in trouble? I can help."

The young woman shook her head with a kind of despair in her tightly closed eyes. "It's you and Nurse Kinley. You have to disappear."

"What?"

The girl gripped his arm with slender fingers, strong and faintly trembling. Her brown eyes pierced him. "You're both in danger. You have to run away. It's the only way you'll escape from them."

Maylin Kinley glared at the harmless green sticky note stuck to the chart of a six-year-old girl who had come into the Free Children's Clinic with a bad cough. The scrawling handwriting on the note was just barely legible: "See G. Whelan if ?s about ABX."

Her coworker, Thea, sighed. "I'd have guessed it was Dr. Whelan just from the sticky note." She pointed to the logo of the Oliver Medical Supply company at the top. "These are new, though. Last week he was using orange sticky notes from Diggle Surgical Tools."

It was a running joke among the nurses that Dr. Whelan preferred leaving notes because he was too snooty to converse with the lowly nurses. Maylin might have believed it of the arrogant Geoffrey Whelan she'd known when she first met him at Merlyn Memorial Hospital in Los Angeles years ago. He'd only paid attention to nurses if they were pretty—everyone else were people he ordered around. A pathetic part of her had been flattered he'd seemed so attracted to her, but even in his flirting, he had that air of condescension that set her teeth on edge. He had seemed to flirt with her even more because she rebuffed him, which made it harder for her to get over her attraction to him.

But since he started volunteering at the Free Children's Clinic a few months ago—helping out until the full-time doctor position was filled—she'd noticed that he was different than he had been before. He was still too handsome for his own good, but the past several years had drastically changed something inside him. He still clipped out orders in that low, confident voice, but he no longer flirted and he'd lost that condescending tone.

Perversely, now that he wasn't paying any attention to her—or any other woman—Maylin found him more fascinating. It seemed as if something haunted him—she could see the shadow of it in his green-streaked brown eyes. It puzzled her. She would have assumed that he'd spent the past few years partying with his doctor friends down in Los Angeles or some other big city.

"I think he leaves these sticky notes to keep us in line," Maylin muttered. Dr. Whelan had been the same way with sticky notes when she worked with him before. Not everything about him had changed.

Thea tilted her head to the side. "Hmm, that's a thought. He's a bit of a control freak."

"Hey, Thea!" An X-ray technician, Laurel, hurried down the hallway toward them. "Felicity and Moira are coming with us tonight, too. I can't wait to try out the new menu at Rock Love ..." Laurel broke off as she suddenly realized Maylin was standing with Thea. Her cheeks went pink.

Thea gave Maylin an uncomfortable glance. Maylin wanted to tell her not to be embarrassed, because she already knew her coworkers thought she was odd. She was used to being the outsider, being alone. It had always been that way with her family, in school, at work. Besides, she had only started working here four months ago, and the women staff in the clinic had already been very good friends long before that.

But Maylin's mouth never seemed to catch up to her brain, and before she could say anything to ease the situation, Thea said in an uncomfortable voice,

"You're welcome to come tonight, too, Maylin. The Rock Love is really trendy."

Was it a music bar? She tried to think of something to say, but the only thing that came out was, "Rock Love?"

"You've never heard of it?" Laurel's surprise was incredulous. "In Napa? Food and wine critics have been raving about it for the last six months."

Yet more proof for these women that she was odd. She didn't keep up with trends—she'd rather bike through the vineyards after work, or spend a weekend up north hiking in the redwood forests.

"No, thanks," she finally managed to say. She wanted to say something about how she appreciated them asking her, but before she could formulate the words, Laurel had left to head back to the X-ray lab and Thea said she had to check on a patient.

In frustration, Maylin peeled off the sticky note from the chart in her hand and crumpled it.

As if in response to her violence to the innocent sticky note, Dr. Whelan's voice sounded from the other end of the hallway. "Nurse Kinley."

She turned quickly to him, hiding the crumpled sticky note behind her back like a child caught stealing from the cookie jar. "Yes, Doctor?"

She had always thought he was handsome, with his angled face and firm mouth. The years had added fine lines to the edges of his eyes, but that only seemed to make him more attractive. She noticed a softening of his expression that hadn't been there when she first knew him. Before, he'd always seemed to be on the verge of a smirk, but now his smile was more genuine. As he drew closer to her, she was again struck by the sadness that shadowed his face.

"Could I speak to you in private for a moment?"

"Certainly." She followed him into the staff break room, an airy space with lots of windows on one wall looking out over the parking lot. A police squad car was pulled up to the curb. Maylin studied it for a moment, noting an officer sitting inside. He seemed to be waiting for something. A police car at the clinic wasn't an everyday occurrence, but it wasn't too unusual, either.

Dr. Whelan gestured for her to sit at one of the small circular tables. "Can I get you any coffee?" He took a step toward the coffeemaker on the counter.

"None for me, thanks."

"You don't mind if I eat, do you?" He went to the refrigerator and removed a container of strawberry yogurt.

Now that she thought about it, she didn't even remember him taking a break for lunch. The nurses had gone on a short break at two, but he'd still been talking to the mother of a boy with a broken clavicle. "Did you get a chance to eat at all?"

He had gotten a spoon from a drawer near the sink and sat down across from her. "Does a Snickers bar count?"

She sighed. "Doctor Whelan—"

"It's just us. You can call me Geoffrey." He looked at her over his container of yogurt with bright eyes, at this moment more green than brown.

She flushed. When they'd first met years ago, he'd half-heartedly flirted with her and she'd rebuffed him easily because she'd disliked his playboy personality. But now, his innocent remark sent her heartbeat blipping erratically.

She'd been alone for too long, that was all. "I hope you're going to eat more than that yogurt." She deliberately didn't say his name, whether Dr. Whelan or Geoffrey.

His expression looked faintly guilty.

She got up and went to the fridge. "I have half a sandwich left over from lunch. Would you like it?"

"If you're sure ..."

As Maylin opened the fridge, she realized she still held the crumpled sticky note in her fist. She hastily dropped it in a nearby trash can and got out her turkey bacon sandwich, wrapped in a paper napkin.

"Thanks."

His smile made faint dimples peep out, and Maylin swallowed, then concentrated on sitting down again without doing something stupid like blushing.

"With my luck, I'd pass out from low blood sugar just as I was treating a child who had diabetes." He dug into the sandwich with gusto.

Maylin tried not to look at him anymore. She was looking at him too much as it was. Her gaze fell on the cop car outside, and saw that the officer was talking in a friendly fashion with two Asian men wearing dark suits and ties. They seemed a little out of place here at this country clinic.

"I had a strange conversation in the hallway a few minutes ago."

That's right, he had needed to speak to her about something. She half-expected him to be annoyed at her inattention, but he wasn't. His face was serious, but also ... confused. "A girl came up to me—no, I suppose she was a young woman. She looked like a student nurse."

Maylin frowned. "But we don't have any student nurses."

"She didn't have the same scrubs as the nurses, either. Hers was pale gray with 'KSN' in red on the pocket. And she wore an expensive Rolex."

Maylin didn't know any nurse who had a Rolex. "Who was she?"

"She didn't say. She just said she had a message for me and for you."

Maylin straightened in her chair. "For me?"

"She said that you and I were in danger."

Maylin blinked at him in surprise for a long moment. Then she realized her mouth had fallen open, and she closed it. "I don't understand."

Dr. Whelan—Geoffrey—shrugged. "I don't either. She said we should disappear, because 'they' were after us."

"Who's after us? And why?" This sounded so ridiculous. She gave a short breath of laughter. "This is a joke, right?"

Geoffrey shook his head. "She looked serious. She looked scared."

Maylin stilled. "What was she afraid of?"

"I asked her, but she didn't answer. She kept looking around as if she didn't want to be seen talking to me. Then one of the nurses entered the hallway and called to me, and the girl turned and left."

"So that's all she said?"

He nodded.

They stared at each other for a minute. Geoffrey looked as puzzled as she did.

"Why would anyone be after us?" she said.

"Your guess is as good as mine." Geoffrey looked away from her. "I've spent the last several years in Japan."

That surprised her. "What were you doing in Japan?"

He hesitated before answering. "Medical missions with a Christian relief organization. After the tsunami."

She stared at him. Volunteer medical relief work was the last thing she'd have expected. "That must have been hard," she said softly. She could only imagine the devastation, the loss he'd witnessed among the survivors.

His jaw clenched, but then he gave a tight smile. "It wasn't so bad."

The way he gave his neutral answer reminded her of her ex, Sebastian, with his iron control over his feelings and over everything else around him. Maylin sat back in her chair, putting distance between them.

Geoffrey hesitated, then added, "I have extended family in Japan, too, so I got to see them quite a bit."

Yes, that made sense. His high cheekbones and something about the shape of his eyes had made her suspect he was part Asian. "What have you done since you came back to the States?"

"I came back to take care of my mom. My brother is an architect, so he's building Mom's house, and I've been helping with that when I'm not volunteering here. I'll have more time to help her when Monica fills the physician position here."

That's right, the nurses had mentioned that Monica Grant, who started this Free Children's Clinic, was some distant cousin of Dr. Whelan. It was one of the reasons Monica had been able to get him to step in so quickly to the vacated physician position.

He cleared his throat. "So whatever that girl was referring to must be something that happened recently, in the four months I've been back in the U.S., but I can't think of what that would be."

She turned her thoughts back to the "threat" against them, away from her unreasonable fascination with Dr. Whelan's history. "The girl said you and me, right? But the only contact we've had has been here at the clinic."

"But there have been hundreds of patients we've both worked with."

"Should we tell the police?" She said it hesitatingly. It seemed like such an improbable story.

"What can we tell them? They'd get a warrant to see our patient records, and it might make the clinic look bad. Monica has had to work hard to get this clinic up and running. I don't want to cause bad publicity, especially when we don't have much to go on."

"I see your point, but it seems wrong to do nothing." She nodded at his half-eaten food. "You should finish that before you get called to another emergency."

He gave a half-smile as he turned back to his lunch, and the laugh lines crinkled at the corners of his eyes. Maylin had to force herself to look away. Hadn't she learned her lesson with Sebastian?

At that moment, one of the triage nurses, Felicity, appeared in the doorway to the break room. "Oh, good, you're both here." She lowered her voice. "There are two FBI agents who want to speak to the two of you."

CAMY TANG

Maylin was so shocked she couldn't speak for a moment, just staring at Felicity. Then she glanced at Geoffrey, who looked as confounded as she felt.

He asked Felicity, "Did they say what they want?"

She shook her head. "They seem pretty impatient. I put them in your office, Doctor."

Geoffrey looked as if he wanted to ask her more, but Felicity was jiggling her foot, and Maylin remembered she was the only triage nurse on duty today. "Thanks, Felicity." Maylin stood. "We'll meet them there."

Felicity nodded and hurried away.

Maylin's stomach curled as she followed Geoffrey to his office. She'd spoken to some of the Sonoma policemen, but never to the FBI. Now, the girl's words to Geoffrey about them seemed more ominous. But maybe the agents could clear up what was going on.

The two men seemed to fill the small office, with their broad shoulders and dark suits. They were the same Asian men in suits whom she'd seen talking to the policeman outside the clinic just a few minutes ago. But something about the way they stood seemed ... rumpled. More casual than she'd have expected from FBI agents. Or maybe she had watched too much TV? But even the policemen who came to the clinic on special cases carried themselves with more uprightness. These agents seemed to almost slouch.

They both flashed their badges. The taller of the two said, "Geoffrey Whelan and Maylin Kinley?" He had a strong Chinese accent.

Maylin's shoulders tightened. Her mom was from Hong Kong, and Maylin was almost positive the accent was Cantonese.

"What's this about?" Geoffrey's voice had a tightness to it. Perhaps he also could sense there was something odd here.

"You come with us. We have a urgent matter to talk about."

Definitely Cantonese. FBI agents were supposed to be American citizens. If he'd earned his citizenship, would he still speak in such broken English? No, there was something wrong here. Should she just outright accuse them of posing as FBI agents? She looked to Geoffrey. He already seemed to sense something was not right, but he also seemed to be sizing up the strength of the two men.

"Why can't you talk to us here?" Geoffrey said.

"Sir, it's private topic."

Geoffrey shook his head. "I'm the only doctor on call today. I can't just leave."

Without warning, the large agent attacked Geoffrey, slamming his head against the wall with a dull thud. Geoffrey crumpled to the floor and didn't move.

Maylin was too shocked to scream. When she moved toward him, the shorter agent grabbed her arm in a painful grip.

He snarled at her, "You come with us now."

Geoffrey hoped his moan wasn't too theatrical as he slowly turned over. His head ached where it had collided with the wall, but he had put up his hands at the last second to absorb some of the force. If the men thought he was more injured than he really was, he could take them by surprise.

The two men were speaking to each other in Chinese. At least, it sounded like Chinese to him. He wished he could understand what they were saying. What did they want with Maylin and himself?

That girl who had warned him had been right. He needed to figure out a way to get Maylin safely away.

"Get up." One of the men kicked his ankle.

Geoffrey peered up and saw the larger man standing over him, but his head was averted from Geoffrey and he spoke to the smaller man, who had a grip on Maylin. Now was Geoffrey's chance, while they were distracted.

He got to his hands and knees, pretending to be shaky. He slid his feet under him in a low, stable stance. He never dreamed he'd actually have to use the mixed martial arts he'd been training in. He bunched his leg muscles, then shot forward, slamming his shoulder at the man's pelvic bone.

His low center of gravity gave him the force to shove the larger man against the far wall. There wasn't enough space in the office for the double-leg take down he'd been trying to do, but the blow seemed to stun the man. While he got to his feet, he looked to the other man, who had Maylin.

But Geoffrey was just in time to see her punch her captor in the throat with her free hand. The man choked, his eyes bugging out of his face.

A massive weight from behind shoved Geoffrey into a wooden bookshelf against a wall. Books fell on his shoulder and back. The Asian man slid to the side of Geoffrey's body, exposing his head. He was a bit too close, but Geoffrey hammered his head with his fists anyway, in short, tight jabs like his coach had taught him. The man grunted and his grip around Geoffrey's torso slackened.

From the corner of his eye, he saw Maylin flinging open the office door. She must have gotten free from the man holding her. Her cries shot down the hallway, "Help! Someone call the police!"

The smaller man said something frantic in Chinese. The larger man straightened and swung a massive fist at Geoffrey's face. Geoffrey arched back and the blow only glanced off his ear.

Then the two men were gone, flying out the open door.

Geoffrey followed. The two men shoved nurses aside as they ran down the hallway, out of the clinic. Maylin lay sprawled on the floor near the wall a few yards away.

"Are you all right?" Geoffrey knelt beside her, automatically checking for blood. As his fingers brushed the bare skin of her neck, his hand tingled. He had never been this close to her before, had never noticed the drifting threads of scent—cherry blossom and pear and redwood forest.

"I'm fine. One of them pushed me as he was running past." She was breathing heavily and her hand shook, but her chin was set at a stubborn angle. She reached up to touch his temple. "How's your head?"

As if in answer, the throbbing suddenly pushed against his eye socket. "I'm fine. I didn't hit the wall very hard."

"You're a lot stronger than you look."

He had to smile at that backhanded compliment.

She blushed fiercely. "I mean ... you punched him like it was nothing."

Geoffrey rubbed his knuckles. He'd become used to the lightweight grappling gloves used when sparring, and when he hit the larger man bare-fisted, he'd felt the blows up his arm. "Since I came back to Sonoma, I've been training at that mixed martial arts gym in town. You reacted pretty well yourself."

She gave a one-shoulder shrug. "I took a few self-defense classes. I had already been planning what I could do when I saw you attack the big guy."

"Can you stand?" He helped her to her feet, and the two of them went to the few nurses who had also been shoved aside as the men made their escape.

A policeman ran into the clinic in less than a minute. "What happened?" He was deeply tanned, with brown hair, and the tag on his uniform said "Malcolm."

"Didn't you see the two men running out of the clinic?" Geoffrey said.

"What two men?"

"They must have run right past you," Maylin said.

"Ma'am, I didn't see anyone." Officer Malcolm spoke in a slightly condescending tone, as if speaking to a crazy person.

"Weren't you parked at the curb?" Geoffrey said. He wouldn't have seen the front door, exactly, but he'd have seen anyone running out to the parking lot.

"No one ran past me," the officer said.

Geoffrey studied him, incredulous. Had he really not seen the two Asian men? How was that possible?

He was about to say something else when he felt Maylin's fingers press into his arm. She gave him a steady look, and he shut his mouth.

They gave their statements to the officer, explaining about how the men spoke with thick Chinese accents, and how one had attacked Geoffrey when he refused to go with them.

"Disgruntled patient?" Officer Malcolm asked in a bored voice.

"We only treat children here," Geoffrey said.

The officer shrugged. "Parent, then."

The policeman had an air about him as if he didn't quite believe their stories, which made Geoffrey's shoulders grow tighter and tighter. It was one of the reasons he didn't tell them about the girl's warning for himself and Maylin.

Geoffrey tried to control his temper and be logical about this. The men had posed as FBI agents, but they hadn't done anything else besides rough him up and shove a few nurses. Everything looked like some men just trying to make trouble. No conspiracy theory or imminent danger to anyone ... except for that mysterious girl.

"Are you two okay?" Officer Malcolm asked. "We can call a paramedic ..."

"We're surrounded by nurses," Maylin said dryly. "We'll be fine."

The officer left to speak to some of the other nurses who had seen the two men, and Maylin said in a low voice, "In your office."

He followed her there, stepping over the books strewn across the floor. "They weren't FBI, I guess," he said.

Maylin partially closed the office door. "They were speaking in Cantonese."

He paused in the act of picking up a book. "You could understand them?" He supposed he shouldn't be surprised. Besides her name, she had an exotic swoop to the edges of her dark eyes, hinting at a part-Asian background. It was similar to the shape of his sister's eyes.

"My mom's side of the family is from Hong Kong," Maylin said. "After the big guy attacked you, they were trying to figure out how to get us out of the clinic without being noticed."

"Did they say anything about why they were trying to kidnap us?"

She shook her head.

"We should tell this to the police—"

Maylin glanced at the half-closed door. "Earlier, I saw those fake FBI agents talking to the policeman in the squad car that was parked outside. They seemed pretty friendly with each other."

"When did you see this?"

"A few minutes before they showed up in your office."

Geoffrey looked out his office window, but his view of the parking lot didn't show the squad car. "Do you know why the policeman was here in the first place?"

"You didn't call the Sonoma PD?" Maylin's brows wrinkled.

"Nope."

The Sonoma police weren't often called here to the clinic, but when they did arrive, they had always been courteous and left Geoffrey with a positive impression of their characters. But this officer had seemed reluctant to believe them, and somehow he had claimed not to see the two Asian men running from the clinic. Was this cop somehow involved with the Asian men?

"That girl who warned you was right." Maylin wrapped her arms around herself.

"She could have been a bit more specific about who's after us and why." Geoffrey nudged at a fallen binder.

"We need to find out more about her," Maylin said, just as Felicity appeared in his office doorway, pushing open the half-way closed door.

"Sorry to bother you, Doctor." Felicity's eyes were bright as she saw Maylin standing there. "The policeman just left."

"Is everyone all right? Those men didn't hurt anyone?" Geoffrey asked.

"We're fine. But we just got a busload of kids—literally. A bus driver accidentally hit a big fallen tree limb and skidded off the road. All the kids came here with minor injuries."

Geoffrey and Maylin headed out to the front area, which was filled with middle-school children, and soon he was immersed in checking scrapes, wrapping sprains, and dealing with a broken foot. The work strangely soothed him, helped him to calm down from the adrenaline rush of dealing with the two fake agents.

Work had always served to focus him. When he had stayed in Japan after the tsunami, the work had helped him stay sane in the midst of all the horrors he'd seen, the tragic stories he'd heard. The loss of his cousin and grandmother had punched a hole in his soul, and nothing he did had helped to heal it. He had thought coming back home would make him feel more anchored, but strangely, he'd only felt more adrift.

He knew this wasn't a way to live, but he didn't know what to do.

He was surprised when Maylin handed him a chart with a green sticky note attached, bearing a message in her handwriting.

"DON'T GO HOME."

Ice water washed down his spine. He looked at her.

Her eyes were dark and serious, but her tone was deceptively light. "Dr. Whelan, how's your mom doing these days?"

He immediately understood what she was telling him. Those men knew their names. They could find their families. Recently his mom and most of his siblings had decided to move back to Sonoma, and he had several second cousins here, too.

"Her house is almost done," he answered, also in that light tone. "All but one of my siblings are living with her there." So she was well protected.

Maylin nodded in a vague manner, but relief flickered across her face.

"Do you have family in Sonoma?" he asked.

She quickly shook her head, then peeled the sticky note from the chart in his hand, crumpling it so no one else could see it. In a more official voice, she said, "This little girl was complaining of chest pains, so I contacted her grandmother ..."

One of the patients was the son of a security guard here at the clinic, and as he spoke to the man about his boy's sprained wrist, Geoffrey got an idea. He had to interrupt his conversation to grab a sticky note from the pad in his pocket to write it down before he forgot, then continued his consultation. Afterward, he went to give the boy's chart to Maylin, but attached the sticky note to it:

"Wait for me after clinic closes. I have a plan."

2

Somehow Maylin felt safer now that the clinic had closed and was empty of everyone except herself, Geoffrey, and the night security guard. She stared out through the slits in the blinds in Geoffrey's office at the deserted parking lot. The summer sunlight was finally fading, and shadows cast long fingers across the asphalt. It would be more obvious if someone arrived who wasn't supposed to be there, especially since the parking lot wrapped around two sides of the building, while the other two sides were surrounded by grassy play areas.

A car's headlights cut through the dusk as it turned from the main road into the parking lot.

"That'll be Monica." Geoffrey got up from his desk.

"No, I think it's the janitor," Maylin said. "It's a white pickup truck."

"Yeah, that sounds like John's truck."

"Wait, there's another car. A blue SUV?"

"That's Monica. She just bought a Jeep Grand Cherokee."

"She got here pretty quick," Maylin said.

"She doesn't live far from the clinic."

Maylin followed Geoffrey to the glass front doors of the clinic, where a woman with dark hair waving around her face headed toward them. Geoffrey went to the nurses' station, a small area with a counter and computers on desks, and disengaged the clinic's silent alarm system. He waved to Monica to let her know the alarm was off.

She waved back as she opened the front doors with her own key, but paused to chat with the janitor, John, who had come up behind her.

"See you later, John," Monica said as the two of them entered the clinic. The janitor nodded to them all in a friendly fashion as he headed through the main doors to the supply closet off the main hallway.

"Hang on, let me reengage the alarm." Geoffrey tapped the code into the alarm panel.

Maylin had a chance to study her boss. Monica dressed more casually than Maylin would have expected of the director of the clinic. She couldn't help comparing Monica's jeans and silk shirt to her sister, a CFO, who always dressed in a power suit even on a visit to her company after hours. And her sister certainly wouldn't know the janitor's name. Maylin had to remind herself that not everyone was as conscious of image as her own family. Still, she smoothed her wrinkled scrubs with one hand as Monica gave Geoffrey a hug.

"Thanks for doing this for me," he said as he released her.

"No problem, cuz." She grinned at him, and then her eyes slid to Maylin. "Maylin Kinley, right? I remember your interview a few months ago."

"Really? I mean, um ... thanks." Maylin's face was on fire. She wished she were as confident and elegant as Monica. As any normal woman, really. She was tired of being such a misfit.

Instead of looking at her strangely, Monica simply smiled at her, a genuine smile that accepted her for who she was.

Maylin felt warm. In a good way. There was just something about Monica that was so different from anyone else she'd ever met. Maylin hadn't really seen it in her interview with Monica, but she could sense it now. It was elusive, something she couldn't quite pin down.

Monica turned to Geoffrey. "So explain to me what you couldn't talk about over the phone. I heard about the police coming to the clinic this afternoon."

Before answering her, Geoffrey surprised Maylin by looking to her first, as if wanting her approval. She nodded to him.

Geoffrey started with the girl who had approached him with her warning. He then told Monica about the two fake FBI agents. "I thought there was something wrong when I saw them. I've met a couple FBI agents, and they didn't carry themselves the way these two men did. These two guys stood like ... gangsters."

"And how would you know how gangsters stand?" Monica raised an eyebrow at him. "Saw a lot of gangsters when you were in Japan?"

"No, but ..." Flustered, Geoffrey frowned at her, but Monica just laughed at him.

Maylin saved him. "I thought there was something wrong when I heard how broken their English was, because I know FBI agents have to be American citizens."

"And then the big guy shoved my face into the wall," Geoffrey said.

Monica's playful attitude disappeared. "What? Are you all right?"

Geoffrey explained what happened, and Maylin added that she had been able to understand their Cantonese conversation. Geoffrey ended with their frustration with the police officer who had responded, and Maylin added how she'd seen the fake FBI agents speaking to the officer beforehand.

Monica looked at them both. "This is really serious. If there are cops somehow involved with those guys ..."

"Isn't Aunt Becca dating a detective?" Geoffrey said. "Maybe she can ask him about that officer."

"They could have just been fooled by those fake agents," Maylin pointed out. "In that case, they were simply ignorant, not involved in anything shady."

"I can call Aunt Becca," Monica began, but Geoffrey interrupted her.

"Actually, I asked you here because I need your password for the security video footage."

"Oh, I get it. You want to see if that girl is on the video."

"We can see who she might have talked to besides me."

Monica led the way to the security office just off of the front lobby. She knocked on the door, which was opened by the guard, Roy.

Monica smiled. "How's your daughter doing? Does she like San Diego?"

"She loves it," Roy said. "She declared her major last week—she's getting her degree in international relations."

Roy shook Geoffrey's hand and said, "Thanks for the recommendation on the short-term missions trip for this summer, Dr. Whelan. My youngest son is applying."

"It's one of the organizations I worked with when I was in Japan," he said. "They'll take good care of your son."

"I know God will teach him a lot and use him, just like he used you," Roy said.

Geoffrey's mouth tightened, and his eyes flickered away. "Your son will enjoy it," he said in a gruff voice.

Monica didn't seem to notice it, but Maylin was puzzled. Geoffrey had said he'd been doing medical missions with a Christian relief organization, so why had the comment about his faith seemed to make him uncomfortable? Not that Maylin knew what she believed, herself.

"Roy, I'm afraid I need to kick you out." Monica nodded at the computer on the desk in the security office. "I need to look at the video from this afternoon."

"Not a problem. I need to do my walkthrough anyway." He grabbed his ring of keys from the desk and headed out the door.

Even with Roy gone, the security office was cramped with the three of them there, but Maylin leaned over to see the screen over Monica's shoulder. Monica logged into the system to access the video files.

"It was the northwest hallway around two o'clock." Geoffrey leaned over Monica's other shoulder, his eyes on the monitor as she searched through the video. "There she is."

The girl who approached Geoffrey almost looked too young to be a nurse, even a nursing student. She had on plain scrubs that showed up light gray in the black and white video. She had a beautiful rosebud mouth and sultry dark eyes, but her movements were furtive, nervous. Fear radiated from her stiff shoulders, her hunched posture. There was no sound, but her conversation with Geoffrey was brief.

"Can you back up and find out when she came in?" Geoffrey asked.

They found her entering the clinic a few minutes earlier. She moved easily through the half-empty waiting room and directly up to Felicity, the triage nurse on duty, as if used to hospitals.

"She didn't even bother talking to the receptionist," Maylin said.

The girl was saying something as she dug out of her pocket a badge and a security card key.

"That badge isn't one of ours," Monica said. "It's the wrong shape."

After looking at the badge, Felicity moved to an empty computer terminal and looked something up. She said something to the girl, who nodded and gave Felicity a smile. Then the girl headed through the main doors into the clinic.

"We have to talk to Felicity to see what that girl said to her," Maylin said. "Something that made Felicity let her walk right into the clinic."

"Where did she go?" Geoffrey said.

Monica switched video files to follow her as she walked down the hallway. She spoke briefly to a nurse, who pointed toward the northwest hallway, probably telling her where to find Dr. Whelan. They again saw her speak to Geoffrey, then Monica switched video files again to follow her out of the clinic.

Except she didn't go straight out. She paused at the water fountain, getting a paper cup of water. As she sipped, she closed her eyes and rubbed the base of her throat.

"She looks terrified," Maylin murmured.

The girl happened to look out a window in the hallway, and suddenly froze.

"That window looks out onto the parking lot," Maylin said. "She'd have seen the police car I saw earlier. And the Asian men talking to the officer."

"So was it the policeman or the Asian men who scared her?" Geoffrey said.

Even with the grainy black and white video, the girl clearly went pale. She ducked into an empty exam room next to the water fountain. A few minutes later, the two Asian men, led by Felicity, walked right past the exam room.

The girl peeked out at the two men, then darted in the opposite direction. Monica tracked her, and they saw her hurry out of the clinic.

"Can you find the video of the two men?" Geoffrey asked her.

The two men entered the clinic and went to the receptionist, who pointed them to Felicity. The men showed Felicity their badges, and the triage nurse seemed taken aback by whatever they said to her, but she went to a computer terminal and looked something up for them, just like she'd done for the girl.

"We really have to talk to Felicity," Geoffrey said.

Rather than letting the men walk through the clinic, Felicity led them to Geoffrey's office. After they walked past the exam room and the girl had run down the hallway away from them, Maylin noticed that one of the men glanced around behind him.

"I wonder if he saw her?" she said.

Felicity left the two men in Geoffrey's office. In a few minutes, Geoffrey and Maylin entered his office and closed the door. A few minutes after that, the door was wrenched open and Maylin came running out, quickly followed by the two men. The smaller one shoved her aside as he sprinted down the hallway. They knocked a couple other nurses out of the way before they ran out of the clinic.

"I wish you had video of the parking lot," Geoffrey said. "I'd like to know what happened when they ran out. I don't know how the two officers could have missed them."

"The video doesn't give us much about them," Monica said.

"But it might give us something about the girl." Maylin leaned forward. "Can you find the video when she went into the exam room?" She pointed to the screen. "She had the water cup when she entered the room, but it's not in her hand when she left."

Geoffrey straightened. "If we can find the cup she threw away in the room, we can get her DNA."

"Let's hope no one else threw a water cup in that room's trash can." Maylin followed him out of the security room, trailed by Monica. There was a good chance that the girl's cup was the only one in that exam room trash can, because there was a larger trash can next to the water fountain where most people threw their used cups.

However, as they approached the exam room, Maylin saw the janitor's cart, and it was parked right next to the water fountain. The light was on in the room that the girl had entered. They sped up, sliding into the room.

"John, wait!" Geoffrey held his hand outstretched, but it was too late. The janitor was just placing the emptied trash can back in the corner of the room. John froze and blinked owlishly at them.

Each trash can had a plastic liner bag, however, so Maylin asked, "John, did you pull out the liner, too?"

The janitor nodded slowly. "But I don't tie the bag if it's not too dirty. I just throw it in my garbage cart." He nodded to the cart parked outside the exam room.

Monica was closest to the cart and peered inside, and Maylin joined her. There were several plastic liners of trash in the garbage bag, but they had partially spilled out and mixed together. There was no way to know which bag was from this exam room, and no way to retrieve the girl's paper water cup.

Maylin sighed. "It was a long shot, anyway. There might have been several paper cups in the trash can in this room, and we'd have never known which was hers."

At that moment, Monica's cell phone rang. "Hi, Roy," she answered the phone. She immediately frowned. "No, don't let them into the security office. Ask them to wait. I'll be there in a minute." She disconnected the call and immediately began dialing another. "Roy said there are two FBI agents who showed up, asking to see the video surveillance of the clinic."

Maylin felt as if she'd been dowsed in ice water. "FBI agents?"

Geoffrey had stiffened, his hands clenching. He looked faintly dangerous.

"I'm calling Detective Carter to ask him to come down," Monica hit the send button on her cell phone. "Just in case ..."

Then the sound of a gunshot echoed down the hallway.

Geoffrey instinctively stepped in front of Maylin and Monica. John started and grabbed his broom tightly.

"Roy." Maylin's hand was in front of her mouth, and the name came out muffled.

Monica's hand holding the cell phone shook, but then the sound of a man's voice coming from the phone brought her out of her temporary shock. She pressed the phone to her ear. "Horatio, come to the clinic quick! We just heard a gunshot."

"Stay here." Geoffrey kicked off his Doc Martins and headed down the hallway toward the front of the clinic, his socks whispering against the industrial tile floor. He stayed low to the ground since the doors up ahead that led to the front lobby had windows on their upper halves. Instead of opening the swinging doors, he cut right into the open doorway to the nurses' station. He heard the sound of breaking glass. He crawled behind the desks until he could peek out behind a corner.

The two men at the front of the clinic had shot a hole in the glass doors and were now smashing a larger opening so they could reach inside to unlock the deadbolts. They were the same two Asian men who had come to the clinic earlier that afternoon.

Movement caught his eye and he eased out further, hoping the shadows in the waiting room would hide him. Roy sat on the floor a few feet away from the door, clutching his arm. Blood ran down through his fingers.

Roy turned and saw Geoffrey, and began shuffling toward him. Aside from the shot to his arm, he looked to be all right.

When he got to the edge of the nurses' station desks, Geoffrey whispered, "Come on, to the back of the clinic." They'd need to lock themselves in a room in order to buy time to patch him up. By now, even if Monica hadn't been on the phone with Detective Carter, the clinic's silent alarm had been triggered when the front door glass was broken. However, the clinic was on the outskirts of Sonoma, and it would take the police a few minutes to get here.

"Wait." Roy got to his feet using his good arm, and dashed to the nearby security office door, pulling it shut. It automatically locked.

"Where's the key?" Geoffrey asked as Roy slipped behind the nurses' station.

"Inside the security room."

Geoffrey helped Roy crawl back to the open doorway, but then Monica appeared with three plastic water bottles in her hand. She cracked open the main doors to the waiting area and rolled the bottles out into the room, toward the two men, who had just entered the building.

"What are you doing?" Geoffrey mouthed to her.

She beckoned to them. Before they could reach her, they were startled by a loud *bang!* from the waiting room. There was a stunned moment of silence, then the sound of men's voices.

"Dry ice bomb," Monica said to him. "To slow them down."

The clinic, like many hospitals, had a dry ice chest that was constantly refilled by a dry ice service. The dry ice was used to keep frozen samples from degrading during transport. Geoffrey remembered making a dry ice bomb or two as a prank in high school and college, but he'd never have thought to use it to surprise the two men entering the clinic.

The other two bombs must have been made to delay in going off. They were out of the nurses' station before two more *bangs!* echoed down the main hallway behind them. A sudden gunshot made the three of them flatten to the floor, but then one of the men began haranguing the other in Chinese.

Maylin came running down the hallway toward them, also without her shoes on. She had two hot water bottles in her hand, both bulging and full.

"Go back," Geoffrey started to say, but she ran past them, crouching behind the main door. She pulled a pocket knife from her slacks and punched holes in the two water bottles. Immediately smoke began to curl from the holes. She cracked the doors and sent them sliding into the waiting room.

"Run!" she hissed as she came up behind them. Geoffrey caught a whiff of acrid pepper that made his eyes start to water.

Geoffrey ran, his arm around Roy. Behind him, he heard painful hacking and coughing.

"What was that?" Geoffrey said.

"Home-made tear gas," Maylin said as she ran. "Cayenne pepper, vinegar, baking soda."

He saw John standing at the end of the hallway, his face white. "Here, take Roy." Geoffrey grabbed a towel from a nearby cart and wrapped it around his injury to keep him from bleeding onto the floor, then pointed down the side hallway. "The medication room is the most secure in the clinic. Lock yourselves in."

"What are you going to do?" Maylin said.

"Misdirection."

The two women headed down the hallway with Roy and John. Geoffrey toppled the cart, using it to partially block the hallway and also indicate in which direction he was running. He kicked over a chair further down the hallway, then turned to his office.

Monica was going to kill him, but it was the only way he could think of to lead the men away from them. Maylin and Monica could treat Roy's wound in the meantime, while they waited for the police to arrive. If only the clinic weren't so far away from the center of town ...

Geoffrey deliberately kept his office door open, then waited and listened. The clinic was silent, not even a scuffle from feet against the smooth industrial floor.

Then he heard it, a muffled grunt. It came from the hallway leading to his office.

He grabbed his office chair and swung it at the large window behind his desk. It bounced off with a heavy *thwack!* and nearly flew out of his hands, leaving a spiderweb in the glass.

He tightened his grip and swung it again. This time there was the sound of cracking glass that he hoped carried down the hallway. One leg of the rolling chair stuck in a softball-sized hole in the glass, and he had to tug to pull it free.

He swung a third time, and the hole blew out to a beach ball size with jagged edges. The legs of the chair stuck and he had to jerk and maneuver to get it out. He then used the chair to smash the glass out to make a hole easily large enough for people to climb through.

Geoffrey set the chair down and waited.

The men didn't even attempt to hide their foot-steps. They ran to the office and hesitated in the doorway. The largest man gave Geoffrey an ugly look, then said something in Chinese to the smaller man, who took off back down the hallway. Geoffrey was guessing he would go out the front doors, thinking that Monica, Maylin, and Roy had escaped through the window and out to the parking lot.

Geoffrey considered diving out the hole in the win-dow to make the man follow him, but he didn't want to turn his back. The office was smaller than the spar-ring ring at his gym, so he'd have to switch up some of his striking moves.

The two of them circled the desk warily, in short jerky movements. Then the larger man sidestepped and swung a beefy fist in a roundhouse punch. Geoffrey twisted easily to avoid it, but the man pivoted com-pletely around in the direction of his swing, bringing his other arm in a spinning backfist.

Geoffrey just barely ducked in time to avoid it, feel-ing the man's hand slice through his hair.

Geoffrey attacked with an open palm slamming into the man's nose, his fingers stabbing into the soft eye sockets. He felt the nose break and the man gave a painful grunt.

Without stopping his forward movement, he lifted his elbow high and brought it down in a *muay Thai* elbow strike to the man's face, a solid blow to the spot between his eyes.

The Asian man staggered back, clutching his face, but a wildly swung arm clipped Geoffrey in the shoulder with a painful crunch. He'd underestimated the length of the man's arm span, and since the man easily outweighed him, the blow felt like an iron hammer.

But he had to shake it off. The man was still blinded by his hand over his pained nose. Geoffrey stepped forward and captured the man's free arm in a clinch that immobilized his shoulder, then pulled the man's torso down as he brought his knee up in a sharp strike. It connected with the man's fingers over his face, and he bellowed in pain again.

But as his cry died down, Geoffrey heard the wail of police sirens through the broken window.

It took the man a few seconds longer to hear it, but when he did, he shoved Geoffrey away and ran out the office door, his shoulders hunched. Geoffrey tried to follow, but his socks slipped on the floor and he almost fell. As he got to the front waiting area, a silver car pulled up in front of the clinic. The smaller man was in the driver's seat, and he leaned over to open the passenger door.

The injured man dove into the car and it took off just as Geoffrey exited the clinic, leaving him only with the heat from the exhaust swirling around his socks-clad feet.

3

Maylin had never met Detective Carter before, but the Sonoma police detective obviously knew Monica well. He cupped the younger woman's cheek. "Are you all right?" he asked in a gravelly voice.

"I'm fine, Horatio." Monica smiled at him. "I hope I didn't take you away from dinner with Aunt Becca."

"No, your aunt and I have dinner reservations at Lorianne's Cafe for tomorrow night, so I was working late tonight."

The officers who arrived with Detective Carter were more like the other Sonoma PD officers Maylin had dealt with when they came to the clinic, courteous and concerned. After they gave their statements to the officers, Detective Carter came to speak to them himself.

He had kind gray eyes under his thinning red hair that made her feel comfortable telling him everything that had happened.

"Why were you all here at the clinic this late?" he asked them.

Geoffrey hesitated, then glanced at her as he had done before. This time, Maylin told him about the girl who had warned Geoffrey about the danger to him and herself. She also explained about looking for her on the video surveillance.

"I'll need to take a look at that." Detective Carter raised his eyebrows at Monica.

"Sure, I have the master key for the security room. I can get that for you."

"As far as we know, she's not involved with the two men," Geoffrey said. "She was trying to warn us against them. But if you discover something about her ..."

"I'll let you know." The detective sighed. "Your family seems to have a track record for getting in trouble."

"But Geoffrey's only a second cousin," Monica said with an innocent look.

"And there are two bullet holes in your clinic," the detective pointed out.

Monica and Geoffrey winced, looking at each other.

"The two men were the same ones who came to the clinic earlier this afternoon," Geoffrey said.

"This afternoon?" The detective obviously hadn't heard about it.

Geoffrey filled him in, mentioning how the officer hadn't seen the men running out of the clinic. As he listened, Detective Carter's mouth grew grim. "I'll talk to Officer Malcolm," he promised, making a note in his notebook.

"Why was he here? We didn't call for any police officers." Sometimes Geoffrey called the Sonoma PD if there was a chance the child they were caring for was in some sort of danger, but that hadn't happened very often.

Detective Carter's eyes grew harder than steel. "I heard rumors he's dating a nurse. He's been reprimanded before about doing personal business during his shift."

Geoffrey wondered briefly if Officer Malcolm's "personal business" had prevented him from seeing the two men fleeing the clinic.

He finished by telling him about what had happened this evening when the two men returned.

Detective Carter asked a few more questions, taking notes in his notebook. He gave his business card to Maylin and Geoffrey, then said, "I'll need your cell phone numbers in case I need to get in touch with you."

They gave the numbers to him. Geoffrey said, "We'll probably be sticking close to each other until this gets resolved."

"We will?" Maylin glared at him. Sebastian had been insistent on keeping her close, saying that he only wanted to protect her. There were some things about Geoffrey that were nothing like Sebastian, but she couldn't help reacting automatically, with suspicion and annoyance. It didn't help that Geoffrey was confident, like Sebastian.

Detective Carter's eyebrows rose again, and then he discreetly sidled away.

Monica gave Geoffrey an exasperated blow to the arm. "Way to not communicate, cuz."

"Hey, I got hit in that shoulder." Geoffrey tried to look like the injured party. "I was busy getting beat up."

Monica threaded her arm through Maylin's in a sisterly fashion. "It's because he's the oldest of his family. He gets a bit high-handed because he's used to being in charge of his siblings and all the cousins, too."

"It's because I was always the only responsible one out of all of us," Geoffrey protested.

"I think that we wouldn't have been quite so rowdy if you hadn't been such a stick in the mud." Monica stuck her tongue out at him.

Maylin couldn't imagine bantering this way with her older sister, let alone any of her cousins. None of them seemed to even want to try to understand her sense of humor. Maybe she was just too odd for anyone to understand.

"I'd better pull up the video for Horatio." Monica's look of concern encompassed both of them. "Be safe. Let me know if there's anything else I can do for you." She had walked away before Maylin could respond.

"I'm sorry," Geoffrey said in a rush. "I meant to talk to you about sticking together, but I forgot. It's why I need to write things down."

While she didn't like having decisions made for her, she also didn't want to be on her own with two mysterious men threatening her. "I guess it would be safer."

"Although I'm sure you'd be fine." There was humor in his voice, and his smile, the teasing tilt of his head, made her breath catch for a moment. "You told Monica to make the dry ice bombs, didn't you?"

"Well, yes, because I needed time to go to the kitchen to make the tear gas bombs." Luckily, she had known for a fact they had all the ingredients because several of the nurses had a fondness for spicy foods.

"I thought so. She'd never have thought of that on her own. How did you know to do all that?"

She shrugged. "I was good at chemistry." Actually, she had a fascination with all things that exploded, but that wasn't something she could put on her resume or mention on a first date.

"Anyway," Geoffrey said, "that's why I know you'd be fine."

She realized he was impressed by her. She wasn't sure how to feel about that.

Geoffrey continued, "But two heads are better than one in figuring out who's behind all this and why."

"You're right," she said quickly.

He was a little startled by her agreement at first, but he gave her that smile that revealed the slight dimples under the dark gold shadow on his cheeks. Then he sobered. "I was thinking about your note, about not going home. What were you going to do?"

The creepy thought of those two men staking out her apartment made her shudder. "Check into a motel room, maybe." Except how long could she afford to stay at even a cheap motel that wouldn't balk at a fake name?

"I have an option for both of us, a place those men couldn't find. My mom and my siblings have moved back to Sonoma because they chipped in to buy fifty acres of land from my mom's aunt."

"That must have been expensive." Especially with the land prices in Sonoma.

"It wasn't, really, because it's almost all wilderness and rocky, not suitable for crops. My mom's uncle only ever ventured onto the property to go deer hunting. But my siblings' businesses can use the space, and Mom is building a house on the best section of it. Mom's uncle built a hunting cabin on the land—it's more like a shack. It's not on any property records. It's completely off the grid. But there's no phone, the electricity comes from a generator and the water is pumped in from a nearby well. How are you with roughing it?"

She almost laughed. "I love camping and backpacking. A cabin would be like a luxury hotel."

"Great." His voice had a tinge of surprise. "We'll be safe for tonight."

"But what about your mom? She'll be alone at her house."

"No, besides me, three of my siblings are staying at the house with her. Your family ..."

"Is down in Los Angeles. I'm living alone." It sounded rather pathetic when she told her coworkers, but now she was glad.

"I thought we could try to call Felicity tonight, even though it's late, to ask her about what she said to that girl and the two men," Geoffrey said.

Maylin shook her head. "She's out with friends tonight at Rock Love."

He looked blank. "Rock Love?"

At least she wasn't the only one. "It's a famous restaurant in Napa."

He shook his head. "Never heard of it."

"Don't worry, I hadn't heard of it, either."

"At least I'm not the only one."

She suppressed a smile. "I thought you were from Sonoma?"

"My family moved from Sonoma when I was five, and we grew up in Arizona. I've only been back here since Mom started work on her house."

Maylin pulled out her cell phone. "Is there a cell signal the cabin?"

"Nope."

"I'll call Felicity and leave a message for her. We can arrange to meet her tomorrow morning, maybe before her work shift starts." And not at the clinic— while she didn't think the men would return here a third time, they might once they realized she and Geoffrey wouldn't be returning to their homes tonight. What would they do then?

She called Felicity's cell phone, and it went straight to voicemail, so she left a message. Meanwhile, she heard Geoffrey on his phone, and it sounded like he was talking to his mom.

He disconnected the call and looked to her. "Ready to go? Okay if I drive?"

"Sure." He knew where the cabin was, anyway.

His car was an older Mustang, not old enough to be vintage, and it badly needed a paint job.

"Sorry for the mess." He swept some newspapers from the passenger seat. "I'm borrowing this car from my brother and never got around to giving it a good clean."

When she'd first learned that this car was his, she'd been surprised, since it wasn't the car she'd have expected of a doctor, but now that she knew he'd been overseas on medical missions, it made more sense.

They stopped at the grocery store briefly for supplies, but the entire time Maylin kept looking over her shoulder, half-afraid the Asian men would have somehow found them again. She started when she saw a large Asian man in a suit smelling the cantaloupes, and Geoffrey laid a hand on her arm. His touch felt warm and tingly at the same time.

"Those men would have had a hard time following us from the clinic because it was crawling with police officers," he said. "I think we're okay for a little while."

"I feel like I'm being hunted."

Geoffrey nodded. "I don't like the loss of control over the situation."

She couldn't help pulling away from him, even though logically she knew that not all men would be like her ex-boyfriend.

The Whelan property was outside of Sonoma, far away from any of the farms and vineyards. Geoffrey drove down a trail that led into dark wilderness, and the car headlights lit on juniper bushes, scraggly trees, and thorny bushes in between stretches of desert sands and rocks. The mustang dipped and bounced along the road, which was little more than a dirt track that wound through the brush.

"Sorry," Geoffrey muttered after a jaw-rattling stretch. "Usually we drive out here in someone's truck or SUV."

The road snaked downward through the rolling foothills until it ended in a little valley between two rocky cliffs. Even this late at night, the residual heat from the day radiated from the hard-packed earth and stones, making the air heavy.

"Watch your step," Geoffrey said as they got out of the car. "The rocks are pretty loose around here."

The pebbles rolled beneath her feet, but it wasn't more difficult to walk than a hike up some of the steeper mountains in the San Francisco Bay Area. Maylin followed him deeper into the brush, and as they emerged from behind some oak trees, she saw the cabin.

It was a solid-looking shack standing in a clearing, with thick trees and overgrown juniper bushes behind it. Moss hung from the roof, but the area around the door had been cleared of weeds and bushes, and there was a footpath that ran around the cabin toward the woods behind it.

Geoffrey frowned at the door. "One of my siblings must have been here recently."

"Is that unusual?"

"Well, I can't think of a reason they'd use the cabin."

He searched under a rock at the corner of the house, finding the key to the front door. Inside, he lit a lamp from a shelf next to the front door and set it on the dining room table.

The small space had a living room/dining room with a fireplace set in blackened stones, an old-fashioned kitchen, and two doors leading from the main area.

"Those two are the bedrooms." Geoffrey pointed to the doors. "And the bathroom is outside behind the house."

He lit another lamp for her and then knelt in front of the fireplace to start the fire. Maylin started putting away supplies. In opening a cabinet, she saw a shotgun lying there.

Geoffrey growled. "They should have put that away in the gun cabinet." He grabbed it and set it on the floor next to the door, then rummaged above the fireplace mantle.

His movements stilled. "The key is missing."

"To the gun cabinet?"

He nodded slowly. "That's odd."

"Maybe the key is in the cabinet?"

He went into one of the bedrooms, but returned a moment later, shaking his head. "And I can't call home to ask my family where they left the key."

Maylin glanced at the shotgun, but unspoken between them was the worry that they would need the guns at all. Surely those men couldn't have followed them through that wilderness in the dark?

"Let me show you how to work the water pump." Geoffrey grabbed several plastic gallon containers and a flashlight and led the way out the backdoor.

The backyard had a small strip of grass and weeds, and then there were trees leading deeper into the valley. A footpath cut through them. Geoffrey picked his way along with Maylin following the bobbing of his flashlight. Every so often, the flashlight fell on a pipe half-hidden in the ground that ran from the house to the well.

They came to a small clearing with brush and trees all around them and a cylindrical water tank partly embedded into the ground in the center, with a motor off to one side. Next to it was a white hand pump and faucet.

"There's a generator-run pump for using the shower, but for other stuff, we use the hand pump." Geoffrey positioned one of the containers under the faucet and began pumping. Soon a stream flowed out of the faucet into the container. He continued to pump, and Maylin replaced the containers as they got full.

"We've got water filters inside," he said as they filled the last container.

They each grabbed some containers and headed back to the cabin. But as they entered the backyard, Maylin happened to look up.

Thousands, millions of stars thickly dotted the blue-black night sky. Out here, away from the city lights that had concealed them, the stars exploded across the sky. They made her breath catch. They always did. She didn't go camping or backpacking as often as she wanted to, but she never missed moments like these, staring up at the sky, drinking in the wonder. She set down her water containers and arched her back so she could take in all of the night sky.

Then Geoffrey was beside her, his water containers also on the ground, and he looked up with her. "They looked different in Japan." There was a sorrowful note in his voice.

He would have seen stars like this on the empty shores of cities washed away by the tsunami.

She reached out to touch his hand. She understood him so much better after only one day than in all the months she'd worked with him. She respected him as a doctor, but now knowing about his last several years in Japan, she respected him as man. She couldn't imagine what he must have seen, and she saw how it had changed him, because she'd known the man he'd been.

They looked at each other at the same moment. His face was shadowed, but she saw a glitter that was his eyes.

Then his hand reached up, touched her cheek. His caress was lighter than a petal against her skin, she wondered if she imagined it. She caught the scent of his musk, and eucalyptus, and cedar.

The way he looked at her made her feel beautiful, and confident, and precious.

And then they heard the low, quiet growl of a car engine out front.

They both froze. Maylin's mind raced. Who would be here? No one else was supposed to know about this cabin.

Then they raced for the back door, leaving the water containers, and into the house. Geoffrey grabbed the shotgun and doused the lamps. Maylin grabbed an iron poker near the fireplace, using it to scatter the small fire so it wouldn't emit as much light, and doused the last lamp.

Geoffrey stood to one side of the front door. Maylin hid to one side of the back door that led from the kitchen, in case someone tried to sneak in that way.

The rocky cliffs on either side of the house seemed to magnify sound. They heard the crunching of boots against the gravel as at least two people approached the cabin. Maylin tried to swallow, but her throat was tight and dry. Her hands clenched and unclenched around the iron poker.

It sounded like the men were going to the front door and not the back. She could only see a dim outline of Geoffrey in the pitch blackness, but she heard his sharp intake of breath as the door handle moved a fraction of an inch, as if someone were testing to see if it were locked.

The wooden door creaked as it opened, and Maylin saw the slash of grayness from the night outside, which was quickly blotted out by a shadow.

Then the sharp sound of the shotgun being primed cut through the air. "Stop right there."

The shadow in the doorway stilled. "You wouldn't shoot your favorite brother, would you?" The man's voice was similar to Geoffrey's but a little lighter.

"I don't have a favorite brother," Geoffrey growled, but she saw movement as he lowered the shotgun from where it had been pointed at the open doorway.

"But he has a favorite sister," said a cheerful woman's voice from behind the man in the doorway.

"I only have one sister," Geoffrey said, still in that low voice.

"That makes me favorite by default."

Geoffrey sighed. "You idiots. What are you doing here?"

"We could ask the same of you."

There was a fumbling sound, then light blazed from the lit lamp.

The man in the doorway had lighter colored hair than Geoffrey, with a more angular jaw and a nose that had been broken once, but his eyes and the smile he gave his brother was the same. As he noticed Maylin, she saw that his eyes were a lighter green than Geoffrey's, with an adventurous gleam.

"Move, you big oaf." Someone behind the man pushed at his back, and he stepped into the cabin. The young woman didn't much look like her brothers except for her eyes. Her small, round face only emphasized the brightness of her wide smile as she threw herself at Geoffrey for a bear hug. Her long, straight hair was a lighter shade of brown, with the faintest hint of red.

There was a strangled sound from Geoffrey at her arms squeezed tight around his neck, then she saw Maylin. "Hi there, I'm Olivia."

Her brother, catching sight of the bruise on Geoffrey's face from earlier that afternoon, interrupted before Maylin could respond. "Whoa, I hope the other guy looks worse, because you look like he chewed you up and spit you out."

Olivia rolled her eyes. "Don't listen to him, Geoff, he's just feeling inferior because I beat him on the rock climbing wall today."

"I'm not feeling inferior," he complained.

"Maylin, the guy with the rude manners and the inferiority complex is my brother, Lincoln," Geoffrey said. "You'd never know we were related ..."

"Because I'm so much more handsome." Lincoln grinned.

Maylin was taken aback by the ache she felt as she watched them. She'd seen close families before, and the comparison with her own bleak one hadn't bothered her. But suddenly she felt the emptiness of having no siblings or cousins who would understand her so well that they could joke with her.

She shook off the feeling. She was being pathetic.

"This is Maylin Kinley, one of the nurses at the clinic," Geoffrey said, "but I have a feeling you already knew that."

"Of course. Monica told us." Olivia backhanded his shoulder. "She was right, you weren't going to involve any of us, were you? But God wasn't going to let you get away with it. He made sure we were at the Den when you called Mom tonight."

God had rolled off of Olivia's tongue as if she was best buds with Him. It was similar to how Maylin's parents spoke about God, and yet different in a way that didn't make her cringe.

"The Den? You mean Mom's house?"

"Blame Liv," Lincoln said. "She's the one who started calling it that."

"Since our name means 'wolf,' it's perfect," Olivia said. "And besides, Mom *loves* it."

Geoffrey burst out laughing. It took years from his face, and for the first time since she'd seen him again, he looked … unburdened.

"Of course she would," Geoffrey said. "She always called us a pack of wild animals."

"Let me take that from you before you shoot your foot off." Olivia took the shotgun from Geoffrey's slack grip.

"I'm not that bad a shot," he said. "And why wasn't it in the gun cabinet? And where's the key?"

"It's filled with our guns," Olivia said as if that were the obvious answer in the world, then took the shotgun with her into one of the bedrooms.

"Why do you need so many guns here?" Geoffrey said. "Why are you two using Uncle Tommy's cabin in the first place?"

"No, way." Lincoln leveled a finger at his brother. "You first. What in the world is going on?"

"Monica didn't fill you in?"

"She said something about guns and Asian hit men at the clinic, and then she hung up. I can't believe she did that," Olivia said as she came out of the bedroom.

"Maylin will tell you while I get the water containers." Geoffrey headed out the back door.

Maylin was faced with two curious and identical pairs of green-brown eyes, and for a moment, she froze. "Uh …"

Olivia smiled at her, nudging her toward the heavy wooden dining table. "I don't bite. Linc might, because he isn't housebroken, but he's had his shots."

Lincoln gave his sister a sour look.

Maylin told the story again, and Geoffrey came in with water just as she finished. His siblings' expressions had grown serious.

"You have no idea who that girl is?" Lincoln asked.

"No clue," Maylin said. "We're hoping to talk to one of the other nurses tomorrow morning."

Geoffrey poured water into a kettle and placed it on the stove, which he'd started. "We didn't want to go home because those men knew our names."

"Don't worry, Chris is at home with Mom," Lincoln told him.

Olivia explained to Maylin, "Chris is our other brother. He's an architect, and he's the one building Mom's house."

"Liv, why don't you stay here with Geoff and Maylin?" Lincoln said. "I'll stay with Mom and Chris at the Den."

"Why are you two here?" Geoffrey demanded. "I almost shot your fool heads off."

"Liv and I are looking over the property," Lincoln said. "We think this side is the best place for our shooting range and training grounds, and the cabin's more convenient since the Den is too far away."

"You're building a shooting range?" Maylin asked Olivia. That would explain why the two siblings had enough guns between them to fill a gun cabinet.

"Linc was a sniper in the army, and I'm a shooting instructor," Olivia said. "We helped Mom buy our great-uncle's property so we can build our own commercial training grounds for maneuvers and a comprehensive shooting range."

Each member of Geoffrey's family certainly had their own unique backgrounds. Maylin's family hadn't allowed her to stray far away from the medical or legal fields when she was in college, since her dad was a surgeon and her grandfather had been a lawyer. They'd been deeply disappointed when she chose nursing over medical school.

"I'm waiting for my thank you." Lincoln cupped his ear and leaned toward Geoffrey. "You could have been chasing gigantic spiders out of this cabin at this moment instead of heating water."

"I was the one chasing out the spiders because you were a wimp," Olivia shot at her brother.

Geoffrey gave them both a smile. "Thank you. Really. I hadn't thought about how bad it would be after being abandoned for so long."

"I would have been fine," Maylin said to Geoffrey. "I've gone backpacking lots of times. Just me and the centipedes."

"You're a girl after my own heart." Olivia grinned at Maylin. "Do you like rock-climbing?"

Lincoln groaned. "You and your rock climbing."

"You're just jealous because Geoff and I are better at it than you are." Olivia turned expectant eyes at Maylin.

"I've never tried it," Maylin said.

"We built a rock-climbing wall a few weeks ago. It's so fun, you would love it. I'm sure you wouldn't fall a million times like this guy." Olivia gave Lincoln a grin.

"On that note, Liv, give me your car keys." Lincoln stood. "I'm heading back to the Den."

"Don't tell Mom about this," Geoffrey warned him.

"Do I look like I want to hear her complain about you all night?" Lincoln's teasing look faded. "Maybe you two should lay low for a while, not venture into town."

"We can't," Geoffrey said.

At the same time, Maylin said, "We have to figure out who's after us and why."

The two of them looked at each other. His face looked as determined as she felt.

"This won't end until we stop whoever's threatening us," Geoffrey said. "I'm pretty sure we'll be safe here. It's not hooked up to the Sonoma water or electric company, right?"

"We hadn't gotten around to calling them yet," Olivia said.

"And the building isn't on any property maps or records. No one can find us unless someone tells them about the cabin."

Lincoln gave his brother a hug. "Stay safe," he said. "Because if you don't, then Liv will take your bedroom and she'll be impossible to live with."

"It's past time you left," Olivia said to him. Right after he'd closed the front door, she added in a yell, "And don't get a scratch on my truck!"

"We bought hamburger patties," Geoffrey said to Olivia.

"Good, I'm starving."

"Then make yourself useful and fix the salad." He headed toward the back door. "I'll get the charcoal grill started and throw the burgers on."

His face was perfectly calm as he glanced at Maylin, as if the moment outside had never happened. He was firmly in control of himself and the situation.

Just like Sebastian, and his impenetrable facade. Later in the relationship, he'd have an expressionless mask on his face even while he said the most degrading things to her.

What had Maylin been thinking in the backyard? She only just got over Sebastian and the number he'd worked on her self-esteem. Did she really want to get involved with another strong, intelligent, alpha male?

No, she should look for some sweet, kind man who would cherish her and wash the dishes.

"So have you worked with Geoff for a while?" Olivia asked as they washed the lettuce and tomatoes.

"A few months. I first met him years ago when he was doing his residency at Merlyn Memorial Hospital in Los Angeles."

"Did you really?" Olivia's gaze wandered to the closed back door. "Jesus has changed his heart a lot since then."

"Yes, it seems that way."

"With his friends, he was kind of wild—he once got spanked because he and his friends had been trying to ride old Mr. Rivers's pigs."

Maylin snorted in laughter. "The pigs must have been thrilled."

"Mom wasn't sure whether to laugh or scold him. But with us, his siblings and his cousins, he was always so strict and trying to tell us what to do. And we always disobeyed him, just because he was trying to be a dictator." Olivia winked at her.

"You have a fun family." Maylin's voice was light, but there was a slight ache at the back of her throat. She wanted a family like that.

"We were a bunch of rascals." Olivia laughed, then started telling a story about how Lincoln had been lying in wait, ready to shoot a fox that was invading the chicken coop, but in reality it was their brother Chris trying to sneak back onto their property after curfew.

The story was funny, especially when Geoffrey returned and told several about Olivia, the two of them laughing and insulting each other in that way that made it obvious how much they cared about each other.

Maylin laughed, but that ache in her throat traveled down to her chest. Who was she kidding? She didn't belong in a family like this. She was too strange, too awkward. She could never fit in with Geoffrey's family.

And why was she even thinking about it? She shouldn't be thinking about Dr. Geoffrey Whelan in any way other than a professional capacity or as a fellow fugitive, because she was just a little too off-kilter for an emotionally healthy relationship.

She had to refocus, try to figure a way out of this dangerous situation. The sooner, the better. Because then she could put Geoffrey Whelan out of her thoughts again.

4

Captain Caffeine's Espresso Shop was bustling with people getting their early morning fix of coffee. Geoffrey hadn't wanted to meet in downtown Sonoma, in case the men after them spotted them, but Felicity hadn't called them back. However, she went to Captain Caffeine every morning as part of her normal routine.

"How do you know she comes here?" Geoffrey sat at a table at the back of the coffee shop, his Giants ball cap pulled down to shade his eyes.

"The more you fiddle with your hat, the more you're drawing attention to it." Maylin gave him an exasperated look that was very like his sister's when he did something to annoy her.

"Sorry." He hunched over his cup of coffee. It was no wonder she and Liv had hit it off last night. And Maylin had behaved as if that ... whatever it was in the backyard hadn't happened. Or hadn't meant anything.

What had happened, really? Nothing. And he needed it to stay that way. He should be glad she wasn't making more of it than it was.

But it had been more, which he didn't want to admit to himself. He had wanted to kiss her, an urge he hadn't felt for any woman in a long time.

He shook off the memory. No use dwelling on it. He had no business being attracted to anyone right now, not with his head such a mess.

"I know Felicity comes here every morning because she usually has one of their cups in hand when she walks into the women's locker room." Maylin pointed to the distinctive logo on the disposable coffee cup in front of her. "Although she's a bit late today. Maybe she was out late last night."

"Maybe you should check your voicemail again, in case she left a message."

She again gave him an exasperated look. In many ways, she reminded him of how his sister, Liv, reacted when he got too overbearing. He knew it was a bad habit, but he did it because he was used to being in charge, whether over the siblings or in his position as a medical professional, not because he got a personal thrill out of dictating to others.

"Please," he added in a more gentle tone. "Just in case. I don't want her to put herself in danger because of us."

Maylin's glare softened, and she nodded, pulling out the disposable cell phone they'd bought earlier this morning. She had been the one to worry about the men being able to track the GPS in their personal cell phones, so they'd taken the phones apart and left them at the cabin.

But before she could dial to check her voicemail, Felicity dashed into the coffee shop and went to stand in line to give her order.

"There she is." Geoffrey got up and made his way to her, trying to appear casual as he got into line behind her. His bulk blocked the view of anyone who might look into the large windows of the shop from the street. "Felicity."

She turned and pulled off her sunglasses. "Dr. Whelan?" Her mouth dropped open.

"I'm sorry to come up to you like this, but I really need to speak to you."

"Of course. I heard about what happened at the clinic last night, too. Are you and Maylin all right?"

"We're both fine. Can you come to our table after you get your coffee?"

When she sat down across from Maylin, Felicity's eyes were wide with surprise. "Did you really set off a bomb in the clinic?"

"What? No."

"Oh." Felicity looked a little disappointed. "I didn't think so, but Thea insisted she heard someone say that you did."

"She set off a dry ice bomb and a homemade tear gas bomb." If Maylin wasn't going to brag about her quick thinking, he certainly would. "It held the men off until the police could arrive."

"Actually, what held the men off was Dr. Whelan attacking one of them in his office," Maylin said. "We were hiding in the medicine room."

He thought Felicity might be more open to speaking to them once they explained what had happened, so they told her a brief account of the attack. They also mentioned seeing the strange nurse and the men talking to Felicity in the video surveillance.

"I don't remember her name." Felicity chewed on her lip. "Katie something? I do remember she had a really nice watch. She was from Kind Samaritan Hospital in Napa."

Kind Samaritan, Napa. That must have been what the KSN embroidered on her scrubs stood for. Something about it struck Geoffrey as odd, but he couldn't put his finger on it.

Felicity continued, "She showed her badge. So did the two fake FBI agents. They said they were FBI agents, although I thought they were a little odd for FBI. But then again, I've never talked to an FBI agent. What was really strange was that the men and that Katie girl both wanted me to look up the medical personnel who worked on a specific patient, Frank Chan."

Geoffrey thought back. He said, "Teenager?" at the same time that Maylin said, "Mountain bike accident, right?"

Maylin flashed him a surprised look, although she looked away quickly.

Felicity looked from one to the other. "Wow, I'm impressed you both remembered him."

Had that been why Maylin had been surprised? He thought back to when he'd first known her during his residency in Merlyn Memorial Hospital in Los Angeles. Back then, he didn't bother to remember a patient's name—he'd more easily recall the injury or illness, instead.

It seemed like a thousand years ago. Or rather, a thousand lives ago.

"I remember Frank," Geoffrey said. "Didn't he have an allergic reaction to Amoxicillin? We had to intubate him and give him shots of Benadryl and Narcan." It had been unexpected because Frank hadn't shown an allergy to that antibiotic before, and they'd had to work fast to counteract the reaction.

"That's him," Felicity said. "That girl specifically asked for the medical personnel who had saved his life. It was kind of an odd request, but we get personnel requests once in a while. I assumed Frank Chan's regular doctor was at Kind Samaritan Napa and the family wanted to know who had saved him."

Geoffrey nodded. He knew that scenario happened sometimes, where a nurse would call an independent clinic to find the names of emergency doctors who had cared for a patient.

"There was one thing kind of weird, though," Felicity said. "Frank's records didn't have his street address—a lot of patients don't give an address, so that wasn't unusual—but he put down San Francisco for his hometown."

"But that girl said she was from Napa?" Maylin frowned.

"Yeah. I didn't do anything wrong in telling her, did I?" Felicity asked.

Maylin quickly said, "Absolutely not. The girl showed a KSN badge, and you wouldn't have known those men weren't FBI agents."

Geoffrey hadn't realized the tension across Felicity's shoulders until they relaxed under Maylin's assurance. "After what happened yesterday, I wondered," Felicity said. "I heard Roy is okay, though. And the clinic is opening later today, but we have to come in for our normal shifts to help clean up and make sure everything is sterile."

"Thanks, Felicity, for everything," Maylin said.

"Hey, no problem. Are you guys going to be okay? What are you going to do?"

"The police are looking into those men," Geoffrey said. "So we'll keep out of sight for a little while." He glanced at Maylin and met her understanding gaze. He didn't want Felicity to accidentally reveal to the wrong people what he and Maylin were doing.

"I'd better get going." Felicity got to her feet. "Please take care. It would be awful if something worse happened to you both."

After Felicity left, Geoffrey sipped his cold coffee. "I wish I'd known earlier that both the girl and the two men had spoken to Felicity—and even asked her for the same information. It was so busy yesterday afternoon after the police left, I didn't get much of a chance to chat with anyone about what had happened."

"I didn't talk to many people about it, but from the little I heard from other nurses, none of them knew the men had attacked you, they only knew the men pretended to be FBI agents and ran out of the clinic. I guess Felicity didn't have a chance to talk to anyone about the connection with the KSN nurse, because no one mentioned it to me. And Felicity and her friends left right when the clinic closed because they had dinner reservations, so I didn't see them in the women's locker room."

"Kind Samaritan Napa isn't far. We can visit them today and see if we can find Katie."

"We should also find an internet cafe and look up Frank Chan," Maylin said. "Maybe we can find something that explains what about him made us a target."

Geoffrey opened the door to the coffee shop, scanning the people on the street. He wasn't sure what he was looking for, but he had to see if those two men had somehow found them. Then a woman who had been walking behind a group of people sidestepped them and saw him.

It was his mother.

His first reaction was to look around again, even though he hadn't seen anyone suspicious when he exited the coffee shop. He'd done his best to avoid his family, to prevent drawing them into this, and here he'd walked right into his mother on the streets of Sonoma.

"Geoffrey, you look like you're ready to bolt." His mom looked faintly disapproving, but more amused than anything else.

"Hi, Mom." With a last look around, he took her arm and led her back into the coffee shop, bumping into Maylin, who had been behind him. "Let me buy you coffee."

"I should hope so." She leveled a highly unamused eye at him. "I heard about the shootout at the clinic. And when you called me last night, you didn't breathe a word. You have some explaining to do."

"It wasn't a shootout, Mom." He led her back to the table they'd been sitting at.

"I heard guns were involved. That says 'shootout' to me."

"Mom, this is Maylin Kinley. She's a nurse at the clinic."

His petite mother studied Maylin like a surgeon in the middle of a triple bypass. "You were at the shootout too, weren't you?"

"It was two men trying to break into the clinic," Maylin said calmly, as if she didn't even know what a homemade tear gas bomb was. "There are a lot of medicines we keep in the medication room, you know."

"Oh." His mother sat back. "Is that all? The rumor mill has it sounding so much more sensational. Multiple gunmen, bullets flying, blood and gore ..."

"Our security guard did get winged by a bullet," Maylin said, "but I think he just got accidentally hit when the men shot through the glass door so they could unlock it. I patched him up myself."

Maylin gave Geoffrey a look of understanding. He could have kissed her for knowing exactly how to ease his mother's wild imagination without lying to her.

"What coffee do you want, Mom?"

"Oh, get me one of those iced white chocolate thingys with whipped cream. *Extra* whipped cream." Her merry brown eyes twinkled.

He hesitated, not knowing if it was okay to leave Maylin alone with his mom, but she smiled at him as if understanding his dilemma. "Nothing for me, thanks," she said to him.

He kept glancing over at them as he ordered and waited for his mother's White Chocolate Macchiato with extra whipped cream. His mom seemed to be smiling a lot, and Maylin looked relaxed. He wondered if under her facade, she wanted to run screaming from the coffee house.

What did she think of his crazy family? He'd almost shot his brother, they had dinner and spent the night with his sister in a dilapidated cabin, and now his mother was likely asking for Maylin's entire life story. If it was him, he'd certainly run screaming from the coffee house.

But she'd seemed to fit, last night. She joked with Liv, she even did her own share of teasing him. He'd

enjoyed talking to her, telling a few stories from Japan
which he hadn't even told his own family. And Maylin
had listened in a way that even his mother didn't, with
eyes that seemed to see into his heart.

"White Chocolate Macchiato with extra whipped
cream," the barista yelled, breaking into his thoughts.

What was he doing, dwelling on Maylin's eyes? If
she knew, she'd definitely run screaming away from
him.

"Here, Mom." He set her coffee drink in front of her.
"And stop being nosy about Maylin."

"I was doing no such thing." His mother's look was
all innocence.

"I know you too well, Mom. By now you're trying to
figure out if you've somehow met Maylin's mom,
what's her name ..."

"Moira," his mother supplied.

"What did I tell you?" He cocked an eyebrow at
her, and she colored.

"There's nothing wrong with being curious about
the first girl I've seen you with—"

"Mom," he said in a pained voice.

Maylin looked like she was going to tear a lung trying not to laugh out loud.

Geoffrey couldn't imagine being more embarrassed.
And yet, there was something about Maylin that made
him want to forget the struggles and doubts that had
been plaguing him since he came home from Japan,
and just enjoy the moment. With her.

"How's your house coming along, Mrs. Whelan?" Maylin asked her.

"Oh, call me Emma," she said. "Geoffrey told you about how we bought some land from my aunt? It belonged to my Uncle Tommy, but my aunt was selling it for cheap since it's not farmland. My son, Chris, is an architect and he specializes in security features in buildings, so he's putting in all sorts of things like a panic room and reinforced doors. As if I could get into any sort of trouble where I'd need a panic room."

Maylin's eyes flickered to Geoffrey, and he knew what she was thinking. Neither of them had ever thought they'd get into any sort of trouble where they'd need homemade tear gas and mixed martial arts fighting moves.

While his mom talked about her house and finished her drink, Geoffrey kept looking out the windows, searching the street. He couldn't see anyone who might be loitering or suspicious, but then again, he didn't really know what "suspicious" was supposed to look like.

Had someone been following his mother, hoping she'd lead them to Geoffrey? Was it even possible? And had they seen him?

He waited for his mom to pause for breath and asked, "Is Chris with you, Mom?" Linc would have told Chris about the situation, and neither of them would have let her go out alone.

"Oh, no. I got up early before Chris or Linc woke up and drove here myself."

They were probably trying to call her cell phone, and she probably forgot to charge it again, since she so rarely used it. "Can I see your cell phone, Mom?"

She gave it to him. Yes, it had run out of power.

He didn't want her to go home alone. He took out his disposable cell phone and texted his siblings:

Met Mom @ CaptCaffeine. Can 1 of U C her home?

Olivia texted back:

We were worried. On the way to town now. C U in 5.

Finally his mother looked at her watch. "Oh! I've been rambling and you two need to get to work, don't you?"

"Liv texted me, Mom. She's heading here right now, so we'll wait until she gets here."

"Why is she heading here? They told me they had work to do at home." Mom gave him a look with a glint of steel. "I don't need a babysitter, thank you very much."

Busted. "She's not babysitting you, Mom. She ... heard I was here with Maylin."

"*Oh.*" His mother gave a coy smile.

Despite himself, Geoffrey's face turned to flame and he studiously avoided looking at Maylin. But his embarrassment was ten times better than the truth, which would go over so well with his mother: *Liv and*

Linc are protecting you because I've got Asian men with guns after me.

"In that case, that means I can get another one of these iced white chocolate thingys." His mom slurped at her macchiato.

"I met Olivia yesterday," Maylin said, laughter in her voice. "She was telling me about how you taught your kids to shoot."

"Well, I learned from their father ..."

Thankfully, Liv and Linc showed up a few minutes later. The skin around Linc's eyes were tight and he strode in swiftly, betraying his worry, but Liv walked with her easy athletic grace, as if she hadn't a care in the world.

"Hey, Mom," Liv said, "you left without us. We wanted some coffee too, you know." She looked at Geoffrey over their mom's head, and her serious expression belied her teasing tone. He nodded his thanks to her.

"We'll be heading out, Mom," Geoffrey said.

"But I thought you were waiting for Liv."

"And she saw us. I never said I was going to stay to get grilled by my sister." Geoffrey kissed his mother's cheek. "Bye."

"Nice to meet you, Emma," Maylin said.

As they left, Geoffrey heard Liv ask, "So what did you and Maylin talk about?" Probably to distract Mom.

Instead of heading out the front door, Geoffrey took the narrow hallway toward the bathroom at the back of the building. Next to it was the back entrance, which led to the small parking lot. He looked around the lot, which was packed with cars, but didn't see anyone. Then he hurried out.

"Do you really think your mom might have been followed?" Maylin asked in a low voice.

He turned to her. "How did you know I was thinking that?"

"You immediately looked around when you ran into her, and I could tell you were worried."

"I didn't see anyone, did you?"

"No."

"Then maybe I'm just being paranoid." He headed toward where they parked their car down a side street. "Let's go to Kind Samaritan Hospital in Napa. The sooner we can find Katie to explain all this, the sooner this will be all over."

The day had turned gray and hot, and as they pulled up to Kind Samaritan Hospital, Maylin thought that the slightly shabby building looked like it came out of Jane Eyre or some gothic novel.

Geoffrey frowned as he got out of the car. "Now I know why I didn't think it made sense, her working for Kind Samaritan."

"When did you think that?"

"When Felicity mentioned she'd flashed a KSN badge. I couldn't quite understand why, but I thought she would have worked for a more upscale hospital, maybe a private institution. Now I remember her watch. Rolex, and a higher-end one, too."

"Maybe a gift from family?"

"But if she had family that wealthy, they might have been able to get her a job at one of the private hospitals that caters to wealthier clients."

"Maybe she didn't want help from her wealthy family." Maylin realized how tart her voice was.

Geoffrey noticed, and shot her a curious look.

She felt heat rising from her neck. "My family wanted me to work for a private hospital, but I wanted to work for Merlyn Memorial, and eventually the Free Children's Clinic. I feel like I'm making more of a difference in the ER than in pampering wealthy patients."

Geoffrey surprised her by coloring under his tan. "I'm sorry. I didn't mean to assume."

"Don't be. I'd probably assume the same thing if I'd seen the Rolex."

Kind Samaritan Napa was a large hospital, but it still retained its small-town feel. The lobby was large but still had sturdy wooden furniture from the seventies, shabby but carefully maintained. Toys scattered across the floor, upended from the large toy bin in the corner, and several children entertained themselves while their parents waited to be called. The walls had old black and white photographs of places around Napa from the turn of the century.

Geoffrey and Maylin went to the receptionist behind the glass-fronted counter and showed their badges. "I'm Dr. Geoffrey Whelan and this is Nurse Maylin Kinley from the Free Children's Clinic in Sonoma."

The receptionist straightened in her chair and her demeanor changed from "empathetic nurse" to a more professional expression as soon as she knew she wasn't speaking to patients. "How can I help you?"

"We had a visit from one of your nurses, but our triage nurse couldn't remember her last name, and we need to speak to her to clarify something. Her first name was Katie."

"Certainly." The receptionist typed into her computer, then said, "A nurse, you said? Not a doctor? We have a Dr. Kathleen Lance."

"No, she said she was a nurse."

Maylin felt a twinge of foreboding in her stomach. Katie had said she was a nurse, but what if she wasn't? What if she wasn't a KSN employee at all? This would be only a dead end. Where could they go from here to figure out what was going on?

"Here we go, Katherine Wilson. She's a nurse in cardiology, on the third floor." The receptionist pointed to the hallway to her left. "Go up the elevator and then turn right."

"Thanks."

Maylin followed Geoffrey to the elevator. Her fears had been for nothing. She was becoming too suspicious after everything that had happened.

In the cardiology department, Geoffrey went up to the nurses' station and showed his badge again. "I'm Dr. Geoffrey Whelan and this is Nurse Maylin Kinley from the Free Children's Clinic in Sonoma. Could we speak to Katie Wilson?"

"I just saw her." The nurse got up and peered around the corner. "There she is." She pointed to a young woman who had just come out of a patient's room.

It wasn't the same woman.

Maylin's gut tightened. This nurse was the same height as the other woman, and had the same dark brown hair, but her skin was much fairer. The other nurse had had that slightly exotic tinge to her eyes and cheekbones that made Maylin think she might have been part Asian, but this nurse had wide blue eyes and a long, slender nose.

Geoffrey had hesitated, also, and he gave Maylin a look that matched what she was feeling. But he approached the nurse with a friendly smile. "Katie Wilson?"

"Yes?" The smile Katie gave Geoffrey had a bit of extra brightness, and she tilted her head to look up at him with hint of flirtatiousness. She looked cuter and more confident than Maylin would ever be.

Maylin looked away, clenching her hands together. She didn't know why she even cared that Katie found Geoffrey attractive. Most women would, with his height and rugged features. She supposed it just emphasized how she wasn't the kind of girl with the self-assurance to be so comfortable when a handsome man walked up to them.

"I'm Dr. Geoffrey Whelan." Maylin was faintly surprised that his smile was purely professional, maybe even a little cool, and even more surprised when he added, "And this is Nurse Maylin Kinley. We're from the Free Children's Clinic in Sonoma."

Katie's eyes flickered to Maylin with disinterest, then back to Geoffrey. "How can I help you, Doctor?"

"One of our triage nurses said that a nurse calling herself Katie Wilson came to the clinic yesterday, asking for some patient information. She even showed your badge."

Katie's eyes widened, making them seem even more blue. "My badge?"

"She had KSN scrubs, also," Maylin added.

Katie barely acknowledged her, and instead addressed Geoffrey. "My badge was stolen yesterday from my locker."

His brows lowered. "When, exactly?"

"The plastic hole in my badge tore from my holder the day before yesterday near the end of my shift, but I didn't have time to go down to security to get a new one right away, so I left in my locker. We only use the picture badge for the cafeteria and the general areas in the hospital, but all the guards already know me, so I didn't need it. I remember seeing it in my locker at the end of my shift. But when I went to my locker the next morning, it was gone. I reported it, but security didn't take it too seriously, because we use a separate security card key for the restricted areas, and I still had that with me on my holder."

"What time did your shift start yesterday morning?" Maylin asked.

Katie again addressed Geoffrey. "I got off work at six at night, and my shift started at seven the next morning, so it was taken sometime between then. There were nurses going on and off shift, so anyone could have taken it and no one would have noticed."

Anyone could have taken it. A dead end. She didn't understand what was going on.

"Thanks, Katie," Geoffrey said. "We'll let you get back to work."

Katie held out her hand. "No problem." Geoffrey hesitated, then took it. Katie held his hand as she added, "If there's anything else I can do for you, you know where to find me."

Maylin refrained from rolling her eyes. This was the cherry on top of her stress sundae, jealousy over a woman ten times prettier and a hundred times more self-assured than she was. She ought to concentrate instead on her current problem of staying alive.

As they turned and walked away, however, she noticed that Geoffrey discreetly wiped his hand on his shirt.

She was trying to understand her muddled emotions when ahead of them, far down the hallway, the elevator dinged and the doors opened.

The two Asian men in suits stepped out of the elevator, turned and saw them.

5

Geoffrey froze. His heart pulsed once, loudly, in his ear.

Then he grabbed Maylin's hand and ran back down the hallway.

He was trying to remember the layout of the hospital from the brief glimpse of the directory on the first floor. He knew each floor had the same general floor plan. Where had the stairs been? He cut right, dodging a nurse who was wheeling a patient in a chair. Maylin gave a small yelp and dodged them, as well.

"No running!" the nurse yelled after them, but then he heard her gasp, probably as the two Asian men shot past her. Geoffrey didn't want to turn around to look.

"Here." He pulled Maylin down a hallway to the left, hoping he wasn't leading them to a dead end. No, there was the door to the stairs.

He yanked open the door and let go of her hand as they pounded down the stairs, their steps echoing against the concrete walls. He jumped the last couple steps to the landing, then spun around down the next flight. He heard Maylin's feet land hard and thought she might have jumped the last few stairs, also.

They were on the first floor landing when they heard harder footsteps above them. The men had entered the stairwell.

He dug in his pockets for his car keys as he opened the door and cut right down the hallway. There was a back door they could use to skirt around the building and back toward the parking lot.

The first floor was busier than the third floor had been, and they slowed to avoid hitting patients, nurses, and doctors in the hallways. They had several people yell at them, but he ignored them and kept going. He hoped the crowded hallway would enable them to hide from the men, so they wouldn't know which hallway they ducked into.

He turned left and then left again, swinging around an empty gurney and then out a small, unmarked door to the right. Warm air rushed at him after the air conditioning of the hospital, but he didn't break stride as he raced for the Mustang. He knew he was outdistancing Maylin, but he would use the extra time to start the car.

He jammed the key into the lock to unlock it, then threw himself into the driver's seat. He'd cranked the engine and put it in gear just as Maylin opened the passenger door and dropped into her seat.

Geoffrey reversed out of the parking stall, and as he looked behind him, he saw the two men running out of the front doors of the hospital. He put the car in gear and headed out of the parking lot as fast as he could.

There was too much traffic on the road. He couldn't speed away from the hospital because of the mass of cars at the stop lights. He used the slower pace to strap in his seatbelt, and Maylin did the same. Within a couple blocks, he spotted the Asian men in a silver Civic several cars behind them.

"They're behind us," he said. "Can you see their license plate?"

Maylin twisted around, then unbuckled her seatbelt and stuck her head out of the car window. She finally sat back down, strapping herself in again. "Can't see."

"How did they find us?" But even as the question burst out of him, he knew. They must have followed his mother, who had led them right to him.

It was as if Maylin read his thoughts. "The fact they're here might mean there's no one following your mom anymore. She might be safe again."

"The problem is that now we need to get safe. We need to lose them."

"Where's the Napa police station?" Maylin said. "They wouldn't follow us if we went there, would they?"

"Let's hope not." Geoffrey used the traffic to his advantage, now. He cut in front of cars and wove through them, finally turning left to head to the police station.

However, he had to do a few extra right hand turns when he realized he was heading in the wrong direction. But the right hand turns made the silver Civic stand out more. Geoffrey could clearly see the driver, who was the smaller man, and the passenger, who had a white bandage over the nose that Geoffrey had broken.

"I got the license plate number." Maylin twisted back around and rummaged in her purse. When he glanced over at her again, she was writing the number on a green sticky pad like the promotional ones Oliver Medical Supply had given to the clinic.

"It's a silver Honda Civic," Geoffrey added.

She nodded and scribbled it down. Then she got on her cell phone and dialed the number on the business card Detective Carter had given to each of them. "Hello, Detective Carter, this is Maylin Kinley. Geoffrey Whelan and I are in Napa and we think we're being followed by the same men who attacked the clinic last night. They're driving a silver Honda Civic, license plate number 5FJI873."

Geoffrey could hear Detective Carter's agitated voice from the cell phone.

"Thanks. We're heading to the Napa police station right now." As she disconnected the call, she said, "Detective Carter is calling the Napa PD to tell them we're coming. We're to park in front and go right inside."

He finally got to the police station and pulled up in front. As he did so, an officer came to the car. Geoffrey hoped Detective Carter's call had gone through.

"Sir, you can't park here."

"My name is Geoffrey Whelan. Detective Horatio Carter from the Sonoma PD should have put in a call to your station. We were being followed by a silver Honda Civic. He told us to park in front."

The officer immediately used his shoulder radio to speak to someone about them, and Geoffrey looked around. The Civic hadn't followed them down this street. Would it be waiting around the corner for them to leave the station?

"I want to keep you safe, but a part of me wants to draw these guys out so I can try to find out what they want," he said to Maylin.

Her mouth quirked in a half-smile. "I'm not sure whether to be flattered or insulted."

He was ready to smile, to assure her to be flattered, but something in him stopped him. Japan had changed him too much, made him realize how much he was lacking. He had no business flirting with any woman, no matter how attractive, until he could put his doubts to rest, find his anchor.

It was strange, because although Katie had been painfully obvious in her flirting, he hadn't wanted to respond to her the way he wanted to respond to Maylin. But he kept his voice neutral as he said, "I wouldn't put you in danger."

"It probably would be better to know more about why they're after us before we start planning dangerous traps for them." Her voice was a bit cooler, but not unfriendly. "And Detective Carter would kill us, anyway."

"Come with me, sir," the officer told him urgently. "We're sending officers to search around the block in case the car parked nearby."

"Thanks." Geoffrey almost grabbed Maylin's hand as they followed the officer into the police station, just like he had grabbed her hand in the hospital when running from the two men. He clenched his fingers instead.

She noticed. "Are you all right?" she asked in a low voice.

"I'm fine."

Her gaze on him was steady. Almost knowing.

"I don't like being followed," he said. "It makes me jumpy." It made him crazy. He didn't like this feeling of not having a handle on the situation, of not being in control of his own safety, let alone Maylin's.

"We'll be safe for a little while," she said.

But what about when they left the station? The girl who warned him hadn't been Katie Wilson. Who was she? How in the world could they find out? Setting a trap for those two Asian men was looking better and better.

The officer sat them at a desk cluttered with paperwork and asked for their identification. Geoffrey and Maylin gave him their drivers' licenses and also their clinic badges. As Maylin handed her badge to the officer, she started, as if she'd been shocked by electrical static.

However, once the officer was gone, she turned to Geoffrey with a thoughtful look on her face. "I think I know how we can find this girl."

"How? I thought we were at a dead end."

"I did, too, until I remembered ... at least, I think I remembered it right. Katie mentioned that only her picture badge was stolen, right? She still had her security card key to the restricted areas of the hospital."

"Yes." He'd had a similar setup at some other hospitals, with a special card key that got him into certain rooms like the MRI lab and the medication room.

"But in the security video at the clinic, when she talked to Felicity, she showed her badge. But she also pulled from her pocket a security card key, didn't she?"

He pulled up the picture in his memory. "You're right. She did."

"At the time, we were thinking she was Katie Wilson and that it was one of her hospital badges. But if it's not Katie's security card key, then what is it?"

It had been small and white, and the video hadn't been clear enough to see the writing on it.

"I know what it reminded me of," Maylin said. "It looked to me like a card key to a hotel room."`

A couple hours went by before the Napa police felt it was safe for them to leave the station. The Napa PD had received the Sonoma police reports of both the attack in Geoffrey's office and the attack of the clinic yesterday, and so they took the matter of the Asian men tailing them very seriously. A search of the license plate number brought up a blue minivan stolen yesterday, which the men had switched with the plate on their Civic. The Napa PD promised to look into traffic cam footage and any security camera video from businesses in Napa on the route that Geoffrey took, but it would take a few days for them to get that. Also, while Geoffrey and Roy had gotten minor injuries, this sort of case was a lower priority than a murder or robbery, and police resources were limited.

By the time they were allowed to leave, Maylin had gotten antsy with her impatience to look for the hotel the girl might have been staying at. They'd used the time in the station, and the station's WiFi, to search for likely hotels in the Napa and Sonoma areas. The expensive Rolex watch made them suspect the girl would choose a higher end hotel, so they ruled out any economy hotels and any B&Bs who didn't use card key locks on their doors.

There were a great number of hotels in Napa, but only three in Sonoma. They opted to check out the three Sonoma hotels tonight, and if they struck out, they'd go to the Napa hotels the next day.

"Number three." Geoffrey pulled his car up to the valet for the Rochev Hotel, which didn't have a self-park lot. It was a mark of good service that the uniformed valet didn't even bat an eyelash at Geoffrey's eyesore Mustang, but treated them with utmost courtesy. The valets at the two other hotels they had visited had looked like they wanted to call a tow truck.

A second valet came up to Geoffrey with a smile and a ready handshake. "Dr. Whelan, nice to see you here."

"Cisco, how are you?" Geoffrey shook his hand warmly. "How's your boy doing?"

"His arm's feeling great. He's already throwing the ball around at practice, but he hasn't played in a game yet."

"Don't let him push himself too much. We want him playing for the Giants in a few years."

"Sure thing." Cisco chuckled. "Anything I can help you with?"

"Yeah, actually." Geoffrey gestured to Maylin, who had been holding back slightly. "This is Maylin Kinley, and she's a nurse at the Free Children's Clinic with me."

"Nice to meet you." Cisco's handshake was firm. "Dr. Whelan, here, set my son's broken wrist."

Maylin felt a stab of shame. She'd been so caught up in remembering how Geoffrey had been when she first knew him, and yet here again was evidence that he'd changed. The old Dr. Whelan wouldn't have remembered a patient's father, much less chatted with him about his son outside of the boy's injury.

"A young girl came to speak to me at the clinic yesterday." Geoffrey showed him a picture of the woman, taken from the clinic's video, which Monica had emailed to his phone while they were waiting at the Napa police station. "She impersonated a nurse, and Maylin and I are looking for her. We thought she might have stayed at the Rochev Hotel."

Cisco squinted at the photo. "Actually, she looks familiar."

"She does?" Maylin stepped closer. "Do you know her name?"

"No, but my manager could probably help you with that," Cisco said.

"Do you mind introducing us to him?"

"No problem." Cisco led the way into the hotel.

The entrance foyer reminded Maylin of a Grecian temple, echoing with marble columns and a marble floor, which was covered with a plush carpet in cream and forest green. Cisco took them directly to the front counter and nodded to a tall, dark-haired man. "Mr. Donner, this is Dr. Whelan and Ms. Kinley. He's the doctor I was telling you about ..."

Mr. Donner's eyes brightened. "The one who set your son's arm? Nice to meet you, Doctor." He shook Geoffrey's hand. "I was watching the game when the accident happened and the boy broke his wrist. It looked really bad. You worked a miracle."

"Not at all," Geoffrey said. "His youth and determination was what healed him so well."

Maylin, standing to one side as the men talked, happened to turn slightly.

A man sat in one of the plush green-striped chairs in a small alcove just off of the entrance. As she looked at him, his head immediately turned away.

She shook off her unease. She was probably just being paranoid. Surely he wasn't looking at them? Had he been sitting there when they entered the hotel? She couldn't remember.

"Mr. Donner, Dr. Whelan's looking for someone who came to the clinic," Cisco said. "I thought I recognized her. Do you think you could take a look?"

"Oh, certainly."

"You're in good hands. Dr. Whelan, Ms. Kinley, I'll see you later." Cisco left to return to his post with a wave to them both.

Mr. Donner looked at the photo and immediately said, "I recognize her, also. She helped a man in the bar who got a bad cut from a wineglass that broke in his hand. Two nights ago, I think."

Maylin's chest was tight with elation. They'd found her.

"She came to the clinic yesterday, asking for information about a patient," Geoffrey said. "She impersonated a nurse, and we want to talk to her, find out why."

"Impersonated?" Mr. Donner frowned. "But she said she was a nurse. And she seemed to know what she was doing when that man was injured."

"She told the clinic that her name was Katie Wilson," Maylin said.

"No, that doesn't sound familiar." Mr. Donner began rummaging through the drawers in the desk. "The hotel sent a small fruit basket to her room as thanks that night, so I wrote down her name. Let me see if I can find it ..."

While he searched, Maylin again looked at the man seated in the alcove. She wasn't sure why she did so, but again it seemed he looked quickly away from her.

Her elation began to dissipate with the nausea in the pit of her stomach. Why was he looking at them? Was it simply coincidence or something more sinister? Who was he?

"Her name was Cassandra Wong." The manager held out a piece of hotel notepaper with her name and room number written down. "The man she helped also wanted to know her name. She might even have prevented it from being a more serious injury. When the paramedics arrived, they mentioned that it was good there had been a nurse in the bar that night."

So maybe she had only given a false name. But if she was a nurse, why had she impersonated one from Kind Samaritan Hospital? Did she work there also? She would have had easy access to the women's locker room to steal Katie's ID badge, and she'd already have had her own set of hospital scrubs.

"Is she still here?" Maylin asked.

"No, she only stayed that one night. I hope she didn't do anything wrong."

"We don't think so," Geoffrey said. "But we were concerned when we found out she isn't Katie Wilson."

"We only want to talk to her," Maylin added.

"Thank you, Mr. Donner." Geoffrey shook his hand again. "I told Cisco to let me know when his son's first game is, so maybe I'll see you there."

"You definitely will. My son plays on the same team."

Maylin looked at the man in the alcove again, but this time he didn't look away. He held her gaze for a moment.

A chill shot down her spine and she turned away from him. She tried to smile as Mr. Donner bid her goodbye, but her mouth felt stiff. She leaned close to Geoffrey as they headed out of the hotel. "Geoffrey, that man sitting in the green striped chair in the alcove … I think he was watching us."

She saw the muscles in his forearm tighten into cords as he clenched his hands.

"Are you sure?" he said.

"Pretty sure."

Outside, Geoffrey didn't need to hand his valet ticket to Cisco, who grinned as he ran to get his Mustang. The other valet was missing, so it was only the two of them standing outside. Maylin tried not to look back in the man's direction, but then they heard the door to the hotel open.

The strange man stepped outside and looked directly at them.

Maylin took a step back.

The stranger was taller than Geoffrey, with dark hair in a steeply receding hairline. The man's chin tilted up in a faintly arrogant angle as he studied Geoffrey beneath heavily lidded eyes. Then his gaze slid to Maylin, and it seemed that a predatory gleam appeared.

A sharp spasm ran through her.

Without warning, Geoffrey lunged at him, pinning him to the wall of the building with his forearm jammed beneath the man's neck. "Who are you?" he demanded.

The man's eyes had bugged out of their sockets, and rather than fighting Geoffrey, his large, knobby hands fluttered helplessly. "I just ... the girl ..."

"What do you want with her? Who are you?"

"I just wanted to ask her out," the man choked.

Geoffrey stiffened. Heat flooded Maylin's face.

"I swear that's all," the man said, his voice high with panic.

Geoffrey released him grudgingly. "Sorry," he mumbled.

The man rubbed his neck. "You're lucky I don't call the police," he said petulantly.

Maylin didn't know whether to laugh or cry. Maybe it had simply been her own paranoia making her suspicious. She was only dressed in jeans and a blouse, the extra set of clothes she kept in her locker at work, nothing particularly attractive. Coupled with the stress of the past two days, the man's attention wasn't as flattering as it might have been. "It would have helped if you hadn't been staring at me like a stalker," she said acidly.

"You were the one giving off signals." The man sounded like a spoiled child.

Maylin didn't bother to respond. Geoffrey looked like he might take offense at that, so she pulled him to the curb just as Cisco drove up in the Mustang.

"I'm sorry," she said as they drove away.

"Don't be." His voice was tight.

"No, I shouldn't have suspected him." She felt guilty for needlessly heightening Geoffrey's already hot stress levels.

"No," Geoffrey said quickly. "If I'd seen him looking at you, when he came outside, I'd still have done the same thing." He looked over at her. She didn't notice her hands were tightly clenched in her lap until he put his warm palm over them.

His touch made her breath quicken, but so did his words. She felt ... safe with Geoffrey.

No, she couldn't start thinking this way about him. How well did she really know him? Sebastian had made her feel safe when she first met him, but she soon learned that he had wanted to control her. And he'd done it, with words that still cut sharply in her memory. In many ways, there were echoes of Sebastian in the tight control Geoffrey had over his emotions.

She couldn't go through that again with another man. She wanted someone ... softer. Not someone strong-willed like Geoffrey.

"Thanks," she said lightly, and then pulled her hands away from his.

He rested his palm against the gearshift. "It's late, but the library is open for another hour. Let's go there to look up Cassandra Wong."

Maylin felt safer at the library since it was so empty. If those Asian men came in to look for them, they would stick out like a sore thumb. "Cassandra obviously didn't want us to know who she was, which makes me think she doesn't work at KSN," Maylin said as they headed upstairs to the computers. "If she was trying to stay anonymous, she wouldn't want to flash a badge from the very hospital she works at."

"But the fact she wanted to hide her identity also might mean she might be easy to find online."

They started off searching independently on two computers, but after only a few minutes, he said, "I found her."

"That was fast." Maylin scooted her chair closer to his computer and saw an obituary pulled up on his screen.

"I decided to start by limiting my search to the San Francisco Bay Area. I figured there was a good chance she was local. And I did an image search rather than just a text search."

The obituary was a long, elaborate piece for Chet Wong, who had died in a car accident that occurred only a few weeks ago. It listed his family and included an old family photo of him, his parents, and his sisters Cassandra and Chelsea. That was definitely the girl who had spoken to Geoffrey. Then Maylin read further down about his family. "Her father is *the* Chester Wong?"

"What do you know about him? This just says he's a successful San Francisco businessman with ties to Hong Kong."

"I only know the rumors," Maylin said, "nothing proven. Most of his money came through his wife, whose father was a wealthy American businessman. She and Chester got everything when he died. Then Chester's money seemed to suddenly multiply even more after that. There were stories about slave labor in his businesses in Hong Kong, human trafficking, all sorts of nasty things."

"He sounds charming."

"All these stories came out when he was involved in a money laundering case. There were rumors that he'd paid off some jurors or killed a witness or something like that. They couldn't prove he was directly involved in any criminal activity, and he was acquitted."

"None of this explains why she came to warn us. Except ..." He ran his finger down the obituary. "Chet Wong was the same age as Frank Chan. I'm going to see if I can find an article about the accident."

While he was searching, Maylin went back to her own search, which had been in social media websites. She followed Geoffrey's strategy and did an image search, and soon found her.

"I found Cassandra on a social media site," Maylin said. "Her profile is private, so it doesn't show much information about her, but it lists her hometown as San Francisco and her occupation as a nurse."

"Does it list her place of work?"

"No." Maylin pursed her lips as she regarded the profile. "But I have a hunch. If she only needed to impersonate someone else to hide her identity, she could have gone to any other hospital in San Francisco or Marin or San Rafael to steal a badge and scrubs."

"You think she went deliberately to KSN?"

"I think she works for Kind Samaritan in San Francisco, where she lives, and so she went to Kind Samaritan in Napa because she was familiar with it and could easily take that badge and those scrubs."

Geoffrey nodded, looking thoughtful. "You might be right. It would be a good place for us to start looking for her. Otherwise we'd be stuck checking every hospital and clinic in San Francisco."

Maylin tried to see if she could find out any more about her, but then Geoffrey said, "I found the article on the car accident."

Maylin went over to read over his shoulder. The car, a recent model SRT Viper, had flipped over the side of the road, and not much was known about the cause of the accident. Chet Wong had been instantly killed when he was thrown from the car—and the other passenger had been a boy named Frank Chan.

"This happened only a few days after we treated him at the clinic," Maylin said.

"Chet died, but Frank survived," Geoffrey said, reading further. "Looks like he was in guarded condition after the accident but was expected to recover."

"I don't understand. Her brother just died. Why did Cassandra come all the way to Sonoma from San Francisco to find out who had treated Frank at the clinic, before the accident even happened?"

"And why warn us we were in danger?"

Maylin straightened and took a deep breath. "Was she really trying to warn us?"

Geoffrey took a deep breath, also.

"All this time, we've been assuming Cassandra was sincere," Maylin said. "She looked so frightened in the video surveillance at the clinic. But now we know who she is."

Geoffrey nodded. "And because of her father's shady reputation, it makes you wonder about her connection to those two men who are after us."

"How did she know they would come for us?" Maylin said. "Until tonight, we never even considered the possibility, but she might be involved with those two man trying to kill us."

Geoffrey's hands tightened on the steering wheel when he saw the light winking in the darkness.

"Is that light from the cabin?" Maylin asked.

"I think so."

"I don't remember Olivia saying she'd come back to the cabin tonight. But who else could it be?"

He didn't know. He wanted to switch off the headlights, but it was too dangerous to drive this trail without them. Then he saw the sleek black SUV parked in front of the cabin, and he groaned. "It's Liv."

Maylin gave him a strange look. "Why is that bad?"

"I just ..." He sighed. "I didn't want to get my family any more involved in this than they already are. I worry that they want to help." He wanted them to stay safe. Even moreso now that he was back from Japan.

"I can understand that you don't want your family in danger," Maylin said, "but your siblings aren't walking into this blindly. They know what happened at the clinic yesterday. They want to help because they care about you."

"I'm responsible for them." His chest felt tight, like he was drowning. "I have to be there for them. I can't have anything happen to them like ..."

The guilt and shame closed over his head like ocean waters. Like tsunami waters. He felt panic that he couldn't do the right thing, that he couldn't do anything to protect them.

Coming back to Sonoma was supposed to help anchor him. Instead, he felt even more as if he was being tossed about in a stormy sea. He wasn't physically injured, but there was a gaping wound in his soul that had only festered after the Japan tsunami, rather than healing itself. He wasn't whole anymore. And yet he had a responsibility for his family, and now Maylin.

Then he felt her hand on his, soft and gentle. She didn't say anything, didn't ask him what he'd meant. She simply held his hand, let him know she was there, imparted comfort and encouragement, whatever he needed from her. Her thumb rubbed his knuckles in a rhythmic gesture that soothed him.

He forced himself to take a slow breath, and the panic eased. He was in control of himself again.

But he couldn't look at her. Didn't want to see what was in her eyes. He schooled his face into a mask of calm. "Let's get inside." He got out of the car.

The delicious smell of homemade stew greeted them as soon as they opened the cabin door. Liv looked up from where she was stirring the pot on the stove. "Hey, you two."

Geoffrey gave a mock groan. "Please tell me you didn't cook." He knew his voice was a little too cheerful, a little too loud.

"You're going to give Maylin a terrible impression of our family."

"Oh, don't worry," Maylin said gaily, her voice also too loud, "I knew I'd like you when you told me you'd filled up the gun cabinet." She headed to the stove to sniff the stew.

Liv's eyes brightened. "Do you have guns?"

"Just a revolver. I took a few classes at a shooting range in San Francisco. It was fun." Maylin's voice was light, but Geoffrey thought he heard a note of strain. What had made her want—or need—the revolver in the first place?

"Good job, bro. You've picked a winner for your partner in crime." Liv gave Maylin a high five.

Maylin looked embarrassed but also pleased by Liv's hearty approval. But Liv always had that effect on people, making them feel accepted. She obviously liked Maylin, and there was a warmth in Maylin's smile that Geoffrey hadn't seen often at the clinic.

Thinking about her at work made him realize that Maylin usually had an air of isolation about her, even among the other nurses. The women didn't really treat her like someone who entirely belonged, maybe because she was a little different. She was shy, and awkward, but she had a calmness and comforting air about her that made her connect with patients better than other nurses. Her coworkers were sometimes impatient with her because while they focused on their tasks, Maylin didn't mind spending a few extra minutes adjusting pillows, picking up toys that had fallen to the floor, playing a little make-believe with a sick child.

He wanted her to know that he understood her and appreciated her, much more now than he had when they first met years ago or even a few months ago when they started working together again. But that was something he couldn't say to her, even if it brought out her blindingly beautiful smile, because he was too damaged. He had to figure out what was wrong with him without involving anyone else in his problems.

"How was Mom after we left the coffee shop?" Geoffrey pulled out some plates from the cupboard.

"She had another macchiato," Liv said. "And after she finished all the whipped cream, she sent me back to the barista to ask for another squirt to top it off again."

Geoffrey shook his head. "That's too much sugar. You couldn't tell her no?"

Liv raised her eyebrows at him. "Would you have been able to?"

"Good point."

"Everything okay after you guys left?"

"Oh, fine." Geoffrey's back was turned to his sister, so Liv didn't see his grip on some spoons tighten briefly.

Then came the sound of a choking car engine outside the cabin.

Geoffrey dropped the spoons. "Where's the shotgun?" he demanded.

"Wait, wait." Liv held up a hand. Unfortunately, it was the one holding the spoon she was stirring the stew with, and hot brown gobs splattered on him.

"Liv!"

"Sorry." Liv put the spoon down. "It's probably Liam."

It took him a second to remember, but then he glared at her. "Liam O'Neill?"

"I asked him to come because he's a skip tracer. Isn't that exactly what you need to find that girl?" She headed to the front door.

"Wait, you don't know for sure that it's Liam."

"Are you kidding? I could recognize that dying engine from anywhere." She flung open the door and greeted the man who had been about to knock. "Hi, Liam. Come on in."

"Hi, Liv." Liam gave her a friendly hug.

How many more people had to know about this, putting themselves in danger? Geoffrey knew Liv only meant well, but he had to tamp down his frustration.

Maylin seemed to know exactly what he was thinking, because she shot him a look that clearly said,

Smile and be polite, you moron. Well, he might have imagined the moron part.

Liam held out a hand to Geoffrey. "Hey, Geoff." Liam O'Neill still had the buzz cut from his days in the army, which emphasized his wide jaw and rugged cheekbones. Geoffrey hadn't seen Liam in a while, and the scars on his shoulder and arm from shrapnel during his tour in Afghanistan had faded from angry red to a pale pink.

He shook Liam's hand. "Glad to see you."

There was a knowing glint of humor in his startling blue eyes. "I hope you will be."

"Liam, this is Maylin Kinley. She's a nurse at the clinic," Liv said. "Maylin, Liam O'Neill is related to us by marriage. His brother married our cousin, Monica, last year."

Maylin shook his hand. Geoffrey's jaw tensed when it seemed Liam held hers a little too long.

"I hope you can help us," she said to him.

"Let's talk over dinner," Liv said. "It's late and I'm starved."

"You didn't cook, did you?" Liam asked.

Liv glared at him. "You don't have to eat."

"I meant ... I hope you didn't slave over that stove all night."

"Good save," Geoffrey murmured to him.

"Nice try," Liv said.

Maylin snorted and tried to turn it into a cough.

Over dinner--which was rather good, indicating Liv hadn't cooked the stew--Geoffrey gave an abbreviated version of how they'd gone to Kind Samaritan in Napa, and skipping the part about being followed, how they'd found Cassandra's name at the hotel. He didn't want Liv to worry, or to want to get involved. If she was safe in Sonoma, he would feel more comfortable, more in control of the situation. She would say he was being overprotective—actually, probably more like pigheaded and insufferable—but he just couldn't accept her help, if it would put her in danger.

He didn't want Liv knowing about Chester Wong's rumored criminal businesses, so he only said, "Liam, since your job is finding people who don't want to be found, we could use your help."

"No problem." Liam finished up his bowl of stew.

Geoffrey would find a chance to talk to Liam alone to tell him what they'd found at the library. Maylin gave Geoffrey a look that was deliberately neutral, but she didn't say anything more about Cassandra.

"You know, her name sounds familiar," Olivia said slowly. "I can't place where I've seen it before."

"Hopefully that means she'll be easy to find." He didn't want Liv knowing about the connection to Cassandra's shady father.

Liv shot him a suspicious look. "You're pretty laid-back about all this."

He shrugged. "So far, it's been fine. We've been keeping a low profile."

"You haven't seen those two Asian men?"

"Well, I've been looking twice at every Asian man I see on the street." Geoffrey nudged his sister's elbow, and Liv seemed to not notice that he hadn't answered her question. "The police will find them. They've got to be on a traffic camera somewhere." He hoped that with both the Napa and Sonoma police aware of the men, they'd find them soon.

"But even if you find Cassandra, figuring out why the men are after you may not help you stop them," Liv said.

"But if I know why they want us, then I can look for leverage against them." There was a dark, intense edge to his thoughts.

Liv frowned. "Geoff, don't do anything reckless."

He forced a careless smile. "You worry too much. I'm the responsible stick in the mud, remember?"

But for Maylin and his family, he would be reckless if he had to. He would do everything he could to make those men stop. Whatever it took.

Maylin awoke with a start. The darkness in the bedroom was deep and black, and for a moment she felt as if she were in a tomb.

Then Olivia, sleeping next to her on the bed, moaned and rolled over.

No, she was in the cabin, not a tomb. After living in the city or the suburbs all her life, nighttime in the middle of the wilderness was too quiet. She had expected coyotes or owls, but there was just ... nothing.

So what had woken her?

Her heartbeat had started to slow, but it ratcheted up again. She got out of bed, shivering in the aching cold of the unheated room, and felt her way to the bedroom door. It was only as she drew near to it that she realized there was a faint glow beneath the crack in the door.

She pushed the door open, wincing as it creaked, and slipped out of the room.

There was a fresh log in the fireplace and it was just starting to flicker. And in front of it was Geoffrey.

He had twisted around when he heard the door creak, but upon seeing her, something deep and intense settled in his eyes, making them seem even darker. She wondered if he perhaps didn't want company, but then he said, "Are you all right? You shouldn't be up, you need rest."

"You shouldn't be up either."

They stared at each other for a few heartbeats. Then he gestured for her to come to the fire. "It's cold."

She hesitated. This wasn't a good idea. Then she realized her feet had brought her to Geoffrey without her knowing about it. She sat.

It was a lot warmer next to the fire, and she stared at the flames in silence for a long time. What was she doing here, with him? She should go back to bed. Then she turned to look at him.

He looked as if he was dying inside.

He had schooled his features into an expressionless mask, maybe because his emotions at this moment were so near to the surface, stirring like a creature beneath black waters. She couldn't forget what he'd said.

"I can't have anything happen to them like ... "

He'd given her a glimpse into the reason behind the bleakness in his eyes that she'd seen since working with him again. Something horrific had happened to him in Japan.

She wanted to take that bleakness away. She wanted to help him find some peace.

But why would he allow her in when he didn't want to open himself even to his family?

He broke the silence. "My sister seems to like you a lot."

"I think she's amazing." Olivia was vibrant and beautiful, and the fact she didn't seem to mind Maylin's oddities and awkwardness made her even more like a rock star.

"The two of you talked a lot after dinner."

"Since she's a shooting instructor, I should have guessed she'd be excited about my revolver."

Geoffrey hesitated, and it looked as if he was wrestling with himself over something. Then he asked, "Why did you buy it?"

"Just home security. I was living alone in Los Angeles at the time." It wasn't a lie, exactly. Sebastian had grown more unstable. While they were dating, even during those last few weeks, he had never hit her, but his words grew more venomous and he began throwing furniture and objects around. After she'd finally broken up with him, she'd taken precautions and bought the gun. Just in case.

Her answer had caused some of the stress lines around his eyes to relax. "Well, be warned, Liv's a bit fanatical about her guns. She especially likes taking out her paintball guns to shoot at her defenseless brothers."

"She already invited me to go paint-balling with you all when this is over." Even though this dangerous situation made her feel like she was running on no sleep and too much caffeine, a part of Maylin had desperately longed for that time of fun with Olivia. With Geoffrey's siblings. With him.

When she'd bought her revolver, her mother had insisted she was being melodramatic about Sebastian, her sister had angrily accused her of deliberately being ridiculous just to embarrass her family, and her father hadn't spoken to her for a few months. Maylin had almost gotten rid of the gun, but then she had found the job in Sonoma and moved away from her family.

In contrast, Olivia had not only praised her for it, she'd been genuinely interested, not just in the gun, but also in her. Olivia made Maylin feel like ... family.

She had been so used to being alone. She began to wonder if she didn't need to be.

No, she shouldn't enjoy this so much. She couldn't get used to it. Because they had to stop the threat against them, and once that happened, surely Geoffrey and his family would realize that she didn't belong. People always came to that realization eventually. It had ceased to hurt her anymore.

It was hard because Geoffrey's family had almost made her think it might be possible for her to have that kind of connection with other people. "I really like your family," she said. "They make me feel like ... it's recess at kindergarten."

He looked at her with a strange expression in his eyes, which had darkened to gray-brown. If she didn't know better, she would almost have thought it was ... longing.

But then he shifted his gaze back to the fire. "Well, sometimes they all act like kids," he said in a mock grumble. "What's your family like?"

"Nothing like yours." Maylin thought about her cold parents, her disapproving sister. "They're pillars in the community," she said bitterly.

Geoffrey gave a bark of laughter. "The Whelans are definitely not that."

"I didn't mean it that way. They're very conscious of how their community sees them. They like appearing to be perfect, someone for others to look up to and envy." She remembered the fight that erupted when she told them about the job in Sonoma. "That's why I left."

"I don't blame you," Geoffrey muttered. "Too much work trying to be perfect."

"I never did. They blamed me for that, too."

"Did you root for the wrong baseball team? Buy the wrong shoes?"

She gave a half-smile. "I was a nurse instead of a doctor."

He blinked in genuine surprise. "There's nothing wrong with being a nurse."

"I love being a nurse. They wanted more." In a way, it was cathartic speaking to him about this, because he didn't know her parents and would never meet them. They wouldn't approve of him anyway—medical missions as opposed to a successful practice.

"That's ridiculous. They can't dictate your career."

"They dictated so many other things in my life. My friends, my school clubs, my boyfriends."

"How can they dictate your boyfriends?"

"I shouldn't say that. They didn't dictate that I date Sebastian, not exactly. But they approved of him. And when I broke up with him, they weren't happy." They'd berated her for her bad judgment in breaking up with a man who would have been able to give her a huge house in Nob Hill and vacations to the Bahamas.

"Why did you break up with him?" Geoffrey's voice was rough, and she thought that redness was stealing up his neck, but in the firelight, she couldn't be sure. She supposed anyone would be curious.

"He was verbally abusive." Her counselor had told her to name it baldly, to not cover it up or make it any softer than what it was, but she still flinched a little as she said it.

Geoffrey had stiffened. "A person doesn't need to strike someone to leave a mark," he said in a low voice. She realized he was ... angry on her behalf.

She didn't answer. She wasn't entirely sure if enough time had passed, if she'd gone to enough counseling sessions, for her to have moved on. Maybe she was attracted to Geoffrey because he was protecting her from the bad guys, making her feel safe, whereas Sebastian had made her feel beaten down.

Then suddenly, she felt the warmth of his hand covering hers where it rested on the rug before the fire. "I'm sorry that happened to you," he said.

"Thank you." She wasn't sure what else to say.

But then his other hand reached up, cupped her cheek, turned her head toward him. And then he leaned in and was kissing her.

She was lost in a forest scented with eucalyptus, fir, and Geoffrey. His mouth was firm and yet gentle at the same time. It was as if he wanted to impart both strength and comfort to her. The touch of his lips sent a fiery tingle throughout her body, filling her with warmth, and a yearning, and a connection.

No, what connection? It was just a kiss and she was being stupid. Geoffrey Whelan would never want her in normal circumstances. She pulled away. "We shouldn't."

He started as if waking from a dream.

And it had been a dream, hadn't it? This wasn't something she needed. Geoffrey wasn't what she needed. She wanted someone less ... confident.

Maylin got to her feet. "You should go to bed." She almost ran toward the bedroom door. "I should go to bed. Goodnight." She closed the door behind her and leaned against it.

She stood there for a long time, listening to Olivia's even breathing and letting the tears fall down her face. She never heard Geoffrey return to his bedroom before she finally crept, cold as a block of ice, back into bed.

Maylin felt a bit dead inside. Unemotional. Maybe it was the lack of sleep making her zombie-like. Either way, she was her calm, normal self to Olivia and to Geoffrey, pretending last night hadn't happened. It was probably best that way. It shouldn't have happened.

Ever since they'd left Olivia at the cabin this morning, Geoffrey had been the same cool, professional Dr. Whelan she'd worked with at the clinic these past few months, but there was a brittleness to his manner when he spoke to her. He was probably regretting what he'd done. She wanted to tell him not to worry, that it hadn't mattered to her, but she didn't want to bring it up at all. And she wasn't entirely sure that would be truth.

Except it *couldn't* matter to her. She had to stay focused.

She had gotten practice in hiding her feelings from her parents, from Sebastian. She used to be good at shoving the emotions into a box and strapping it shut. It was a little harder now, but she had to do it.

"When we get to Kind Samaritan Hospital in San Francisco, if we mention who we are, I worry Cassandra would bolt," Geoffrey said as he drove.

"Do you really think she'd suddenly leave work?"

"Maybe not, but she could hide from us. She could get her coworkers to cover for her."

"She may not have a shift today," Maylin said. "She might be at home or out."

A muscle in his jaw worked, then he said, "When I called him this morning, Liam mentioned he would be able to find her home address, among other things."

"I know you don't want to involve other people—"

"It's too dangerous," he said.

She continued, "We did all right by ourselves, but it's Liam's job to find people who don't want to be found. I'm glad Olivia called him." She looked out the window and added softly, "It might help this to end quickly."

She meant it, and yet she didn't.

Kind Samaritan Hospital, situated on the edge of South San Francisco, was much larger than the one in Napa. They had to park several blocks away and walk past warehouses, small businesses, and a few diners.

There were a few dozen people milling around the waiting area just inside the first floor entrance, some standing around, some sitting, most going to and fro. Some patients, some nurses and doctors. Maylin and Geoffrey waited in line to speak to the receptionist, a woman with a pinched mouth and a long nose through which she heaved forceful sighs quite often as she listened to patients. When it was their turn, they immediately showed her their clinic badges, but it seemed to only make her annoyed.

She huffed a nasal sigh. "What is it you need? We're very busy, here."

"We need to speak to a nurse, Cassandra Wong," Geoffrey said.

Another long-suffering sigh. "I can't look it up on this computer. You'll have to go to Human Resources on the eighth floor and ask them."

Maylin eyed the computer. The woman probably could look it up, but it would take a few steps.

Geoffrey apparently suspected the same, because his eyes glittered coldly. He opened his mouth, but Maylin grabbed his arm and said to the receptionist, "Do we need any sort of visitor's badge to go to Human Resources?"

"Of course not," she said as if Maylin were an idiot.

"Thank you." She dragged Geoffrey away.

"For nothing," Geoffrey muttered.

"It wouldn't have been any use to talk to her any more," Maylin said. "She's the kind of person who believes everyone is out to make her life a living hell. We could have showed up with a fruit basket for her, and she'd still have blamed us for the trash she'd have to throw away."

"So how do we find Human Resources? The eighth floor must be full of offices."

"I have a better idea." Maylin led the way to the directory next to the main bank of elevators and searched. She found Internal Medicine on the fourth floor and punched the button for the elevator.

When they entered the wing for Internal Medicine, it was full of people, but they were almost all seated and waiting to be called for their appointments. The nurses behind the reception desks bustled about carrying charts or working on computers, but there wasn't any of the air of panic or uncertainty that had pervaded the first floor.

"Why Internal Medicine?" Geoffrey asked.

Maylin shrugged. "At Merlyn Memorial, the Internal Medicine department was just as busy as the other departments, but it also tended to be the calmest department. I thought I'd try this one."

They approached a reception desk, and the nurse, working on the computer, glanced at them and said, "Just a minute, please, and I'll be right with you."

"Take your time," Geoffrey said.

She typed for a little while, printed out a few sheets of paper which she clipped together, then finally turned to them calmly. "How can I help you folks?"

They showed their badges and introduced themselves. "One of your hospital nurses came by to see us two days ago. We need to speak to her to clarify a few things."

"She didn't give her department to our triage nurse," Maylin added. "Her name is Cassandra Wong."

"Sure, give me a second to look her up."

Maylin held her breath as the nurse searched on her computer. Would Cassandra be a nurse here?

"Cassandra Wong, you said?" the nurse asked. "Not Fong?"

"Wong," Maylin said.

"Okay, here she is."

Her heart beat fiercely. They'd found her.

"I'll write down her department and the wing number." The nurse scribbled on a pad of sticky notes—the same green promotional ones from Oliver Medical Supply that they were using at the clinic. "Here you go."

"Thanks," Maylin said with a smile. As they walked away, she looked at the paper. "I should have guessed. She works in Cardiology, same as Katie."

The Cardiology department was busy with nurses and doctors walking down the hallways. The nurses' station, however, was empty, and they waited for a few minutes before a nurse returned to the desk. "Can I help you?" she asked.

"We're looking for Nurse Cassandra Wong," Geoffrey said.

The nurse frowned slightly. "Can I ask what this is about?"

They introduced themselves and showed their badges. "She came to the clinic two days ago, asking for some patient information. We just need to clarify a few things with her."

"Which doctor requested the information?"

CAMY TANG

"I'm afraid we don't know," Maylin said. "She spoke to our triage nurse, who gave her the information."

The nurse looked even more concerned. "That's really odd."

"It is?" Maylin said.

The nurse leaned in toward them. "Cassandra had a day off two days ago. And then she didn't come in for work yesterday and today. Our supervisor is furious."

Why would Cassandra not show up for work? Was she in danger, or was she involved with the two men after them?

"No one knows where she is?" Geoffrey said.

The nurse shook her head. "That's what's weird. If she were sick, she'd call in."

"You said she had the day off two days ago?" Maylin asked. "When did she ask for that?"

"I think it was last minute. You'd have to ask our supervisor about that."

"Where is she?"

"She might be in her office." The nurse pointed down the hallway to her left. "Go to the end and turn right. Room 1226, last door on your right. If she's walking around the wing ..." The nurse shrugged. "If I see her, I'll let her know you're looking for her."

"Thanks."

They went down the hallway, and then turned right into a short hallway that dead-ended. The last door on the left had a red exit sign above it, indicating it was the stairs. Maylin could see that the last door on the right was open, with light streaming from the doorway. And at the very end of the hallway were two chairs against the wall.

A dark-haired man lounged in one of the chairs, looking bored, maybe waiting for someone. These chairs might have been for nurses waiting to speak to the supervisor, for there wasn't a side table with magazines next to them, like the chairs in typical waiting rooms, so he was staring into space, his elbow on the arm of the chair and his head propped up in his hand.

It was one of the Asian men from the clinic.

Geoffrey stiffened. The man, the tall one with the bandage on his broken nose, hadn't seen them yet. He grabbed Maylin's arm in a tight grip and began pulling her back around the corner.

Then the man's gaze wandered up, and he saw them.

He started, his legs kicking out. His wide eyes met Geoffrey's for a half a heartbeat, then he was shooting to his feet.

Geoffrey cut right and pulled Maylin with him, back down the hallway.

They couldn't run because of the people in the hallway, but they moved quickly toward the nurses' station. Geoffrey's brain ran through their options. He had glanced at the directory but wasn't sure where the other stairwells were. As he dashed past the nurses' station, however, Maylin's voice sounded behind him. He stopped and turned.

She said urgently to the nurse they'd been speaking to earlier, "Call security. We just saw an Asian man in a dark suit, and he has a gun. You don't have any patients who needed a bodyguard, did you?"

"No." The nurse's face paled, but she immediately reached for the phone. While her attention was distracted, Maylin pulled Geoffrey away.

Good thinking. But it would take security several minutes to get to this floor. If they tried the elevators, they'd be exposed while waiting, so they needed to find a way off this floor without the man seeing them.

Maylin and Geoffrey exited the Cardiology wing and he spied a sign pointing to the Lab. He'd interned at a lab one summer in high school. He had an idea. "This way."

He walked into the Lab wing calmly but with purpose, as if he had a right to be there. Maylin followed his lead. He passed the tiny waiting area, which was only a handful of chairs and a small window to an administrative office, and strode down one of the hallways.

"What are you looking for?" Maylin said.

"Break room."

"What? Why?"

He found it at almost the end of the hallway, an open doorway into a large room. There were three circular tables with chairs, each with one or two people sitting, and at the far end of the room, a refrigerator stood next to a sink and counter.

And directly to the side of the door were hooks with white lab coats hanging there. None of the people in the break room wore their work coats.

Geoffrey had been hoping for that.

He walked casually into the room toward the water cooler next to the counter. Two women chatting next to the coffee pot on the counter stopped to glance at him.

"Do you need some help?" one of them asked.

Geoffrey smiled and shook his head. "Just getting some water. We're waiting on samples."

"Oh, go ahead. Want any coffee or tea?"

"No, thanks."

He filled a paper cup with water from the cooler, and Maylin copied his actions. They drank, threw away their cups, and then headed back out the door.

But as they passed the hooks with lab coats, Geoffrey snagged one. Maylin did the same.

They threw the lab coats on just in time. As they exited the break room, Geoffrey caught a glimpse down the hallway of the Asian man.

Geoffrey immediately turned his back to the man, shielding Maylin's face, making it look like he was chatting with her. The hallway wasn't as crowded as the other areas of the hospital, but there were a couple other people entering and exiting lab rooms.

"Is he gone yet?" he asked her.

She peeked around him. "Yes."

"Let's go."

They hurried down the hallway and stopped at the corner to look around. The Asian man was walking down one of the other hallways.

"This way." They exited the Lab wing and Geoffrey led them back to Cardiology. Keeping their heads averted, they passed the nurses' station and back to the supervisor's office, and the stairwell. It was the one stairwell the Asian man wouldn't look at right away, because he had been sitting next to it when he saw them. The only hitch to his plans would be if the man's partner had been speaking to the supervisor and was still there.

No, the supervisor's door was closed. They hurried down the hallway, past patient rooms, and into the stairwell. They passed a few people using the stairs between floors, but didn't see either of the men who were after them. The stairs led directly outside, so they ditched the lab coats over the railing just before exiting the hospital.

"How did you know the lab coats would be hanging there?" Maylin asked.

"I worked in a lab one summer, and because of the chemicals and cancer cells the technicians worked with, they were required to take off their lab coats in the break room. I knew the coats look enough like doctors' coats to disguise us."

They got to the car and drove away, but Geoffrey's relief was dampened. "All that for nothing. We couldn't find Cassandra."

"Not nothing," Maylin said slowly. "Did you notice the man's reaction when he first saw us?"

"He was surprised."

"And before he saw us, he was bored and waiting for something or someone. He wasn't there looking for us, for a change."

"He wasn't expecting to see us there."

"Which makes me wonder what he was doing there in the first place."

"Something to do with Cassandra," Geoffrey said. "I thought maybe his partner was speaking to the supervisor, since he was waiting there and the supervisor's office door was open."

"Were they looking for her, too? Was it just bad luck they were at her workplace the same time we came looking for her?"

"If they were looking for her, maybe she isn't involved with them after all," he said. "Maybe she found out they were after us and wanted to warn us."

"If that's the case, then are they after her because she tried to help us?"

"I hope not," he said in a low voice.

"We have to find her," Maylin said. "If she's in trouble ..."

This was getting more and more complicated, and the danger was eating at him like battery acid in his esophagus. It seemed as if the more he tried to stop the threat against them, the worse everything got.

He was starting to feel like he did right after the tsunami, when he was working tirelessly with the relief workers, rescuing people and providing medical services to survivors who had lost everything.

In it all, God was silent. The God he'd believed in since he was a child—he didn't know Him anymore.

And the more he worked to help people, the more there was to do, the less impact he had on the situation. He had driven himself harder than he ever had, trying to expunge his grief, and it had never seemed like enough.

Like now, no matter what he did, it wasn't enough.

His sense of helplessness caused panic to claw at the base of his throat.

He felt a softness on his hand, and realized Maylin was smoothing his white-knuckled grip on the steering wheel. He forced himself to relax.

"We just need to take this logically." Her voice had the same calming quality as her touch. "We'll find her and figure out what's going on. At least now we know what to do."

There was something about her that made his whirling brain slow down and focus. He took a breath, then another.

He peeled his fingers from the steering wheel and closed around her hand. Her touch was soft, but ... solid. He'd been feeling so lost, so adrift. Maylin was like an anchor.

Except that he knew he shouldn't have to burden her, any one, with his problems. A part of him knew he should go to his family for help, but Liv would want to pray with him, and he didn't want to admit that after everything he'd been through, he was starting to have doubts about God, too.

He just needed to keep it together until they were both safe.

"Let's call Liam and see if he's found anything yet," he said.

Maylin dialed his number and put the phone on speaker. "Liam, it's Maylin and Geoffrey. We've just left KSSF, and she's been missing from work for two days."

"Hmm. That explains some things." He seemed to be typing something on his computer. "I noticed something odd earlier this morning, but I wasn't sure if it was related to Cassandra or not. One of her friends from high school, Jean Loring, suddenly stopped posting about herself on social media two days ago, a few hours after Cassandra spoke to Geoffrey."

"That's not really that unusual, is it?" Maylin said. "Maybe she lost her phone, or lost internet access."

"Jean has still been posting, but she's only been sharing funny pictures or quotes that she finds. She hasn't posted any pictures of her cat, which she usually does at least once a day from what I can see, and she stopped writing status updates."

"If I had a fugitive at my house, I'd probably stop posting personal photos in case it gave away that my friend was staying with me," Geoffrey said.

"I would think as long as you didn't post a photo of your friend, that would be okay, right?" Maylin said.

"Actually, Geoffrey's right," Liam said. "I've found people because of a purse or personal belonging in the background of a photo of someone's kids or their pets. If Cassandra's missing, there's a possibility she's staying with Jean."

"Where does Jean live?" Geoffrey asked.

Liam gave them the address. "But I'll keep digging, in case she's not there."

Jean's address was a Craftsman house on a narrow street, surrounded by both modern buildings and a couple Victorian homes. The paint was weathered from the sea air, and the moulding under the eaves had cracks.

Geoffrey managed to parallel park between a beat-up Ford pickup truck and an ancient Honda on the steep street. They walked up the creaking steps to the front door and rang the doorbell.

A young man answered. "Yeah?"

"Is Jean home?" Geoffrey asked. He guessed that using only her first name would give the impression they knew her.

"No."

"When will she be back?"

"Who knows?"

"Could we leave a note for her?" Maylin asked.

"Look, she and I only rent rooms from the lady who owns this house, we're not buddies," the man said.

"Does your landlady know where she is?" Geoffrey pushed.

The man sighed. "No. We're not her kids, she doesn't keep tabs on us."

"Listen," Geoffrey began, but the man interrupted.

"Jean hasn't been home for a few days. Sometimes she does that. And no, I don't know where she goes. Sorry, but she's just not here."

And he closed the door.

Geoffrey stared at the door as if his frustration would force it open again. Maylin, however, pulled him away while taking out her phone and dialing, putting it on speaker as they walked back to the car.

"Liam," she said.

"Way ahead of you," Liam said. "Jean's at her boyfriend's house in Daly City."

Maylin did a double take, frowning at the phone in her hand. "How did you—?"

"I found a message to Jean from one of her friends posted on her Twitter, saying he went by her house and she wasn't there. So I started looking for places she might be if she wasn't at home. Jean's boyfriend is a painter. He isn't active on social media, but online he lists his studio address, which looks like it's also his apartment."

Jean's boyfriend lived in a residential section of Daly City, south of San Francisco, where the street was quiet and the houses decidedly different. The architecture was a mix from every decade, and most of houses were in need of repair, but painted bright colors, including some with designs like ladybugs on a green background, and one yellow house with a rainbow in shades of purple. One house had an attached garage with shingles missing from the roof, but some sort of tree growing through the hole.

Jean's boyfriend, Quentin, lived in a tiny two-story adobe-style home painted nacho-cheese orange with teal trim. It didn't have a garage, but a rusty Gremlin was pulled up on the sidewalk and partially blocking the teal front door, so Geoffrey assumed that belonged to Quentin and he was home.

The street sloped downward at a gentle angle, and Geoffrey parallel parked almost at the bottom, before it T-junctioned with a two-lane highway. They walked up toward Colin's house, eying the eclectic homes of his neighbors.

They circled the front hood of the Gremlin and were about to knock on the front door when the side gate— also teal-colored—opened and a woman stepped out.

It was Cassandra.

8

Cassandra froze in place like a rabbit about to bolt.

Geoffrey was trying to think of what to do when Maylin quickly said, "We're not here to get you in trouble. We just want to talk."

"How did you find me?" Cassandra demanded.

"A skip tracer," Geoffrey said.

Cassandra dropped the garbage bag she'd been carrying and pressed her hand to her mouth, her body shaking. She muttered as if talking to herself, "He can find me. I need somewhere else, somewhere safe."

"You came to the clinic to help us," Geoffrey said. "We can help you. We have somewhere no one could find you."

"It's where we've been hiding," Maylin added.

Cassandra's brown eyes were wide. "Did he come after you?" she whispered.

"Some men came after us," Maylin said. "We don't know who they are. We're hoping you can explain."

"Hey, Cass—" A young African American woman came through the side gate and stopped at the sight of them. She immediately grabbed Cassandra's arm, dragging her behind her. "Who are you?" she demanded. Geoffrey guessed she was Jean.

"I'm Maylin, and this is Geoffrey. The same people who are after Cassandra are after us."

The woman's rigid stance relaxed a fraction. "What do you want?"

"Answers," Geoffrey said. "So we can stop all this."

Cassandra choked. "You can't stop it."

"You don't know that. Tell us what's going on. We have resources you may not have."

"You won't have more resources than *him*."

"Cassandra," Maylin said gently, "what have you got to lose by talking to us?"

There was a few seconds of silence, then Jean touched a hand to her friend's shoulder. "She's right, Cass. What have you got to lose?" Jean picked up the dropped garbage bag and motioned toward the open side gate with her head. "Come on back."

The backyard was a square of brown grass, framed by a weathered wooden fence. A plastic patio chair and a pool lounge chair sat around a wicker circular table where there were two coffee mugs. Jean moved a motley-colored cat from another plastic patio chair and carried the chair to the table. "Have a seat. I'll make more coffee and tell Quentin." She disappeared into the house.

Cassandra perched on the edge of the lounge chair. "Jean's boyfriend is working." She pointed to the second story, where the top edge of an easel could be seen through the large window.

"Have you been hiding out here since you spoke to me?" Geoffrey asked.

Cassandra nodded, her eyes on the ground. "I was afraid."

"Of what?"

"My father."

Geoffrey hadn't expected that. "I don't understand."

"Is he the one after us?" Maylin asked.

"You both saved Frank Chan's life, right?" Cassandra said. "A few days later, he killed Chet."

"He killed your brother?" Maylin asked.

"I thought it was a car accident." If Geoffrey remembered the news article correctly, a couple witnesses said that the car had been swerving recklessly, then hit the side rail and flipped over down an embankment.

"Frank was driving his father's car," Cassandra said. "Frank and Chet were both drunk. They were thrown from the car because they weren't wearing seat belts, Frank had head trauma and broken bones, but Chet died almost instantly. Chet was my father's only son, and he went crazy with grief," she said with an edge to her voice. "And now he's out to kill everyone responsible."

Geoffrey was shocked and incredulous at the same time. "How do you know this?"

"Frank died a couple weeks ago."

"What?" Geoffrey and Maylin looked at Cassandra, then each other.

"I can't believe it," Maylin said in a faint voice. "I talked to him at the clinic only a few weeks ago. He was shy and sweet."

And now he was dead.

"It was made to look like a mugging, but I think my father arranged for his men to kill him," Cassandra said.

"You don't know that for sure," Geoffrey said slowly.

"My sister, Chelsea—she's in high school—called me about a week ago. She was so scared." Cassandra's voice quavered. "She had overheard our father ranting that he'd kill everyone involved in saving Chet's murderer. A couple weeks later, she heard about a rash of home invasion murders, but the victims were Frank's parents, and the doctor and nurse who had taken care of Frank in the hospital after the accident."

"You're right, it's coincidental," Geoffrey said. "But are you sure it's your father?"

"No," Cassandra said, "but even if it isn't, I knew your lives would be in danger. Our family knew that a few days before Chet died, Frank had gone to some clinic in Sonoma or Napa after a mountain biking accident, and that he'd almost died from an allergic reaction to an antibiotic. I couldn't just sit here and do nothing when I knew that you two might be next. I thought you might have more time before my father's men went after you."

"So you stole that Kind Samaritan Napa badge so we wouldn't know it was you?" Maylin asked.

"I wasn't afraid you'd know who I was. I was afraid my father would find out I'd warned you." Cassandra shivered, even in the summer sunlight. "And then he'd come after me."

"But surely he wouldn't hurt his own daughter?" Maylin said.

"You don't understand him. I'm not important to him. Neither is Chelsea, because we're girls. Chet was everything to him."

"He'd really hurt his own family?"

There was a bleak emptiness to Cassandra's eyes as she said in a low voice, "His younger brother, my Uncle Charles, was in charge of one of his Hong Kong businesses when it was under suspicion of using slave labor. My sister and I think our father had him killed."

Geoffrey was shocked. He couldn't imagine that sort of man.

But Maylin had sympathy in her eyes as she reached out to touch Cassandra's hand. "It didn't matter that you didn't have proof. You couldn't take the chance that your life might be in danger if your father found out you were betraying him."

"He might have found out anyway." Cassandra's voice had tightened. "I saw those men at your clinic. I didn't recognize them, but I think my father hired them. And I think they saw me."

Geoffrey remembered the security video. One of the men had turned back and might have seen Cassandra as she was hurrying out of the clinic. "That's why you disappeared."

"I panicked. I've spent the last couple days trying to figure out what to do next. But I don't know how I can run away without my father finding me."

"You'll be running for your entire life if you don't find a way to stop him," Geoffrey said.

Cassandra gave a bark of laughter. "You can't stop my father."

"What if we can prove Frank didn't kill your brother?" Maylin said.

There had been something niggling at the back of Geoffrey's mind since listening to Cassandra's story, but only at Maylin's words did he understand what it was. "You're right," he murmured.

"You're crazy," Cassandra said. "What are you talking about?"

"When Frank first came into the clinic, he listed two medications he was on, which were for seizures," Geoffrey said. "He also didn't have a driver's license. Most people with seizures have to be seizure free for at least four months before they can get their driver's license, at least in the state of California. I have a hard time believing he was driving that car. He wouldn't have even taken lessons if he couldn't get his license."

"Lots of kids learn to drive from their friends," Cassandra said. "Just because he couldn't get a license doesn't mean he wasn't driving."

"But he also didn't strike me as the reckless type who would drive knowing he could have a seizure at any time," Maylin said. "He was a quiet, easygoing kid. He'd struck me as a bit of a pushover, the type who would follow stronger personalities."

"If he could have a seizure anytime, that's probably why the car went out of control that night," Cassandra said.

"There's another reason I don't think he was driving," Geoffrey said. "We treated him and know exactly how severe his injuries were after that mountain bike accident. He had bad sprains on his right hand and left ankle. The car that crashed was an SRT Viper, which is a stick shift. He couldn't have driven that without a great deal of pain."

Cassandra seemed more doubtful after hearing this. "But why wouldn't Frank be driving? His father's car was fast and powerful."

"You said both boys were drunk," Geoffrey said. "Maybe Frank was worse off than Chet."

"If we can prove that Frank wasn't driving, would it stop your father?" Maylin asked Cassandra.

"I don't know. It might not."

"Your father's a businessman, so he should be used to making decisions based on facts, not emotions," Geoffrey said. "Even killing your uncle was based on logic, to protect himself and the company. So far in hunting down everyone related to Frank, he's been very methodical."

"Well, normally he's cold, ruthless, and unemotional," Cassandra said thoughtfully. "I'm just worried that Chet's death has made him unhinged, so that even if he knows it wasn't Frank's fault, he might still want to kill everyone connected to Frank just to make himself feel better."

"We won't know for sure unless we try. Present him with evidence Frank wasn't driving."

"And if it doesn't work?" Cassandra asked.

They were silent for a long moment. The heat of the afternoon drenched the small yard. He realized Jean hadn't returned outside—probably to give them privacy.

Geoffrey's mind was whirling, but he couldn't come up with any ideas—except one. He said in a dark voice, "If it comes to it, we can always set a trap. Catch your father trying to kill me, red-handed."

"That is ridiculously dangerous," Maylin snapped.

"He'll kill you," Cassandra said.

"I am not going to run from him for the rest of my life." He wouldn't be bullied by a man like that. He felt like a gigantic slab of granite. He wasn't going to move on this point. If he had to, he would do this, with or without anyone's help. "It may not come to that," he said, trying to dissolve the tension.

But Maylin still looked troubled. "For now, let's get you safe," she said to Cassandra. "We have a place to stay that's off the grid. No one can find it because there's no phone or internet."

Cassandra made a face, but nodded. "Thank you. Until you showed up, I didn't really think about the danger to other people." She gestured with her head back toward the house. "I don't want Jean or Quentin to get in trouble."

"Pack up your stuff and tell Jean you're leaving," Maylin said. "We'll wait out here."

As soon as she was gone, Maylin said, "We need to call Liam."

At the same time, Geoffrey said, "We need to call Detective Carter."

"Why Detective Carter?" "Why Liam?"

At the same time, both of them opened their mouths to talk, but neither spoke.

Finally Geoffrey gestured with his hand. "Ladies first."

"Why Detective Carter?" she asked.

"To see if we can get information on Chet and Frank's accident."

"But that report was the San Francisco PD. Detective Carter could request it if he were investigating something involving Frank or Chet, but we have no proof it's Chet's father behind all this."

"But Cassandra could request the information because it was her brother. Also, if the request comes through Sonoma PD, if her father is monitoring that sort of thing, it'll tell him she's no longer in San Francisco, so Jean and Quentin will be safe."

"That'll relieve Cassandra's mind," Maylin admitted.

"Aside from the fact it was Frank's father's car, I want to know why Chester Wong thinks Frank was driving and not Chet."

"Do you think Frank confessed to driving?"

"I hope not." Geoffrey flexed his jaw muscles. If Frank had confessed to driving, then even if they found proof to the contrary, it wouldn't stop Chester Wong from his vendetta against them. "Why Liam?" he asked.

"We have to stay at the cabin with Cassandra, at least tonight. We're certainly not leaving her alone, and no, before you suggest it, I'm not letting you go alone into town to do internet research."

Geoffrey opened his mouth to protest, but closed it again. He should have known she'd never agree to something like that.

"So let's call Liam and ask him to look online to find out what the boys were doing before the accident," Maylin said. "If we know where they went, we might be able to find something to tell us who was driving."

"Liam might be busy with other cases ..."

"Utilizing Liam's talents is the smartest way for you to protect your family."

He was quiet for a long moment, trying to formulate his thoughts. "I just don't want to get anyone else on Chester's radar. I'm only hoping he won't find out Jean and Quentin helped Cassandra for the past couple days."

"That's why time isn't on our side. And Liam could probably find more information faster than we could."

"All right." Geoffrey sighed. "You call Liam, I'll call Detective Carter."

Detective Carter promised to contact the SFPD today. Geoffrey said he'd get into range of a cell tower and call him tomorrow morning.

On the drive back to Sonoma, Maylin made conversation with Cassandra. Turning in her seat in the front, she asked her, "How old is your sister?"

"Chelsea's a junior in high school," Cassandra said. "She's really good at art and wants to become a graphic designer, but our father would rather she go into business or medicine or law." The way Cassandra said "our father" was odd, a hollow note to her voice.

Maylin had stiffened. "She should do what she wants, what she's good at."

"Mom understands," Cassandra said. "She was so proud of me when I graduated nursing school, she gave me this watch. But our father has always wanted us to be a credit to him. Chelsea is so much smarter than I am, so he expects more from her."

"He's not living her life for her," Maylin said." My parents wanted me to become a doctor, and when I went into nursing instead, they threatened to not pay for schooling."

What kind of parent did that to a kid? Nursing was a respectable, worthy profession. Maylin had told Geoffrey that her parents hadn't approved of her career choice, but had they really cared that much about a doctor's paycheck and the prestige of a doctor's title that they'd financially try to prevent her from pursuing her dreams?

"My father wouldn't pay for her schooling if Chelsea went to art school," Cassandra said in a low voice.

Maylin said, "You never know, it might all work out. My father eventually paid for my nursing school when people from my church made comments about it. It would have been embarrassing for him to deny my schooling."

Her parents had only paid for her schooling because it was embarrassing for them not to? Geoffrey's hand tightened around the steering wheel. What kind of a family did she have? He wanted to take her from people who didn't appreciate her, who had threatened to abandon her, and give her the support of his family, his friendship.

Except he wanted to give her more than friendship.

Yeah, well, we don't always get what we want.

Japan had changed him, and coming back hadn't helped him in the way he'd wanted it to. He needed to find out if he would always feel so meaningless and empty, or if there was a way to find something more.

He was too much of a basketcase to even think about bringing someone else into the twister that was his life.

Except ... Maylin calmed his storm.

She turned and caught his eyes. There was something in her that made him think she wanted to reach out to him, to take his hand, to anchor him. But then something clouded over her features, and she looked away.

Cassandra was asleep in the back seat when they finally arrived at the cabin. Geoffrey parked next to Liv's SUV. "I hadn't really expected Liv to be here." She had been looking over the property today with Linc, and so she'd been out of cell tower range all day.

"I'm glad she is," Maylin said. "I like her."

"You just like hearing embarrassing stories about me," he said.

"No, I like chatting about books and movies and TV shows." She gave him a sidelong glance. "In addition to embarrassing stories about you."

"I only wish I had more embarrassing stories about her. She was a hooligan as a kid, but she was disciplined as an adult. That's probably why she was so successful on the National Shooting Team."

"I was surprised when she told me about how she'd missed qualifying for the Olympics team by only a few points. That's amazing. I had no idea she was so good."

"She's not one to brag. She doesn't let any of us tell people about that."

As they walked into the cabin, Liv looked up from slicing some bread. "Hey guys, you're late."

"We took a different route to the cabin, just in case," Geoffrey said.

Liv nodded toward a bag on the couch. "I brought you both some clothes. But maybe I should have brought more?" Liv's eyebrows rose in Cassandra's direction.

"Thanks." Geoffrey was glad his sister always flowed with new people and new situations without batting an eyelash. "This is Cassandra Wong, the girl who warned us about those men at the clinic."

Liv's eyes grew serious as they settled on Cassandra. "Are those men after you, too?"

Geoffrey explained about Frank and Chet's accident, and how Cassandra's father seemed to be after her, also, for warning Geoffrey and Maylin. He could tell that Liv was annoyed that he had kept from her the connection to Chester Wong, but she wouldn't chew him out in front of Cassandra. He was grateful for the temporary reprieve, but he'd do it again—he didn't want his family involved any more in this if he could help it.

Liv put her arm around Cassandra. "You poor thing. The past couple days must have been awful."

"I just feel terrible that I might have gotten Jean in trouble," Cassandra said. "I never wanted to put anyone else in danger."

His thoughts immediately landed on his family. Geoffrey's gaze flicked to Liv. "How's Mom doing?" His voice was light, but he hoped Liv would see the unspoken worry in his gaze.

"Chris has been sticking so close to her that she's getting highly annoyed. And Linc is staying there tonight. He said he didn't want to risk being poisoned by my cooking." Olivia rolled her eyes. "I'm only making sandwiches."

"Well, we stopped off at a grocery store in Petaluma," Geoffrey said quickly, "so no need for you to do anything."

"I'm starving," Cassandra said.

Maylin cut up the roast chicken they'd bought while Cassandra made a salad, and Geoffrey built up the fire.

It was as they sat down to table that he suddenly heard the sound of a car engine. Slowly coming closer, as if trying to sneak up on them.

They all froze for a second. Maylin noticed that Olivia and Geoffrey both had wary expressions on their faces.

"Were we expecting anyone?" Maylin asked.

"No. Linc said clearly he was going to be staying at the Den tonight," Olivia said.

Geoffrey and his sister got to their feet, their expressions tense.

"Maybe Liam?" Maylin said.

"It's not the sound of Liam's dying engine," Olivia said.

"It's coming slowly, as if the driver isn't sure of the way," Geoffrey added.

"Who else knows about this cabin?" Maylin asked.

"No one." Liv's mouth was grim. "Not even Chris remembers exactly where it is."

Cassandra grabbed Maylin's hand. She was trembling.

"Let's be cautious, just in case." Geoffrey grabbed the shotgun, which had been stowed in the corner of the room because the gun cabinet was still full.

Olivia grabbed the gun cabinet key from the fireplace mantle. "Follow me into the bedroom."

Maylin grabbed a lamp, and following Olivia, ushered Cassandra into one of the bedrooms. Olivia opened the cabinet and handed Maylin a pistol.

At the feel of the cool metal from the pistol in her hands, her breathing calmed as she remembered her instructors from the classes she'd taken. She loaded the magazine, then pulled back the slide.

Olivia gave her a nod of approval. "Stay in the corner." She grabbed a rifle from the cabinet and left the room, closing the door behind her.

Maylin and Cassandra knelt on the floor in the far corner, only the bulk of the bed between them and the door, and she doused the lamp. She steadied her hand on the bed, aiming the gun at the shadow that was the bedroom door.

Her heartbeat was loud in her ears, but calmer than she would have expected. Next to her, Cassandra's breath came in gasps.

"Try to calm yourself or you'll start to hyperventilate," Maylin whispered to her.

Cassandra nodded and squeezed her eyes shut, focusing on her breathing.

Maylin heard the creak of the front door opening, and she could also hear the car engine, even through the bedroom door. She guessed that Geoffrey and Olivia had put out all the lamps and the fireplace, and then snuck out of the house. They wouldn't be able to see well in the pitch dark outside, but Geoffrey wouldn't need perfect aim with the shotgun, and Olivia could probably hit a squirrel with her eyes closed. Also, outside the cabin, they wouldn't need to worry about any stray bullets penetrating the walls into the bedroom. Maylin suppressed a shiver at the thought of bullets—from their guns or someone else's—raining upon Cassandra and herself.

The car engine faded away, and the silence was terrible. Even the sound of cicadas would have eased the tightness in her chest. All she heard was hers and Cassandra's breaths.

Then she clearly heard Lincoln's irate voice shouting, "Geoff, if you have a gun pointed at my head again, I swear I'm going to punch you in the face."

Maylin gave a gasp of laughter that sounded half like a sob. "It's all right. It's Geoffrey's brother."

Cassandra let out a long, forceful breath. "When this is all over, I'm going to learn how to shoot a gun."

They exited the bedroom just as Geoffrey was re-lighting one of the lamps, bathing the room in a soft orange glow. Lincoln and Olivia were entering the cabin.

"We need some kind of signal to let you know it's family," Lincoln said in a peeved voice.

Olivia patted her brother's cheek. "You're just upset because you had a gun pointed at you again."

"It should be equal opportunity endangerment."

"Is that even a word?" Geoffrey said. "And I said I was sorry."

"You had the night-vision scope," Lincoln said accusingly to Olivia. "You could have told Geoff it was me."

"It was too fun watching him sneak up on you."

"He could have shot me."

"There's only rock salt in that shotgun." Olivia grinned.

Lincoln glowered at his siblings, then gave an apologetic look at Maylin. "Sorry to give you guys a scare."

Maylin realized she was still clutching the pistol and went to return it to the cabinet while Geoffrey introduced Cassandra to Lincoln.

"Why are you out here?" Geoffrey asked.

Maylin returned to the living room in time to see Lincoln's shoulders tense. "Well ... here's the thing ... first of all, it's nothing to worry about."

"When you say that, of course I'm going to worry," Geoffrey said. "What's going on?"

Lincoln looked like he was wishing he wasn't the one who had to explain.

"Any day now," Geoffrey said.

Lincoln sighed. "It was tonight just after dinner. Mom let them in because they flashed their badges."

Maylin suddenly felt cold. "Badges?"

"Asian FBI agents?" Geoffrey guessed. "With heavy accents?"

"You never told her about them," Lincoln said. "Chris and I were too late—Mom had already let them in the house."

"They didn't hurt her—?" He was so tense that Maylin could see his back muscles bunching beneath his shirt.

"No, she's fine," Lincoln said quickly. "Chris and I were down at the front door in a heartbeat."

This situation had put Geoffrey's mother in danger. Those men had been in her house. He must be feeling sick.

"Things, um ..." Lincoln rubbed the back of his neck. "... got a little hairy."

Olivia glared at him. "You are the king of understatement."

"It was hardly a fight," Lincoln said. "The big guy went after Mom but Chris tackled him and yelled at her to go to the panic room and call the police. And you know Mom, she's smart enough to go without asking questions. When they realized they wouldn't get past us before she got into the panic room, they took off."

"Are you okay?" Geoffrey reached for Lincoln as if he was going to examine him right then and there for bruises.

"Leave off, I'm fine." Lincoln twisted away from him. "Chris got a shiner, though."

Olivia pinched her brother's cheek. "At least the guy's punches missed your pretty face."

Lincoln made a disgusted noise. "I landed a pretty good blow that had to have bruised that Asian guy's ribs."

Maylin gave him a stern look. "All kidding aside, you've got a doctor and two nurses here. If you need any medical attention, you'd better speak up."

"No, I'm good."

"And ... Mom?" Olivia asked.

"Mom was ..." Lincoln looked pained. "...A little upset. I had to explain and do damage control."

Geoffrey bowed his head and rubbed his forehead. "You shouldn't have had to. If you hadn't arrived when you did ..."

"Hey." All traces of teasing gone, Lincoln went to his brother and cupped Geoffrey's neck in a brotherly gesture. "Mom is fine. Thank God Chris built that panic room in the Den—it's got security features up the wazoo. She's going to be perfectly safe, especially now that she knows what's going on."

"I know what you're thinking." Olivia stepped up to Geoffrey, too. "So I'm telling you to stop it. This is not your fault."

"We're going to find a way to stop this," Lincoln said firmly. "All of us. We're here for you."

"We're always here for you, Geoff." Olivia put her arms around her two brothers, and Geoffrey gripped his brother's shoulder.

The sight of the siblings and their obvious love for each other almost undid Maylin. Their solidarity and confidence in each other was something she'd never experienced with her parents and her sister. Never. They would have been more likely to heap blame and criticize.

The Whelans were a real family.

The ache welled up in her, pushing against her lungs, against her throat. She had gotten to know Olivia and Geoffrey, she knew their love for each other was genuine. She knew their loyalty was strong. It made the moment even more beautiful. She looked away.

Cassandra only looked slightly embarrassed to be a stranger witnessing this tender scene. She had a loving relationship with her younger sister and her mother, from what Maylin could tell. She had no reason to feel like Maylin was feeling now, to tremble with longing at something she'd never had.

The siblings broke apart, although Lincoln slapped Geoffrey's face affectionately before stepping back. Lincoln said, "Mom sent a pot of chili. We only need to warm it up. But she was so hopping mad when she was cooking, she might have added extra cayenne, so be warned."

"We have food," Geoffrey said.

"So now there's enough for me," Lincoln said with a grin.

"Didn't you say you ate?" Olivia asked acidly.

"I'll make more salad." Cassandra went to get it while Lincoln went out to the car to get the pot of chili.

Maylin needed to get out of here. "I'll get some water." She grabbed the water containers and escaped out the back door.

But instead of making her way down the dirt path to the well and the water pump, she stopped and stared up at the stars. They were thrown across the sky above her, looking both far away and close enough to touch. They were still and quiet. They looked content.

She felt small. She thought she would feel peace, but instead she saw the picture of the three siblings, arms around each other. And she felt alone.

The back door opened, but she heard Olivia even before she turned around. "You doing okay?"

"Yeah." Maylin couldn't have forced a smile even if she tried, but she also somehow knew that Olivia would've preferred she didn't. "I just needed some air.

Everything that happened today, and tonight, and then hearing about your mom ... I'm just so sorry."

"What for?"

Maylin struggled for words. "I know logically that it's not my fault, but I can't help but feel guilty that your family is in danger."

"You're right, it's not your fault. But I know Mom will be okay. I have to trust God to take care of her."

Olivia's easy reference to God evoked two different emotions in Maylin—the old habitual dislike, because her church-going parents were such hypocrites, and that desperate longing for a God like the God in the Bible.

"What is it?" Olivia asked.

"Nothing."

"No, I said something to upset you."

Maylin winced. "I just have a complicated relationship with God, that's all."

Olivia gave a smile. "It sounds like you broke up with Him and now you can't figure out if you want to stay friends."

Maylin couldn't help but laugh. "That actually describes it pretty well. I grew up in church, but my parents' religion was so cold. They professed one thing, but their actions were selfish. The church members I knew were manipulative. I left as soon as I graduated high school. I tried all kinds of religions, but I kept coming back to Christianity. I .... missed Jesus. The one in the Bible, not my parents' version of Him."

Maylin sighed. "Now I don't know what I believe. You're the first person I've known who talks about Him the way you do."

"What way?"

"Like you ... like Him."

Olivia laughed. "I do like Him. I like the version of myself that I am with Him."

"I've never liked any version of myself." Maylin didn't know why she said it, it popped out before she could stop herself. Tears pricked the backs of her eyes.

"Oh, Maylin ..."

"I didn't say that to get sympathy or anything like that. It's a fact I've come to accept about myself."

"But I like you." Olivia sounded confused. "Why wouldn't you like yourself? You're strong, and calm, and brave."

Maylin wanted to laugh. "Thank you, but ... I'm a lot of other things, too."

"I haven't seen it."

But she would, if she got to know Maylin better. "I'm a lot of things God wouldn't like. Maybe that's why He's so far away from me."

"He's not." Olivia said it so firmly, Maylin turned to look at her, saw the fierceness glittering in her eyes. "It might feel that way sometimes, but He's not far away. He's always been there for me. Whenever I felt awful or afraid, I knew He was there. I wasn't alone."

Maylin had spent so much of her life feeling alone. Misunderstood. Unwanted. Her friendships were casual ones, shallow, with people she didn't have much in common with. Her family was disappointed in her.

A God who wouldn't feel the same way about her as her coworkers, her family, her acquaintances—that seemed too good to be true. A God who would ... *love* her—that seemed unreal.

"Maylin." Olivia took her hand, and Maylin felt the callouses on her palm. "I'm not saying this because I feel sorry for you. I'm saying this because I really do like you. And I'm saying this because the fact you kept missing Jesus—maybe it means that He misses you, too."

Maylin didn't know what to say about that. She wanted to believe it, and yet she didn't. She didn't know how to think about Jesus.

"Look, I'll be praying for you," Olivia said. "And if you have any questions, just ask me. No judgment, I promise."

"Oh, I believe you." Olivia seemed the least judgmental person she'd ever met. She was an oasis compared to the sandstorm of Maylin's parents' criticism.

Olivia smiled at her, a smile that touched her eyes, and she squeezed Maylin's hand before releasing it.

The back door opened and Lincoln stuck his head out. "Not to ruin your girly-girl chat, but I'm starving. C'mon, Liv."

Olivia rolled her eyes. "You're such a bottomless pit."

"I need sustenance to feed this powerhouse metabolism."

"The only power you have is your inflated ego," Olivia said as she headed inside.

While Maylin couldn't imagine teasing around with Jesus like the Whelan siblings did, she wanted that kind of love and loyalty. She wanted someone who would always be there for her, who'd instantly come to help when she called, who'd lay down their lives for her ...

Jesus had died for her.

The Jesus she'd learned about in church was different from the Jesus she'd read in the Bible, and the Jesus that Olivia Whelan knew. She wanted to know more, and yet ... did she want to become a Jesus freakazoid? Would He just fail her like so many other people in her life? Was He just a figment of her imagination?

She was hesitant, and afraid. And she was also filled with an aching longing that made her want to know more. Maybe when all this was over ...

Who was she kidding? When all this was over, things would go back to the way they were. Except that she wouldn't be quite the same person. And she wasn't sure how she felt about that.

And in thinking about when this was over, she couldn't shove away her fear about how this would end. Would they be able to stop Chester Wong? Or would he find a way to enact his revenge?

Geoffrey had just pulled the car in front of Liam's house when he heard a gasp from the back seat. He and Maylin both turned.

Cassandra sat pressing the prepaid mobile phone they'd given to her up to her ear, her knuckles white. "We have to go to San Francisco," she said. "We have to go now."

"What happened?" Maylin asked.

"My sister." Cassandra bowed her head, her eyes squeezed tightly shut. She took a deep breath and looked up at them. "Someone tried to kidnap her on her way to school this morning."

It was the last thing Geoffrey would have expected, now that they knew it was Chester Wong after them. Geoffrey wasn't entirely sure Chester was really after his daughter Cassandra, but he knew Chester had no reason to have his younger daughter kidnapped. "Who would do that?"

"And why?" Maylin sounded as confused as he was.

"You can listen to her voicemail message." Cassandra pressed some buttons on her phone. They'd had her discard her mobile phone in case Chester found a way to track it, and they'd given her the prepaid phone. After hearing about Geoffrey's family last night, Cassandra had been adamant about going into Sonoma with them to call her sister, Chelsea, to make sure the girl was all right. She was also going to check her phone's voicemail messages.

A young girl's voice sounded over the phone's speaker, trembling as if she was trying not to cry. "Cass, something happened this morning ... I was walking to school and these two men tried to grab me." There was a muffled sob, then Chelsea's voice came on again, stronger and composed. "I got away because someone on the street saw them and helped me. Cass, they spoke Cantonese, but I didn't understand them very well. I don't know why they wanted me. I ..." She heaved a breath. "I went home and told Dad, and he ... it was like he didn't believe me. He looked right through me and asked if I was sure it wasn't all in my imagination."

Geoffrey's hand against the back of his seat clenched hard.

Chelsea continued, "Please come get me, Cass. I'm scared." Then the message ended.

"We have to get her," Cassandra said. "Bring her to the cabin."

Geoffrey decided quickly. "Okay, we'll go to your house today."

"Wait a minute," Maylin said. "You can't remove a teenager from her father's home without his permission."

"But her mother can give permission." He looked at Cassandra, who nodded firmly. "Cassandra, come inside with us. We have to find a way to talk to your mother without your father knowing."

Liam rented one side of a dilapidated duplex with white-washed wooden walls. Three steps led up to a door with a ripped screen, which Geoffrey opened and then knocked on the wooden door behind it.

Liam opened almost immediately, but there was something urgent about his stance, and tension made the cords in his neck stand out. "Come in."

"What's wrong?" Maylin asked.

"Detective Carter just called." Liam returned to his seat in front of his computer, which sat on a card table in his living room. The only other furniture was a sofa with a sheet thrown over it, which didn't completely hide the ghastly roses on the fabric. "He's coming over with an abduction case for me to work on for the Sonoma PD. A young girl."

"That's awful." Maylin's hand covered her mouth.

"We won't take up too much of your time, then," Geoffrey said. "We need to head to San Francisco immediately. Liam, this is Cassandra Wong."

Liam shook Cassandra's hand. "I'm glad you're safe."

"We need to get her sister to safety, too," Maylin said.

Liam's brow wrinkled. "Why? What happened?"

"Someone tried to kidnap her this morning," Cassandra said. "I need to talk to my mom without my father knowing, so we can bring her to Sonoma."

"Sure. Let me get an encrypted phone." Liam went to his bedroom and returned with a cell phone. They all listened to the one-sided phone call between Cassandra and her mother, who was apparently now home with only Chelsea. Cassandra had to explain why she'd suddenly disappeared, because apparently her workplace had called her mother yesterday. When she told her mother about the two men seeing her at the clinic a few days ago, her mom grew silent. Cassandra then explained she'd found somewhere safe for Chelsea.

Cassandra nodded. "We're coming right now, Mom." She hung up and nodded to them. "She said it's all right. She was worried after Chelsea told her what happened this morning, especially when Dad seemed so unconcerned about it."

She said it casually, but Geoffrey saw the pain flash across her eyes. It must be torturing her to witness how indifferent her father was to the safety of his two daughters.

"I think you should ask Liv and Linc to come with you," Liam said. "They can take care of Cassandra and

Chelsea. Geoff, there's something you're going to want to look into in San Francisco."

"You found out where Frank and Chet went before the accident?" Maylin asked.

Liam pulled out a folder from the neat stack on the table and handed them some pieces of paper. "I did my digging mostly in social media. On Chet's online profile, there are lots of posts from friends, mourning his loss. But there was one post from a girl who mentioned she'll always treasure that last dance with him *that night*."

"Dance?" Geoffrey said. "They went to a party?"

"I went to the girl's online profiles, and she had posted some pictures from that night. None of the pictures showed Chet or Frank, but in the comments, someone asked where she was, and she said she had been at the China White."

"I know that club," Cassandra said. "It's a high end dance club. You need membership or a voucher to be allowed inside."

"Are you sure Frank and Chet were there that night?" Geoffrey asked.

"I went searching for other pictures of China White from that night, and found one with Frank in the background," Liam said.

Maylin smiled. "Liam, you're awesome."

"Do you speak Chinese? A lot of the people who posted photos from China White posted messages in

Chinese characters. It looks like a majority of people who go there speak Chinese."

Maylin nodded. "My mother's family speaks Cantonese, and I took Mandarin in college."

Geoffrey was torn. He didn't want Maylin in more danger, but at the same time he wanted her close to him because it made him feel like he had a better handle of the situation, was better able to protect her.

Or maybe, he just wanted her close to him.

Maylin gave him a hard look. "I wouldn't have let you go there alone anyway."

The woman could read his mind way too easily.

He knew it was illogical, but he didn't want to involve Liv and Linc. He wanted them to be safe at the Den with Mom. But he also knew he couldn't investigate this lead with the two young women tagging along. He needed help, and Liam was going to be busy.

"I'll call Liv and Linc," Geoffrey said grudgingly. He had to hope that the cabin's remote location off the grid would keep them all safe.

If Liv knew about his fears for them, she'd scold him and tell him to trust in the Lord. It was already hard for him to do after the doubt that had filled him during his years in Japan, but the past few days had made him feel even more distant from God.

He realized that he had assumed coming back to the U.S. would help him to find his faith again, but it hadn't happened. And if Asian hit men hadn't made

God more real to him, was there anything that would? He didn't know if he wanted to know God anymore.

Maybe when this was all over ... if this would ever be over.

They drove into San Francisco and into an area of rows of "painted ladies," Victorian-era rowhouses, all beautifully maintained, in bright colors. Some had ground floor garages, while for others, the ground floor was first floor and the front door sat at the top of a flight of steps on the second floor. The architecture varied from Stick houses to Queen Annes, but most had elaborate bay windows, gable roofs, and ornamentation. The street screamed money.

Parking along the street was a problem, and Geoffrey had to park farther from Cassandra's house than he would have liked. As he got out of the Mustang, a chill swept across his shoulders.

He looked around the street. All he could see were houses rising above the cars parked in front of them, with the occasional open space in front of a garage. He couldn't see anyone.

But he couldn't shake the feeling they were being watched.

Liv and Linc had driven in her black Suburban, and she had to park even farther away since some of the closer parking spots were too small for her monster of a truck. Geoffrey, Maylin and Cassandra waited for them rather than going into the house first.

Linc and Liv came walking up the narrow sidewalk toward them, and Geoffrey gave Liv a significant look. Then he said to Cassandra, "Let's go to your house."

He fell behind, and so did Liv. He was surprised to find Maylin fell behind, also—she must have caught the look he gave his sister.

"Were you watching for anyone following us?" he asked Liv in a low voice.

She gave a disgusted snort. "Of course," she said, as if he were an imbecile.

Maylin's eyes were sharp on his. "Did you see anything?"

"No. But I'm getting this weird feeling."

"Indigestion from that breakfast burrito?" Liv elbowed him.

"Seriously, I feel like we're being watched."

Liv and Maylin exchanged concerned looks, then they both looked around the quiet street.

"You're not one to have 'feelings,'" Liv said.

"I know," Geoffrey said. "I can't explain it."

"Let's keep our eyes open," Maylin said.

Cassandra's home was a Victorian Stick house that had been elaborately remodeled to include a more spacious garage than most of the Victorians on the street. A metal gate stood sentinel in front of a flight of stairs. Cassandra unlocked it and they trooped up to a balcony over the garage with an elaborate railing, and then to the front door under a small portico.

Cassandra unlocked the front door, but it swung open in her hands. A teenage girl stood in the doorway, and Cassandra immediately folded her into a tight embrace. "You're all right?"

The girl nodded.

"You're here." An older woman was coming down the stairs, which stood directly across from the front door. "Come inside, quickly."

It was a tight squeeze for them all to gather in the front foyer, with the three Wongs, the three Whelans, and Maylin. Cassandra led the way through a doorway on the left into a large living room. There weren't enough chairs, but Linc and Liv stood on either side of the bay window, looking out into the street.

Geoffrey stood in front of the marble fireplace. "We shouldn't stay long. We need to get Cassandra and Chelsea to our safe house."

Their mother nodded, an anguished expression on her face. "I don't understand why this is happening."

"I think Dad has always been emotional," Cassandra said in a low voice, "but he was always holding it in. And now he's snapped."

"Don't say that," her mother said. "If anything, he's been ruthless and ... *orderly* about all of this." She shuddered.

"You and I have been walking on eggshells since Chet died," Chelsea said. "You can't tell me you're not afraid, Mom."

"I was afraid for you," Mrs. Wong said to Cassandra. "Why did you have to involve yourself?"

"How could I not involve myself?" she demanded. "There is nothing right in what Dad's doing."

"She did what she had to do, Mom," Chelsea added.

Their mother sighed helplessly. "I suppose. I just didn't expect him to react the way he did this morning. It was as if ..."

"As if I didn't matter to him," Chelsea said, an edge to her voice. "Except Cass and I have never mattered to him, Mom."

"He didn't care some men had tried to kidnap you?" Maylin asked.

"He was curious," Chelsea said. "He asked if I'd gotten a good look at them. He was surprised. Then he said I must be mistaken, that I was letting my imagination run wild."

"He said there was no reason you should be in danger," their mother said.

In a way, he was right. The people after Maylin and Cassandra and himself were Chester Wong's men. They wouldn't go after Chelsea.

Unless they weren't Chester's men.

"After your son died," Geoffrey said, hoping he was phrasing this delicately enough, "who are the people who have died since?"

"Dad killed them," Chelsea said, her voice tight. "I know he did."

"You haven't any proof," her mother said.

"It's too coincidental," Cassandra said.

"Who were they?" Maylin asked in a gentle voice.

"Well, Frank's parents. The doctor and the nurse who were in charge of Chet."

"Did any of them have ... illegal connections?" Geoffrey asked.

"Illegal?"

"The two men who tried to kidnap Chelsea spoke Cantonese, right?"

Chelsea nodded. "I don't understand it very well, but I can recognize it."

"Was it possible that one of the people killed had some powerful connections who are upset about the murder?"

"You mean a Chinese gang?" Mrs. Wong was horrified.

"Or a Chinese businessman with a powerful reach," Geoffrey said. "In which case, the people after Cassandra are not the same people after Chelsea."

Chelsea shuddered. Cassandra put an arm around her.

"Linc and Liv will keep them both safe," Geoffrey said to their mother. "They'll keep watch for whoever might be after them."

Linc and Liv both nodded from their positions on either side of the window.

"We need to go," Maylin said softly.

Cassandra and Chelsea both embraced their mother. "Stay safe," she said to them. "I'll tell your father you're staying at a friend's house."

They hurried back to their cars, all of them looking up and down the street to see if anyone was observing them. Geoffrey again felt that prickling feeling at the back of his neck and shoulders, but try as he might, he couldn't see anyone on the street or in any of the cars who might be watching them. Maybe he was being paranoid. After all, who could have followed them? If Chester's men knew Maylin, Cassandra, and himself were at the cabin, they'd have attacked them there. They wouldn't have simply followed them back to Chester's house in San Francisco.

"Take care," Geoffrey said to his siblings.

"We'll expect you at the cabin later," Linc said.

"It's going to be a little tight." Liv nudged Linc. "You and Geoff will have to Rock-Paper-Scissors for the couch."

Linc groaned, then waved goodbye to them. Liv had her arms around Cassandra and Chelsea and led them away to her Suburban.

"I feel better knowing they're with your siblings," Maylin said.

"I do, too." Even though he worried about them, he knew Linc and Liv were capable and could protect Cassandra and Chelsea while he and Maylin tracked down the events of the accident.

And if it didn't make a difference to Chester Wong's murderous actions? Then he'd go with plan B, whether Maylin liked it or not.

Either way, after all the trauma and devastation he'd witnessed in Japan, after all the heartache and loss he'd seen over the past few years, Geoffrey wasn't going to let Chester Wong threaten him or the people he cared about, the people he'd come home to be with. He'd die first.

"Are you ready to go?" Maylin stood next to the open passenger side door.

"Yeah."

As she got into the car, the San Francisco breezes caught her brown hair, lifting it up and caressing her face. He wanted to touch her. He wanted to kiss her again.

And he realized with a start that he would die for her, too.

The thought shook him, and he had to pause before opening the car door. He'd worked with her for months, but he'd only really gotten to know her the past few days. Could he really feel that way about someone so fast?

But in working with her, he had gotten to know her. He knew she would take the time to chat with a frightened child and adjust their pillows just right. He knew she could ease a child's tears faster and better than the other nurses, and sometimes even better than the anxious parents. He knew she always had a kind word for her coworkers, despite the fact she seemed to not be close to any of them.

And she had been concerned about him the past few days. She'd seen deeper into the maelstrom inside him than anyone else, despite his efforts to hide it from everyone. She reached out to him with compassion and understanding, but respectful of his dignity.

And he ... he had nothing to give her. She deserved a man with a whole and healthy mind, someone who knew what he wanted, someone who didn't feel so broken inside.

"Geoffrey?" she called from inside the car.

He got in. "Sorry, I was just looking around. I didn't see anyone."

She could tell something was wrong. Her brow wrinkled and she touched the back of his hand. Her fingers made his skin tingle with warmth.

"I think I'm just jumpy," he said. "You really don't feel like anyone's watching us?"

She shook her head, and withdrew her hand. "Now we're off to China White? I'm not exactly sure what you hope we can find there."

"We know Chet and Frank went there. I have a hunch."

"About?"

Geoffrey fired up the engine. "I think I can find out who drove the car."

It was too early for a crowd to have gathered at China White, the upscale dance club a few blocks away from Chinatown. With parking always at a premium in San Francisco any time of the day or night, the club had a valet service at the front of the building, a former warehouse that had gotten an extensive and expensive facelift. White columns with red and gold Chinese decorations marched all along the front of the building, broken only by the front doors in the middle.

As Geoffrey had expected, there was no one at the valet station this early in the afternoon.

"There's a parking spot." Maylin pointed to a spot about a block away on the opposite side of the street.

He parallel parked the car easily. But as he got out, he again felt that uneasy prickle across his shoulder blades. He looked around, but couldn't see anything except a few ladies with grocery bags, one homeless man in a doorway, and a mother and son loaded with bakery boxes. There were lots of cars along the street, and he couldn't see inside all of them because of the glare of the sun, but nothing seemed to be out of the ordinary.

"Do you see anyone?" Maylin didn't even question his suspicion.

He shook his head. "You know what? I'm just being paranoid. Chester Wong might be trying to kill us because we saved the life of the boy who he believes killed his son. We've been chased by Asian men in suits for three days, now. It's just making me crazy."

"But we're not imagining this threat to us. Maybe we are being watched."

"Why would they watch us?" Geoffrey said. "They've been trying to kill us."

Maylin frowned, then sighed. "You're right. Maybe we're both paranoid."

They headed to the club, but instead of going in from the front door, they went around the building to the back. An open door led to what looked like a small kitchen, and they headed inside.

The staff bustled around, preparing for the club's opening in a few hours. The club apparently offered some sort of food, because Geoffrey saw people chopping vegetables and stirring sauces.

One of the staff noticed them. "Can I help you?" She had a slight Chinese accent, but not as heavy as the fake FBI agents who had come to the clinic.

"We wanted to know when your valets get in," Geoffrey said. "I wanted to ask them about a car."

"Are you police?" the waitress asked.

"No, just investigators," Geoffrey said. It was true, in a way. They were investigating Chet's death.

The waitress looked wary. "The valets are already here, but I think you should talk to the manager, before you talk to the valets."

"No problem," Geoffrey said, unperturbed.

After she went to get the manager, Maylin leaned close. "Do you really think the valets would remember Frank's father's car?"

"It was a very expensive car. And out of everyone, the valets would be most likely to remember who drove it."

"They may not."

"I know. But they might remember something. And if this doesn't pan out, we'll try to find that girl who danced with Chet."

Maylin suddenly had an intent look on her face, as if she were listening to an irregular heartbeat. Her eyes were unfocused.

He realized that some of the cooking staff were talking to each other in Chinese a few feet away. They were making dumplings, folding small spoonfuls of some meat mixture into thin dough squares. They were so fast that Geoffrey could barely follow their movements.

"What is it?" he asked after a few minutes.

"It might be nothing," Maylin said slowly. "Those girls live in an area near the marina where there are Triad members."

Geoffrey immediately thought of the Chinese men who had tried to kidnap Chelsea. Were Chinese gang members somehow involved in this? Were they behind the unease Geoffrey felt, suspecting they were being watched? But why would Triad want to watch Geoffrey and Maylin?

"The girls are saying that the Triad seem stirred up this past week because one of their captain's family members was killed." Maylin's eyes were wide as she leaned closer to him. "Do you think one of the people Chester had killed was connected to Triad?"

"It might explain why they tried to kidnap Chelsea, for revenge against Chester." Except the Triad couldn't know that Chelsea's father would be so uninterested in his own daughter's safety.

Maylin then sighed and shook her head. "Maybe I'm making connections where there are none. Just because the men spoke Cantonese doesn't mean they were Triad."

"True, but it doesn't hurt to ask Liam to look into it, right?"

"I'll call him." Maylin nodded over his shoulder. "You talk to the manager."

Geoffrey turned to see a round Chinese man striding between the workbenches toward him. He had deep jowls and looked annoyed to be interrupted. "Yes?" he barked when he was near to Geoffrey.

"I'd like your permission to speak to your valets," Geoffrey said. "I want to know more about two men who came to your club a few weeks ago."

"What about them?"

"Your club isn't in any trouble," Geoffrey said. "I'm not the police."

The man seemed to relax a fraction, but his frown didn't go away. "So? What do you need from them?"

"I just want to know who was driving the car, and I'm hoping the valets remember."

The man's eyes flattened. "Good luck with that," he muttered.

"Do I have your permission?"

"Sure, sure. They're in the bar right now." He waved toward a side door that seemed to lead into the main part of the club. Then he turned and walked back to his office. Geoffrey supposed the manager wasn't too concerned because Geoffrey's question for the valets seemed so unimportant.

Maylin appeared at his elbow. "I spoke to Liam, but he says it might take him a while before he has time to look it up. He's doing research for Detective Carter for an abduction case."

That's right, Liam had mentioned that.

"It might not be connected to the Triads after all," Maylin said. "And even if it was, what can we do? We can't take on the Triad."

But it bothered Geoffrey that Chester Wong was having people killed, and now Chinese Triad members might be threatening the safety of a teenaged girl, and there wasn't anything he could do about it. It was the same frustration of working in Japan and yet being unable to do more than offer comfort and medical expertise in the midst of so much tragedy. He hadn't done any good. And he had been helpless, like he was now.

No, he wasn't entirely helpless. He could find out what happened to Frank and Chet, and maybe make

Chester Wong see reason. "The manager gave us permission to speak to the valets."

He walked through the swinging door and entered the bar area of the club. The dance floor took up most of the vast space, but the bar ran along an entire wall. A cluster of men sat on stools at the bar, but it looked like all of them were drinking only water or sodas.

Geoffrey went up to them. "Hey, guys. We're investigators who need to know about a patron's car a few weeks ago, an SRT Viper. You're not in trouble, and we're not the police," he added.

The men had stopped chatting and now looked to Geoffrey, some a little blankly. Then Maylin translated in Chinese, and several nodded their heads.

One man spoke up in Chinese, and Maylin said, "He remembers that car."

"Driven by two boys?"

Maylin translated, and the valet nodded. He said something in Chinese and laughed, and some of the other valets laughed, too.

"He said they tipped well," Maylin said.

"Who tipped you, the driver or the passenger?"

"Passenger."

Geoffrey held up his right hand. "Did he have a bandage on this hand?"

The valet nodded, and then pointed to his left foot, speaking in Chinese. Maylin didn't have to translate.

"Thanks," he said to him. The man nodded.

"It was Chet driving the car," Geoffrey said as they walked back toward the kitchen.

"I can't believe they remembered Frank's bandages," Maylin said.

"I was a valet for a little while in high school," Geoffrey said. "I remember two things—the really cool cars, and the drivers who tipped me, especially the ones who tipped well. I wasn't sure if the boys would tip the valet, but if they did, there was a chance the valet would remember them."

They exited the club, but rather than that uneasy prickle, suddenly Geoffrey's nerves went on high alert. He looked around.

There was an Asian man leaning against the corner of the building, smoking a cigarette. He looked at Geoffrey and took a long draft. Unlike the other Asian men in suits, he had on comfortable khaki pants and a snug-fitting T-shirt that showed off hard muscles. He looked almost ... bored, and yet Geoffrey knew something wasn't right.

"Get to the car, quick," he murmured to Maylin.

They walked quickly toward where he had parked the Mustang. Geoffrey looked around, but the people who had been on the sidewalks were gone. Even the homeless man had disappeared.

He got his keys out of his pocket and passed them to Maylin. "Go." Then he turned around.

The cigarette man was behind them, closer than Geoffrey had anticipated. He still had that lazy look in his dark eyes, as if Geoffrey were a fly he was ready to swat away.

"What do you want?" Geoffrey said through stiff lips.

The man stopped a few feet away. He seemed to be assessing Geoffrey. Finally he tossed his cigarette to the ground and stepped on it with his Doc Martins. He said in a drawling voice with a Chinese accent, "So Chester Wong wants you dead?"

"What?" Was he questioning it? Was he confirming it?

"You mentioned it a few minutes ago," the man said. "Outside the club."

Geoffrey felt as if ice water had been dumped down his shirt. There had been someone watching them, but not Chester Wong's people.

"Geoffrey!" Maylin's scream cut through him, and he half-turned.

Another Asian man, dressed in jeans and a black leather jacket, had grabbed Maylin near where they'd parked the car. He had an arm around her waist, and his other hand pressed a gun to her side.

Anger and fear both boiled up inside him. He couldn't let them hurt her. "Let her go," he said through gritted teeth.

The man holding Maylin said something in Chinese to the other man, and Geoffrey turned back to the other man just as he grabbed his shoulder. The man swung a fist at him, and Geoffrey blocked it.

"Let me go!"

Maylin's cry made him want to turn around. Instead, he brought up his other arm to block the man's other fist at his head. Then the man made a quick jab that landed hard on Geoffrey's side. The blow sent pain up his ribs.

He set his jaw and began returning punches, just like his mixed martial arts trainer had been teaching him. The man brought his arms up to block Geoffrey's blows.

But then Geoffrey and the man both swung at the same time. The man had a slightly longer reach, and his fist connected with Geoffrey's jaw.

He saw darkness and stars. He thought he was still standing, but then he felt the cement slamming into his back, felt the back of his head ricochet hard. An angry voice in Chinese, sounding like he was cussing.

He heard Maylin, as if from a great distance, "Geoffrey!"

Footsteps next to his ear, then running away.

Geoffrey couldn't make his body respond to him. He tried to roll over, to get to his feet. He rolled to his side, pulled his head up, looked down the stretch of sidewalk.

They were gone. And they'd taken Maylin.

10

When Geoffrey turned his attention from the man in the T-shirt, Maylin realized she'd shouldn't have called his name. Stupid, stupid!

"Let her go." Geoffrey's eyes were blazing green-gold. She'd never seen him look this way before, like an avenging angel.

Then the man holding Maylin said in Cantonese to the one behind Geoffrey, "Grab him and let's go."

Geoffrey began struggling with the larger man. Maylin began struggling, too. "Let me go!"

The man pressed the gun hard into her ribs. "Stop or I shoot."

She stopped, but her mind seemed to suddenly focus with absolute clarity. If they'd wanted to kill her, they already would have. They wanted her alive.

When Geoffrey fell to the ground, her heart stopped. Pain and pressure in her chest made her realize she'd stopped breathing, too.

She gasped in air and began struggling again, but the man grabbed her arm hard. Pain shot up her shoulder, and she stilled.

The man standing over Geoffrey cussed in Chinese.

"What did you do that for?" snarled the one with the gun. "We needed him. We can't move him if he's unconscious."

"Shut up, I know that. This was your brilliant idea in the first place. You're too impulsive."

"Let's just go."

So the plan to kidnap her—and Geoffrey, apparently—had been a spur of the moment thing. The men had overheard Geoffrey mention, just before they entered the dance club, that Chester Wong wanted them dead.

And they wanted Geoffrey and Maylin, because Chester Wong wanted Geoffrey and Maylin.

"Take her," said the man with the gun, and shoved her in the direction of the larger man. He holstered his gun under his leather jacket. The man in the T-shirt put a hand on her upper arm in a firm but not tight grip. She knew she couldn't fight him, and he did, too.

They walked only a block and turned down a narrow street that ran behind a row of restaurants and along the blank side wall of another warehouse. There was a rank smell like a dumpster. Their car was parked there, blocking the street.

The man in the jacket opened the trunk of the car, and Maylin tensed at the thought of being shoved inside. But then she noticed something.

The trunk was a mess of receipts, jumper cables, an umbrella, a tire iron. They hadn't prepared the car for a passenger, and the man in the jacket reached in and removed the tire iron and jumper cables.

And she was still holding Geoffrey's car keys.

She had to act now, before he took that umbrella.

She dropped Geoffrey's keys while at the same time kicking out at the man in front of her, shoving him a foot or two away. The larger man's hand on her arm tightened, but she slammed her foot hard on his instep, then elbowed his solar plexus. His grip loosened slightly, and she reached into the trunk, grabbing a handful of receipts and the umbrella.

She swung the umbrella at the larger man, but he caught it easily and wrenched it from her hands. Then he backhanded her.

She fell to the asphalt, her entire head throbbing. The smell was horrendous—rotting food, urine, motor oil. But through her half-lidded eyes, she saw the receipts scattered on the ground.

That had been her main goal.

The larger man hauled her to her feet, making the pain explode in her head like a bomb had gone off. She only barely registered the pain from her shoulder as he threw her into the trunk, shoving her legs inside.

The trunk smelled better than the asphalt, but the air also felt close, even though she knew logically she couldn't suffocate in here. The matted carpet of the floor scratched her cheek, a counterpoint to the throbbing.

The men started the car and they drove away. Away from Geoffrey, away from help. She was all alone.

The pain was receding, but the darkness in the trunk, punctuated by the light glimmering from between cracks on the edge of the cover, felt heavy and thick.

She needed light. She needed air. She needed to tell someone she was in this trunk.

She began kicking at the taillights. She could kick it out and signal to someone driving behind them that she was there.

But in a few minutes, the car pulled over and parked. Footsteps crunching on gravel, then the trunk opened.

She immediately kicked out, but the larger man grabbed her ankle. Then he pulled back a beefy arm and darkness descended.

Maylin woke with her head pounding even worse than it had before. The pain was so intense that she couldn't open her eyes for a long time. She was still in the trunk, and the bumps in the road were like hammer blows to her skull.

Oh, God. It came out like a sob. What did they say? No atheists in foxholes. Or car trunks, apparently.

He's not far away. He's always been there for me. Whenever I feel awful or afraid, I knew He was there. I wasn't alone.

Olivia's voice echoed in the trunk so loudly that it was almost as if she were right there, speaking it into Maylin's ear. She'd seen another side to God in Olivia's kindness, echoes of the one she'd read about in the Bible. And right now, she was all alone, with only a slim chance Geoffrey could rescue her. She had no one, but God.

God, please help me. I'm so alone.

The prayer brought tears to her eyes. The sobs came from deep in her gut, all the loneliness she'd ever felt, all the pain that her family and Sebastian had dealt to her. It was more than the stress, more than the situation she was in. It was like irrigating a wound.

And when the tears had faded, she was still in that trunk, still being driven to who knows where. But suddenly she became aware of a Presence there, something she couldn't see or hear or touch. But she just knew He was there with her, against all logic.

She wasn't alone. Jesus loved her and He would stay with her.

She rested in that Presence for a long time, that balm to her heart. She didn't know what would happen next, but she wasn't alone.

Then she became aware of a change in the road. They'd left a freeway and now drove on side streets. They'd soon reach their destination.

Against all odds, could God lead Geoffrey to her?

And then she had an idea.

She reached into her pocket, where she still had the pad of sticky notes, the green promotional ones from Oliver Medical Supply. She pulled one off and began folding.

She'd learned how to make paper cranes, strangely, in Sunday school at her parents' church. Not as part of the curriculum, but because one of her Sunday school classmates was a Japanese girl who was helping to make cranes for a wedding. She'd taught Maylin, and Maylin had helped her to fold cranes, because the bride needed a thousand of them, for good luck.

The sticky note was almost a square, just right for a crane. She folded, hampered by the jostling of the car, and not a perfect crane, but good enough.

When the car stopped, she held her breath. She needed to time this right.

The trunk opened, and the light speared her eyes. She closed them and pretended to be groggy. The air smelled of fish—she was near the bay, maybe in a marina.

One of the men grabbed her around the waist and dragged her from the trunk. She kept her hand curled around the crane. He hoisted her onto his shoulder, and the force shoved the air from her lungs. She grunted.

Perfect.

Where was the other man? Behind them or in front of them?

"Come on," said the voice of the man with the jacket. He was in front of the larger man, who was carrying her.

She opened her eyes and saw warehouses and empty streets, a dingy looking gas station, an exterminator business, a wholesale boating supply store. She couldn't see where she was carried, but when the larger man stopped, she heard the creak of a metal door being opened.

She dropped the crane, bright green against the gray and black ground. Would they notice it?

She kept her eyes on the crane as she was taken through a doorway into darkness. Then the door closed behind her.

It was all his fault. Again.

Geoffrey dully answered the officer's questions about the attack. He'd already answered them earlier, but they were repeating the questions. Maybe to see if he remembered something different or changed his story.

The hole in his gut was familiar to him. It was the same feeling he'd had when he'd heard about the tsunami hitting the shores of Tōhoku. He'd been at his uncle's home in Yuzawa, sleeping off a late night of drinking with his cousins, when they'd felt the earthquake. Then had come the news about the tsunami heading toward the coast within the hour. One of the places affected would be Ōfunato, where Geoffrey's cousin, Noa, had gone early that morning to visit their grandmother.

Geoffrey hadn't gone with her as planned because he'd been too hammered to get up, so Noa went alone. And she died with his grandmother in the tsunami that destroyed the city.

He had failed her. She had died alone, trying to get their grandmother out of the city. If he'd been there, he surely could have helped her. They might have survived. But he'd been too sloshed and selfish.

So he'd stayed in Japan, trying to purge the demons from his soul. He'd joined a medical missions team and saw the devastation in the wake of the tsunami, tried to help patch up bodies where hearts were already rent apart.

The ache from that hole had faded, but now it came back, the wound ripped open again. He hadn't been able to save Noa or his grandmother. He had thought he'd changed, but he hadn't been able to keep Maylin safe.

After he'd come to, he'd called Detective Carter, who was still in the middle of the abduction case he was working on with Liam. But the detective had called the San Francisco police department and officers had met Geoffrey at the dance club within a few minutes. They were going over the area where the men had been, had even taken the cigarette the one man had been smoking, but Geoffrey knew DNA tests would take days if not weeks. Geoffrey hadn't seen the men's car. There weren't any banks along the street which had ATM cameras that could have caught the men on film.

She was lost to him.

Geoffrey had called his brother Chris, who was still at the Den with his mom, and asked him to drive to the cabin to tell Linc, but he was surprised when his brother arrived barely an hour later. Linc must have been speeding to get to San Francisco so quickly.

The policemen had finished talking to Geoffrey and were getting ready to leave, so he was sitting on the curb when Linc pulled up in Olivia's Suburban. He parked as Geoffrey got to his feet and dusted off his jeans.

"You okay?" Linc's eyes were intent as they studied Geoffrey's face.

"Yeah, the paramedics looked at me. I'm fine."

"Thank God." Linc pulled him into a fervent hug.

Geoffrey slapped his brother's back, surprised to find comfort in the embrace. His siblings tended to be more physically affectionate than he was, but right now, he needed his brother's shoulder to lean on. He found his hands were shaking—he hadn't noticed it before now.

"Tell me what happened," Linc said.

Geoffrey told him, reliving the frustration and horror in his mind at the sight of Maylin with the gun pressed to her side. Was she all right? She had to be.

"I don't know what to do." Geoffrey ran a hand through his short hair. "I want to be doing something, going somewhere, but I don't know where to go."

"Can you go to Chester?"

"They weren't his men. They wanted us because they overheard me saying that Chester wanted us dead."

"Enemies of Chester? I guess he's got a lot."

"I think he murdered someone he shouldn't have." Geoffrey told Linc about what Maylin had overheard about the Triad captain out for revenge for a murdered family member.

"Would Chester really be that stupid to murder a Triad's family member?" Linc looked appalled.

"He probably didn't know he was doing it, he was so focused on getting revenge for his son's death."

Linc began to pace on the sidewalk. "You have no leads, no ideas?"

Geoffrey shook his head. "If it was Triad, they could have taken Maylin anywhere." The bleakness settled on him again, a black weight against his chest. "Oh, God, help us," he groaned.

Linc looked at him, concern but also surprise in his green-brown eyes, but he didn't say anything.

"What is it?" Geoffrey asked.

"Look, I didn't want to pry ..." Linc sighed. "This should be Liv and not me saying this, but we've noticed, you know? Since you've gotten back. You and God."

"What about me and God?" He knew what Linc was talking about.

"You haven't been on speaking terms. It's like God's the ex-girlfriend you're desperately trying to avoid."

"Now you sound like Liv."

Linc grimaced and rubbed his hand against his forehead. "I don't know what I'm saying."

Strangely, Geoffrey knew exactly what he was saying. In Japan, he'd come face to face with a God he didn't know anymore. The God he'd grown up with hadn't been the one who decimated Tōhoku. The God he'd known hadn't been the one who let Geoffrey live, too far away to help his cousin, in a horrific twist of fate.

Coming back to his family in the U.S. had only emphasized that he didn't know God anymore, and he was wondering if he ever had.

He hadn't lived the life God wanted him to, but he had at least believed. Now he didn't know what he'd been believing for so long.

"Geoff." There was a determined cast to Linc's face. "You know I don't normally say this, but I think we should pray."

It was the last thing he'd have expected of his brother, and his heart quailed.

"It's the third down, no timeouts, ten seconds on the clock," Linc said. "Time for a Hail Mary."

"Prayer isn't a football play."

"Don't be stubborn. You know what I'm talking about."

Geoffrey turned away from his brother. He muttered, "God won't listen to me."

"He always listens," Linc said quietly.

Hadn't that been what his mother always told him? And his Sunday school teachers. Faith like a child.

"Come on, brother," Linc said. "We need to pray. I really feel we need to pray."

Geoffrey closed his eyes. Took a deep breath. He turned around.

They sat on the curb, Linc's hand firm on Geoffrey's shoulder. And he began to pray.

"God, You are Lord of this universe. You are over everything, including all the things we don't understand."

Geoffrey had had a hard time with that in the days after the tsunami, when he was climbing through rubble, trying to help find survivors, when he was working in a medical tent without sleep for days at a time. Later, the work had been routine, but still difficult emotionally for him to understand. Yet in his years in Japan, who had he been trying to atone to, if not God?

Much good that did. Maylin was gone, and it was his fault.

Linc prayed, "We know You are in control, even if we can't see it. We know we need to completely give up control to You."

Give up control? His iron self-control had been the only thing keeping him from shattering into pieces in Japan, where everything had been falling down around him.

Like right now.

He was holding tight. He was afraid to let go.

"Lord, we trust You completely," Linc prayed.

Geoffrey had sung "Trust and Obey" hundreds of times, but now, here at his lowest point, he turned the word in his head, trying to understand its true meaning.

Obey he understood. He'd tried to be the good son, the responsible one with his family. His social life had been a bit wild, but he'd always come through for his family. It had been his duty.

Had his faith in God been a duty, too?

Since the tsunami, he'd tried to always do the right thing. Hadn't that been like a duty? He knew faith wasn't a duty. It was something stronger, more real.

Was God really real to him? Did he know how to trust God, especially now when he had no one else to turn to?

He hadn't admitted that to himself until this moment.

Now was the time to lay it all on the line and just jump.

Or rather, throw the Hail Mary pass.

God, forgive me, he prayed. And he just ... let it go.

Suddenly there was a powerful hand that was gripping his heart, holding him, supporting him. God was here. Geoffrey was so small, and yet God was here.

Please help me to find her.

"Amen," Linc said.

"Amen," Geoffrey said automatically.

They sat in silence, Linc's hand still on Geoffrey's shoulder. Geoffrey didn't realize he had tears on his face until one dropped from his nose. He wiped his face with the collar of his shirt.

He sat there waiting. He started to think, *What am I doing? This is stupid,* but then he thrust it aside and continued to wait. To trust. He had to trust, for Maylin's sake. Not because Geoffrey had been the good son to God, but because Maylin's life was in danger.

And if God didn't answer? He had to trust God would take care of her. Save her.

Geoffrey hadn't told her he loved her.

He remembered his last sight of Maylin, held by that man with the gun. Walking away from him.

Wait a minute.

Walking where?

He'd told the police about the men walking away. They'd canvassed the streets, but of course Geoffrey hadn't known where the men's car was parked, and it was long gone by now.

He got up, looking down the sidewalk in the direction they had been taking.

"What is it?" Linc got up also.

"Where did they park?" He started walking. "They had to have been able to see us go to the backdoor of the dance club."

"You'd have seen them if they parked on the street, wouldn't you?"

"They had to have parked close enough to be able to get out and follow us on foot." Geoffrey paused at the entrance to an alley, but it was too small for a car. He continued walking. "If they parked too far away, by the time they walked to where we were parked, they wouldn't have seen us head toward the back entrance of the club. And that one guy was waiting for us at the corner of the building."

There wasn't anywhere on this side of the street where they could have parked without Geoffrey seeing them. He and Linc crossed the street and began walking back toward the club. Maybe the men had parked further up the street rather than down near where Geoffrey had parked.

The stores and restaurants—mostly fast food hole-in-the-wall joints—were packed closely together on this side of the street. They walked past the dance club about a block, pausing at the corner of where a side street T-junctioned with the main one. Geoffrey peered down the side street, and then he saw it.

A narrow street that ran behind the restaurants, parallel to the main street. He headed toward it and turned the corner.

It was more like a back alley than a street, with barely room for a delivery truck. It was apparently used often because it was clear of any Dumpsters or trash cans, although it smelled like a sewer.

Geoffrey walked down the street, not sure what he was looking for. There wasn't any mud or grass or anything to indicate a car had been parked here. But if the men had been following him and Maylin, they could have parked here once they saw Geoffrey park the Mustang along the street, and they'd have been able to stand at the corner and see them head for the back door of the dance club.

"Geoff." There was urgency in Linc's voice. He stood, holding a set of keys.

"Those are my car keys." His pulse began to race. "I gave them to Maylin. Where did you find them?"

"Here." Linc studied the road, which was rutted with potholes and dotted with gravel. It was also littered with paper.

"These receipts haven't been here long." Geoffrey knelt to pick some of them up. A few for fast food restaurants, a few gas station receipts. "Do you think these could have come from the men's car?"

"From their trunk, maybe?"

Geoffrey's jaw tightened at the thought of Maylin being shoved into a car trunk. "If these belong to those men, maybe they can tell us where they've been. And one of those places might be where they took Maylin."

Geoffrey collected all the receipts he could find while Linc checked the web on his smartphone. "There's an internet cafe a few blocks from here."

Good thing he'd gotten his car keys back. "We'll both drive."

As they headed out of the alley, Geoffrey paused to look back. *Thank You, Lord.*

He almost thought he heard, *You're welcome, my child.*

The internet cafe was busy, but they had free WiFi, so Linc used his phone to connect to the internet and look up the addresses of the places on the receipt. The addresses clustered in three spots—the busiest areas of Chinatown, a residential neighborhood in South San Francisco, and the Slade Street Marina in Oakland.

"Chinatown and that part of South San Francisco have too many people around," Linc said. "If I had kidnapped someone, I'd want to put them somewhere that no one could hear their shouts for help."

"What's the area around Slade Street Marina look like?" Geoffrey asked.

Linc pulled some photos up on his phone. "It looks like warehouses, some wholesale stores, a few diners, a gas station."

"There were three receipts from that gas station," Geoffrey said. "Let's start there first."

On the drive to Oakland, all Geoffrey could do was grip the steering wheel and pray. *Lord, please help us find her. Please let her be all right.*

Then he'd remind himself to trust God. And then he'd start worrying all over again.

The gas station, Smoak's, was in an industrial neighborhood near the Slade Street Marina, surrounded by some warehouses, an automotive body shop and wholesale store next door, an exterminator business, and a boating supply store. The streets were quiet since it was late in the day.

They parked and looked around. "It'll be dark in a few hours. We need to move fast," Geoffrey said.

"If I brought a captive to one of these buildings, I'd probably take her in from the backside where no one can see me."

"Then let's look."

They wandered by the backside of the automotive store, but there were still people in the store. Unless they were connected to the two Asian men, Maylin wasn't in that building.

The boating supply store had security cameras all along the perimeter, and they couldn't do more than tug at the locked back door. It was next door to the exterminator business, which also still had employees there, so they moved to the warehouse across the street, a freestanding building which was for a steel manufacturing company. As they approached the back door to the warehouse, that's when Geoffrey saw it. A speck of bright green on the ground.

It was right outside the back door to the warehouse. He bent to pick it up.

It was a folded paper crane, a bit crooked. He and his siblings had been forced to learn to make them because they'd had to help make cranes whenever a relative had a wedding. This was made from green paper, and he could see printed on it, "Oliver."

He unfolded the crane. Oliver Medical Supply. There was a sticky strip on the backside.

This was from a sticky note pad like the ones they used at the clinic. He'd used them only a few days ago.

Maylin had had a sticky note pad like this. She'd used it to take down the license plate of the car that had been following them in Napa.

"Maylin's here," he breathed.

Linc's face grew grave. "You're sure?"

"Yes. We have to call the SFPD." Geoffrey got out the card of the officer who had been in charge when he'd met Geoffrey near the dance club. He made the call and spoke to the officer, who said he'd get some squad cars to their location from the Oakland police department.

But just as Geoffrey hung up, a gunshot echoed. Geoffrey and Linc instinctively ducked.

It had come from inside the warehouse.

11

Maylin ducked her head as the gun went off, but Szu Wen, the gunman who had held his pistol to her side, was struggling with another Chinese man, who was apparently one of Chester Wong's bodyguards.

"Don't move!" shouted Chester's other bodyguard in Cantonese as he aimed his gun at the other man who had captured her, Ying-Chieh.

The bodyguard, who outweighed Szu Wen and Ying-Chieh by at least fifty pounds of muscle, over-powered Szu Wen rather quickly and took away his gun. Szu Wen staggered a few steps away, slapping at his leather jacket in frustration.

"You really thought you could ambush me?" Chester climbed the metal stairs until he was on the second floor of the warehouse with them all. His two bodyguards held both Szu Wen and Ying-Chieh at gunpoint.

"We weren't trying to ambush you," Szu Wen said in Cantonese.

He was lying. They'd called Chester as soon as they'd tied Maylin to the wooden chair she now sat on, saying they had the woman he was after, but they'd only give her to him in person, not to his bodyguards. Then they'd hidden behind the wooden shipping crates dotting the room, so they could fire at Chester as soon as he showed his face. But they'd only gotten one shot off, and Chester's bodyguards had been faster.

Maylin's ears were ringing from the sound of Szu Wen's gun discharging in the vast space. The second floor of the warehouse was the top floor of the building, with exposed metal rafters above. There was a large square hole in the floor near where Maylin sat tied to the chair, with a pulley and crane system to raise and lower heavy objects all the way to the first floor. The Triad were apparently using the warehouse as storage for their illegal import/export business dealings.

Chester approached her, his half-lidded eyes assessing her. "You've been giving my men a great deal of trouble."

"Well, I kind of object to being murdered," she said.

Chester gave a half-smile. "It's your own fault. You saved Frank Chan's life."

"He wasn't driving the car. Your son was."

Chester's face grew stone cold. "Shut up."

"The valet at China White remembers that Frank was the passenger. He had bandages and couldn't drive the stick shift."

"It was his father's car," Chester spat out.

"Frank had seizures. He couldn't get a license."

"He could still drive. And he killed my only son."

"You have two beautiful, brilliant daughters—"

"He was my *son!*" Chester's voice echoed against the rafters. Then he composed himself again, smoothing his maroon tie. "My daughters will never be able to do what he could have done with my companies. And Cassandra is dead to me. She betrayed me."

"What about Chelsea?" Maylin looked at Szu Wen's ugly face. "These men may have been the ones to try to kidnap her this morning."

"Of course they were."

Maylin choked.

"How did you know about that?" Chester asked. "Oh, Cassandra. Of course."

Maylin finally was able to croak out, "Why would they do that?" And why didn't he care?

"He killed my cousin!" Szu Wen hissed in Cantonese.

Maylin had managed to hide the fact she could understand Chinese, so she put on a confused mask.

"She deserved to die!" Chester shot back at him, also in Cantonese. "Just like her son."

Frank's mother had been related to Triad. It was as they had suspected, and Chester had enraged Szu Wen, causing him to try to enact revenge. He'd wanted to use Maylin as bait for Chester, but it was starting to look like Chester would simply get rid of him.

But would he risk starting a feud with the Triad? From what Szu Wen had said, it sounded like only he and his partner were involved in dealing with Chester, maybe because Frank's mother was only Szu Wen's cousin, not one of the Triad. If Chester killed these two men, however, he'd have to deal with the Triad leaders.

"And I know you can speak Chinese," Chester said to her. "After you and Dr. Whelan escaped my men at your clinic, I looked you two up."

"What?" Szu Wen glared at her.

"Now, you're going to tell me where my daughter is."

"I don't know. We haven't seen her since she warned us."

Chester reached into his pocket and pulled out a knife. With a flick, the blade snapped out. He leaned close. "I think you're lying."

"You've been watching too many movies," Maylin said. Then she smashed the hardest part of her skull, her forehead, directly into Chester's nose.

He howled.

She stood up, taking the chair with her since her hands were still tied to the back. She swung around in an arc, slamming the chair hard against Chester. He stumbled and fell.

Szu Wen and Ying-Chieh used the distraction to attack the bodyguards. A gun went off, and she flinched. She heard the sounds of struggling, and the sound of metal impacting flesh.

She needed to break the chair somehow. She looked for something hard to smash it against, but the chair was heavy, and she was awkward on her feet.

Strong arms wrapped around her. One of the bodyguards had come up behind her. She twisted left and right to break his hold. She found herself standing in front of Chester, who had shakily gotten to his feet. His nose was bleeding where she'd slammed her forehead into it.

She leaned back into the bodyguard and brought both legs up, bending her knees. The sudden weight surprised him and his knees buckled, but she quickly kicked out with both legs and caught Chester squarely in his stomach. He coughed and staggered back, and the force of her blow made the bodyguard stagger backward also. They both fell to the ground.

But the impact wasn't enough to break the chair. One of the crossbars on the wooden legs broke when it impacted the bodyguard's bent knee, but nothing else broke loose.

It looked so much easier in the movies.

She rolled to one side to try to get her legs under her, but the bodyguard grabbed the chair back, efficiently snagging her. She tried to kick at him, but couldn't because he was behind her and the chair hampered her. He managed to climb to his feet while she was still lying sideways on the floor, then he hoisted her back up by grabbing the wooden chair.

Szu Wen and Ying-Chieh hadn't been successful, either. The remaining bodyguard aimed a gun at where they both lay on the floor, Ying-Chieh slack and moving slowly, his eyes closed, and Szu Wen groaning, clutching his stomach where the bodyguard must have kicked him.

Chester swore at her and swung a punch. Maylin had already been hit today, and she hadn't thought the pain could be any worse, but this time, there was a sharp pulsing in her cheek. Then she felt liquid trickling slowly down her face. She was bleeding. She looked at Chester and saw that he had a large gold ring on his right hand, the one he'd used to hit her.

He looked down at her with burning eyes. "Forget Cassandra." He turned to his bodyguard. "Kill her."

At the sound of the first gunshot, Geoffrey had grabbed at the handle to the door. It was locked. But it was a flimsy doorknob and lock, loosely fitting in the doorframe. He grabbed his wallet and extracted a plastic card, then began working the card between the frame and the lock.

"It won't work," Linc said just as Geoffrey jimmied the door open.

"How do you think I broke into your bedroom all those times?" Geoffrey jammed the card into his back pocket and was about to head inside when Linc put a hand on his arm.

Linc had pulled a pistol from a holster under his jacket.

The sight of the gun made Geoffrey focus. "I hope you got your Conceal and Carry license."

"Last week. And you should be thanking me."

Geoffrey gave his brother a long look. "Thanks, Linc," he said.

"Follow me, okay?"

They headed into the warehouse, which was filled with shipping boxes, both cardboard and wooden, rather than anything to do with steel manufacturing. One strange aspect of the building was a hole in the ceiling at the far end, but then he saw, through the hole, the pulley hanging down from the ceiling on the second floor. Voices carried clearly down through that hole.

A man shouted something in Chinese, and all sounds of movement stopped. Then the sound of shoes against metal steps, and a man's voice saying, "You really thought you could ambush me?"

Geoffrey and Linc crept further into the warehouse. The wooden crates rose toward the ceiling, and above, the steel support beams were exposed. In studying the criss-crossing beams, Geoffrey realized it was like the rock-climbing wall they'd built on their property.

Then they heard Maylin's voice. "Well, I kind of object to being murdered,"

"We have to get up there," Linc whispered.

"They'll hear us if we use those metal stairs." Geoffrey nodded toward the stairs along the wall that went up to the second floor.

"Do you have a better idea?"

Geoffrey nodded toward the hole in the ceiling.

"Are you crazy?" Linc hissed. "That's a twenty-foot drop if you fall."

"No, there are crates stacked underneath. Besides, I don't intend to fall." Geoffrey began searching for the best way to climb the crate to get close enough to climb onto the exposed beams.

"You'll be hanging in mid-air," Linc said.

"The rock-climbing wall has that overhang section where I've hung mid-air lots of times." Geoffrey was the best out of all his siblings and had passed through that section without problems.

"What about the police?" Linc said.

"Linc, I have to get to Maylin." Geoffrey shucked off his shoes. "We don't know when the police will get here, and we don't know what those men will do to her once the cops arrive. I have to be in place so that I can protect her when that happens."

"I have an idea." Linc pointed to the stairs, which were in the opposite direction of the hole in the ceiling. "I'll take cover behind some crates and fire at the stairs. It'll distract them from you when you swing up through that hole."

"Got it."

"Geoff." The skin around Linc's eyes was creased with worry. "Please be careful."

"That's my line." Geoffrey squeezed his brother's shoulder.

He climbed several crates, carefully so that he wouldn't give away his presence with the sound of his feet on the wood. The crates were stacked high enough that he only needed to reach up to grab the lowest beam, hands on either side of it. He began inching his way along to an intersection with another beam that would take him right to the edge of the hole. The steel beam was easier to grip than his rock-climbing wall, but he still moved carefully. There was no Liv to belay him here, although the crates below him would make his fall only about ten feet.

He switched to the second beam and swung toward the hole. He could hear Maylin more clearly now, and he realized she must be speaking to Chester.

He had reached the hole and he swung his feet up to grip the beam in addition to his arms. He studied it and saw that it wouldn't be hard to pull himself up through the hole, as long as no one was looking in his direction. He still couldn't see anything aside from the pulley and crank in the ceiling above the hole.

Then he heard sounds of struggling. A gunshot went off, and more struggling.

He was torn. Should he swing through the hole to help Maylin, or would that only get him captured, as well? Was she in danger? He wished he could see what was happening.

It ended quickly, and then he heard a soft blow and the sound of Maylin grunting. Geoffrey's hands clenched, and he had to breathe to stay calm.

Then he heard Chester say clearly, "Kill her."

Apparently Linc heard it, too, because he chose that moment to start shooting. The sound echoed through the vast space, and when Geoffrey glanced down, he could see sparks where bullets ricocheted off the metal stairs at the far end.

Men shouted, then suddenly gunshots blared from the second floor.

Geoffrey pulled himself up in one smooth motion, hooking his leg up to help pull himself over the edge of the hole. He rolled to his side to get himself fully onto the second floor.

Maylin sat tied to a wooden chair a few feet away from him. Her cheek was bloody from a cut just below her eye. Geoffrey growled when he saw her.

The rest of the floor was in chaos. Three men in suits and one Asian man had all taken cover behind wooden shipping crates. The other Asian man was on the floor, slowly crawling to safety. They fired at each other as well as at the empty metal stairwell. None of them had noticed Maylin or Geoffrey, and luckily none of the shots fired was in their direction on the other side of the room.

Geoffrey ran to Maylin and grabbed the chair, pulling her behind a nearby crate so she wouldn't be hit by stray bullets

"Geoffrey! Where did you come from?" Her voice was sharp, and aside from the deep cut, she seemed otherwise unhurt.

"I'll explain later." He worked on the duct tape that strapped her arms to the sides of the chair back.

Then he suddenly heard shouting from below. "Police! Put down your weapons!"

The men hesitated. From around the edge of the crate they hid behind, Geoffrey could see Chester's face, and he'd gone red with anger. "What's going on?" he shouted.

Then there was the sound of boots on the stairs, coming up the second floor. Geoffrey peered around the crate and saw the flash-bang grenade just before it exploded in a deafening explosion, with a sharp flash of light and smoke seeping in all directions. He wrapped himself around Maylin to protect her.

Boots rattling the floor. Shouts. The sounds of scuffling.

He pulled back to peer into Maylin's face. "Are you all right?" His voice sounded far away to his own ears.

She nodded. Her dark eyes were shining as she stared at him. "I knew you'd come," she said.

Geoffrey kissed her.

Epilogue

Four weeks later

Maylin peered inside the doorway at the newly furbished panic room, which more resembled a luxury hotel room. "Very nice, Emma."

"Let's hope I never need to use it. Again." Emma Whelan patted the shoulder of her architect son. "Chris even installed an espresso machine."

Geoffrey gave Chris an incredulous look. "You didn't."

Chris gave a helpless shrug. "She insisted."

"Now that your mom's house is done, are you going back to Arizona?" Maylin asked Chris.

"I might stick around," he said. "I have a couple of bids in Napa." He nudged Linc. "And I still haven't tried the rock-climbing wall yet."

Linc looked disgusted. "I don't see what the big deal is."

"Ignore him, it's fun," Geoffrey said to Chris. "He's still hurting from that bruise on his—"

"I wouldn't have gotten hurt if you hadn't 'forgotten' to belay me," Linc snapped. "You're supposed to keep me from hitting the ground."

"I didn't expect you to fall when you were only five feet up."

"It's because Maylin was ahead of me and you were distracted," Linc said.

Geoffrey grinned. "Guilty."

Suddenly the fire alarm went off. Everyone looked at each other. Then Emma asked, "Where's Olivia?"

Chris and Linc's eyes grew wide, and they tore off down the hallway, leaping down the stairs toward the kitchen. Emma, Maylin, and Geoffrey followed quickly, but at less of a break-neck speed.

Black smoke billowed from the kitchen doorway. From somewhere inside, Linc yelled, "Liv, what are you doing, *cooking?*"

"I was only trying to sauté zucchini." Liv's voice came from the depths of the smoke.

"Oh, goodness, my wok! That's from China!" Emma plunged into the kitchen after them.

Maylin and Geoffrey looked at the smoking kitchen, then each other. "Let's air out the house," he said.

They raced through the house, opening doors and windows, and finally met out in the balcony, with the smoke seeping out the glass doors into the cloudless night.

Maylin coughed. "I didn't quite believe you when you said your sister could burn water."

"There are certain things we don't exaggerate about, and one of them is Liv's cooking." Geoffrey coughed, too. From the house, the fire alarm suddenly went silent. Since there was still smoke, he guessed one of his brothers turned the alarm off manually.

But once the alarm was off, they could clearly hear four raised voices talking—or rather, yelling—at the same time.

Maylin winced. "Do you think they need our help downstairs?"

"You couldn't pay me enough to walk into that kitchen right now."

The stars were beautiful, as always. She would never get tired of seeing them out here on the Whelans' property, far from the lights of Sonoma. They were still vast, and they made her feel small, and they were glorious in their beauty. But now, they also reminded her that she was not alone. Jesus loved her. Jesus would always be with her.

She had thought God hadn't been there as she grew up in a church full of hypocrites, in a vain family steeped in censure, as she unwittingly got involved with a supposedly Christian man whose words flayed her very soul.

But then she'd met Geoffrey and his family, people who really loved God. And she realized she'd been disappointed in people who claimed to be His. She had needed to make that distinction. She'd been so focused on how people didn't seem to want to understand her or accept her, and yet she'd ignored the God she'd known since she was a child who loved her already.

God had been there for her, in that car trunk, in that warehouse. She would never be alone again.

"I heard from Detective Carter," Geoffrey said. "I wanted to tell you in private, because it's not common knowledge yet, but Chester Wong is being indicted for money laundering."

"What? Not ... everything else he did?"

"When the police investigated him after the shootout at the warehouse, they found evidence of international money laundering that more directly implicated him than the men who were after us and Cassandra. The FBI stepped in. They're still investigating him on charges of attempted murder, but the evidence on the money laundering is solid. They think he'll plead guilty if they drop the assault charges." Geoffrey's eyes darkened. "I don't think it's right, after what he did to you, but it'll put him away for a long time."

She shouldn't be vindictive—after all, look where that got Chester—but it seemed almost wrong that he'd be going to jail for something unrelated to the four days of danger and pursuit a month ago. She would always hold the scar on her cheek in the shape of Chester's ring, where he'd hit her.

Chester had refused to believe Frank hadn't been driving the car, because according to the police report, which Detective Carter had acquired for Cassandra, when Frank had first woken up after the accident, he hadn't remembered who'd been driving. Apparently he did take the Viper out for a spin occasionally, even though he didn't have a license. The police had assumed Frank was driving since it was his father's car, and Frank hadn't denied it, since he couldn't remember anything that had happened that night. He'd been charged with DUI, driving without a license, and manslaughter, and he'd been out on bail a few weeks later when he'd been killed.

"It doesn't matter what he's charged with," Geoffrey said. "He's out of our lives."

Our lives. And how long would Maylin and Geoffrey's lives intersect?

It was uncanny, the way he could almost read her thoughts. He said, "I've decided to take the permanent physician position at the Free Children's Clinic."

She turned to him with a gasp. "Really? I thought ... the offer from that private hospital in Arizona, and the one from Merlyn Memorial in Los Angeles ..."

Geoffrey cupped her cheeks in his hands. They were warm against her skin, and she breathed deep. It was like walking through a cedar and eucalyptus forest, with that under-note of musk that was pure Geoffrey.

"I still don't understand God's will entirely, but I'm learning to trust in Him more," he said. "I'm learning to give it up to Him, rather than using work to forget my problems. But it's an ongoing process. That's what my counselor said yesterday, anyway."

Geoffrey had told her about what had happened in Japan, about losing his cousin and grandmother, about the guilt that still crushed him at being left alive. Maylin suspected he still had some post-traumatic stress to deal with and had suggested counseling, and his cousin, Monica, had given him the name of a Christian counselor.

His weekly sessions were helping. The haunted look was fading from his eyes. There were times she still sensed the twist of anguish in his heart when he remembered his time in Japan, but he would reach for her hand, squeeze it tightly. She gave him her shoulder to cry on, her silence to help him collect his thoughts, her ear to listen.

And she prayed for him, and with him. Prayer was still new for her, but it also filled her with wonder, because she knew God could hear her.

"I don't want you to stay just for me," she told him. "Take the opportunities you've been given."

"That's exactly what I'm doing."

And then he pulled from his pocket one of the green promotional sticky pads from Oliver Medical Supply, one of the same ones that had led him to her. She felt a mixture of confusion and disappointment at the broken moment.

He started scribbling.

She sighed. "You're always using sticky notes rather than just talking to the nurses."

"It's because I don't always remember to talk to them, so I write it down before I forget. But this time, I think maybe it'll be okay." He ripped the note from the pad and handed it to her.

It said, "I love you."

Her breath caught. She looked up at him, meeting his eyes, which had turned to green-gold. She smiled, and it was like her heart was being filled with liquid joy. "I love you, too."

And then he was kissing her, his lips warm and fervent. His hand cupped her face, pulling her closer to him. He rested his forehead against hers, and she breathed him in.

"I thought I was too wounded to get involved with anyone," he said. "I had lost my faith in Japan, and I didn't even know what I wanted to do with my life in the States. I had nothing to offer someone."

"I don't need anything from you," she said.

"I had to empty myself to God before I found what I'm supposed to do."

"The Free Children's Clinic? Are you sure?" He wouldn't be paid as much as some of the other places he could go.

"I think this is where God wants me to serve him."

She smiled and kissed him. "I'm glad."

He looked intently at her, and there was uncertainty in his eyes. "Are you sure? I know that after Sebastian …"

"You're nothing like Sebastian," she said. "I knew it by instinct when we started working together again, but I was still too afraid because I didn't know you that well. But you risked so much for me, and all you wanted to do was protect me. Sebastian would only have thought about himself. That's when I knew you had a higher nobility of soul."

He smiled against her mouth. "I'm not a knight. Far from it."

"Certainly not, because I'm no lady." She laughed. "But you fit me."

He kissed her again, his mouth lingering, spreading a tingling to her fingertips and toes. He was strong, and brave, and someone she could trust.

"We fit each other," he said.

And then the world fell away for a long while.

Connect with Camy

Dear Reader,

Thanks for joining me on this suspenseful ride through Sonoma and San Francisco!

The story of Liam's adventure—and how he stumbled upon love—is in *Treacherous Intent* (published by Love Inspired Suspense).

You also can read about the danger (and romance) that Monica encountered when she started the Free Children's Clinic in *Stalker in the Shadows*.

You can find out more about my entire Sonoma series at my website (camytang.com). While you're there, download my FREE romantic suspense novella, *Necessary Proof.*

If you enjoyed this book and you'd like to know each time I have a new release or a sale on one of my books, you can sign up for my newsletter (eepurl.com/ qT7ZD).

And on the next page, I'm also including the recipe to the stew-that-Liv-didn't-cook. :)

Camy

P.S. If you find any errors or typos that got past me and my proofreaders, please do send me a message at my website.

Unshakeable Pursuit is book #4.2 in my romantic suspense Sonoma series, although each book can be read alone.

Sonoma series:
#1 Deadly Intent
#2 Formula for Danger
#3 Stalker in the Shadows
#4 Narrow Escape
#4.1 Necessary Proof (novella)
#4.2 Unshakeable Pursuit (novella)
#5 Treacherous Intent
#6 Gone Missing

The Stew That Liv Didn't Cook

Since Olivia Whelan is the world's worst cook, she got her mom to make the stew that she brought to the cabin with her the second time.

Also, since I (Camy) am the world's laziest cook, I adopted "Mrs. Whelan's" excellent recipe into something I can throw into the slow cooker. The original recipe was from my friend Mrs. A. Wong.

- About 4-6 pounds (whatever's in one package) oxtail (I love oxtail, but if you don't care for it, substitute about 2 pounds stew meat)
- 2-4 tsp minced garlic
- 1 bunch parsley, chopped (I know this seems like a lot of parsley, but after that time in the slow cooker, it doesn't taste as strong. However, if you dislike parsley, feel free to eliminate it. I personally love cilantro and will substitute that here instead of parsley.)
- 2 tsp dried thyme
- 2 bay leaves
- 4 tsp salt
- 2 tsp pepper
- 1 tsp cayenne pepper (optional)
- 1.5 cups red wine (If you use a decent wine, it tastes better. And you can have a glass while cooking the mushrooms. :)

- 1 pint beef stock (or use beef bouillon and water)
- 1 pound mushrooms, sliced
- 1 onion, chopped
- 1 Tb butter
- 1 tsp sugar

Throw everything except last 4 ingredients into slow cooker on low for 10 hours or high for 6 hours (or until the meat is tender). If you are not as lazy as me, brown the oxtail/meat in a pan on the stove with a little oil, add it to the crock pot, then deglaze the pan with the beef stock before adding the stock to the crock pot.

About 20-25 minutes before serving, sauté the last 4 ingredients in a pan, add it to the crock pot, and cook for another 10-15 minutes.

Serve with noodles or over rice.

ABOUT THE AUTHOR

Camy writes Christian contemporary romance
and romantic suspense as Camy Tang and
Regency romance as *USA Today* bestselling author
Camille Elliot. She lives in San Jose, California,
with her engineer husband, and they both used to
be staff workers for her church youth group and
play on one of the Sunday worship teams. Visit
her websites at http://www.camytang.com/ and
http://www.camilleelliot.com/ to read free short
stories and subscribe to her quarterly newsletter.

CPSIA information can be obtained
at www.ICGtesting.com
Printed in the USA
FSHW011953280521
81935FS